AENIGMA

Book Four of

Geo the Space Explorer

by

CL FOOT and EA HICKSON

The characters and events portrayed in this book are fictitious. Any similarity to real persons, living or dead, is coincidental and not intended by the authors.

NATIONAL LIBRARY OF AUSTRALIA

A catalogue record for this book is available from the National Library of Australia

ISBN-13: 9781764360821

Cover design by: The House of Hickson Pty Ltd

To the winemakers

who create

magic potions

on Earth.

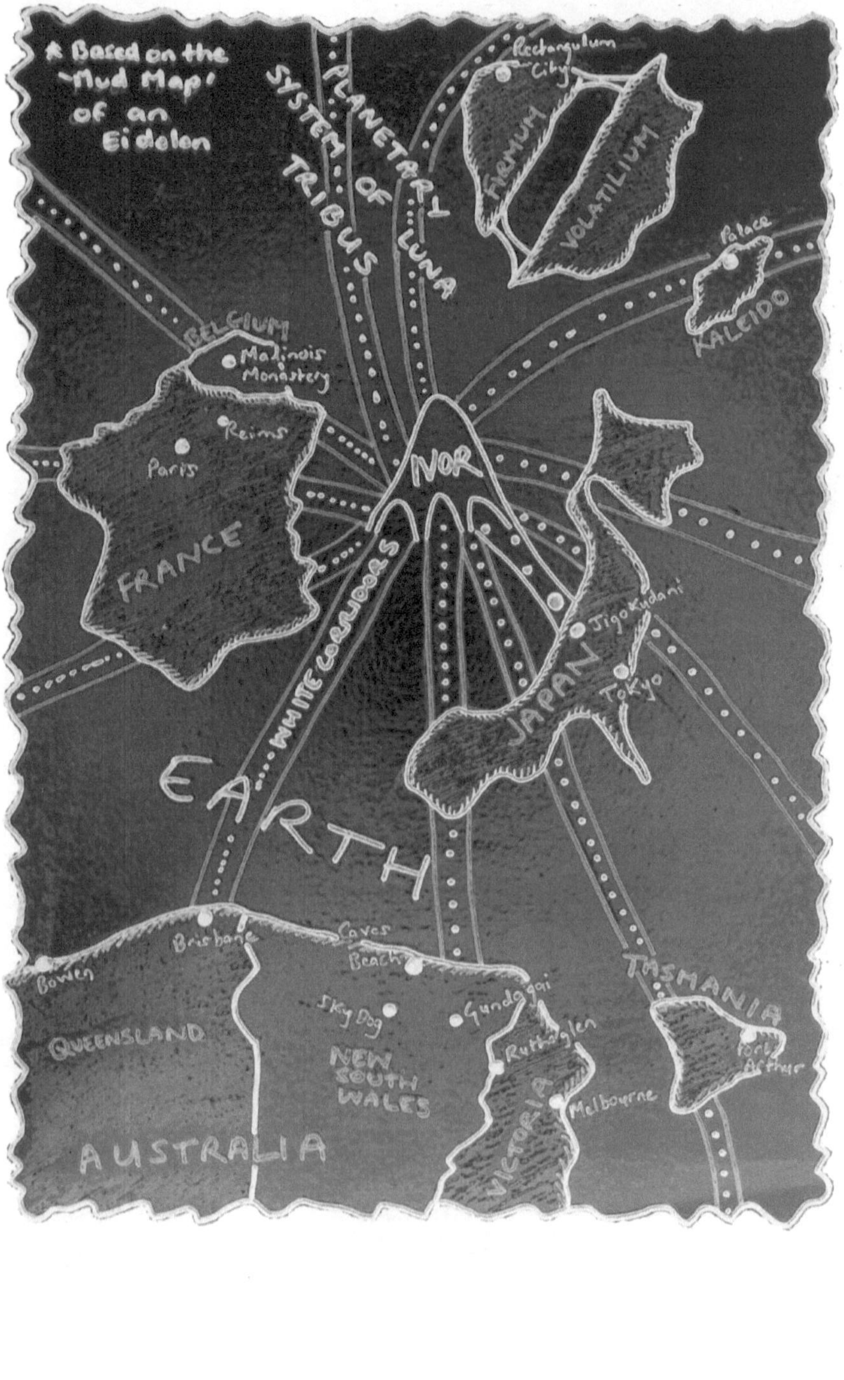
* Based on the 'Mud Map' of an Eidolon
SYSTEM OF TRIBUS
PLANETARY OF LUNA
Rectangulum City
FIRMUM
VOLATILIUM
Palace
KALEIDO
BELGIUM
Malinois Monastery
Reims
Paris
FRANCE
IVOR
WHITE CORRIDORS
Jigokudani
Tokyo
JAPAN
EARTH
Brisbane
Caves Beach
Bowen
Sky Dog
Gundagai
QUEENSLAND
NEW SOUTH WALES
Rutherglen
Melbourne
VICTORIA
TASMANIA
Port Arthur
AUSTRALIA

PRINCIPAL CHARACTERS

Tobias.. Malinois monk

GJ.. Chocolate Labrador

Kalan..King of Kaleido

Viz..Brother of Kalan

Menagerie... A lion

Master Sabi... Head Magician

Ellie.................................... Praeceptorum of Rectangulum City

Ro.. Husband of Ellie; Son of Kalan

Eff...Son of Ellie and Ro

Big Timmy...Albino rat

Snuggles.................................Rodent brother of Big Timmy

Annie... Caves Beach resident

Sandy... Daughter of Annie

Kate...Daughter of Sandy

Mikey... Son of Sandy

The Prof...Former ESA scientist

Gavin...Veterinarian

Octy...Octavian explorer

Beauty...Magical vehicle

The Oneidon.................................... Head of the Compasse

Sir Geo.. Chocolate Labrador

Flanders...Malinois monk

Smiley..................................Staffordshire Bull Terrier

Orizuru..Crane

Chapter 1
KALEIDO

A cold, wet nose sniffed vigorously at the slippery, mossy ground. Nostrils twitched furiously. The stench was vile, causing Geo Junior's starving belly to churn with revulsion. The young Chocolate Labrador, known as GJ, had picked up the trail of a creature known as *Felis catus*, or on Earth, simply as a cat. In the not-too-distant past, back on his home planet, a dog such as himself might have contentedly, albeit with an occasional kerfuffle, been raised in a human residence alongside such a creature. Both animals would have fondly been classified as family pets.

This was no longer the case. The unforgiving Praeceptorum Mergen of the Planetary System of Luna Tribus, known as Luna Tribus for short, had commanded his powerful Head Magician, Master Sabi, to travel to Earth and turn humans against pets. He had successfully achieved this; an enduring, spiteful act of revenge against 'Geo the Space Explorer' for stealing his daughter. A singular act of magical malevolence, had played on the intrinsic biases of some humans towards animals.

GJ's first and only prior encounter with a feline had been during a tousle with an egregious tabby cat named Ginger. He could still hear her nasty hissing and recall the disgusting taste of the orange tuft of fur that had filled his mouth and almost choked him. These vivid memories, imprinted while feeling afraid, had sensitised him to the feline pheromonal odours that were now pervasive. He was certain that multiple cats were now skulking around them. This time he was more prepared to tackle them.

He thought of Geo, the warm-hearted, pragmatic adventurer who had triggered an unabated cascade of events through a simple act of curiosity. This was the dog he proudly called his father. He felt grateful for all he had been taught in his formative months by the formidable canine; along with Big Timmy and Snuggles, the charismatic albino rat brothers. In the dark, shadowy woods where he now found himself, he wished Geo, with his unrivalled optimism and unerring capacity to always know what to do, was padding along at his side.

On Kaleido, a small planet incalculably far from his home, GJ now travelled with a different pack. Walking with him were two different brothers: Kalan, the former King of Kaleido and the magician Viz. He knew the entire human Page family on Earth would be proud of him, if they knew that the fully grown dog had bravely volunteered to accompany these humanoids on a perilous mission. They were unaware that the rightful Praeceptorum of Rectangulum City, Elektra Heredis, less formally known as Ellie, had barely returned from exile and started to rule, when new disturbing intelligence had reached her palace.

'Having enslaved a population of cats, Master Sabi has converted our palace into his new residence and operational base,' Viz had reported. Ellie had exchanged a knowing look with her husband Ro, his nephew,

The Prince of Kaleido, and said, 'it's time your family took back their home. Kaleido must be restored to its former glory. King Kalan must return to his lands and reclaim his throne.'

Ro had been convinced it would require an army, in contrast to his father, who said quizzically, 'no one knows Kaleido like Viz and I. We should use stealth rather than muscle. Dear brother, wouldn't you relish the opportunity to bring our nemesis and your previous torturer to justice?'

Viz had nodded, and at this point, GJ had insisted that he would *need* to accompany them.

'I wonder how Tobias is going with his task?' Kalan asked his brother, as they paused to rest in the forest where they had played as boys. After significant protest from their friend about being left behind, the canine-humanoid, hybrid monk, who was the leader of the Earth based, Order of the Malinois, had been charged with a vital task. His assignment was to collaborate with their most trusted allies in devising an impenetrable prison for when they returned victorious with their captive. Developing a fail-proof strategy for capturing and containing the treacherous Master Sabi had become an obsession for all involved.

The trio set off again, contending with gag-inducing waves of nausea. After another brief rest stop, GJ suddenly moved forward on high alert, sensing they were being watched. The confidence that he had felt at their grand send off, had now faded. He shivered in the cold, damp, musty, ammonia infused air and tried to push fear to the back of his mind. The dog reminded himself that once Master Sabi had been removed as a threat, he could safely leave his friends, able to return to the family he had left behind on Earth.

'I'll make you proud,' he inadvertently thought out loud, imagining the moment when the evil magician was locked up.

'Hush!' Kalan whispered, worried that if they were detected, they might lose the element of surprise, crucial to their plan.

'Sorry!' GJ cried, feeling guilty.

Viz placed a firm hand on his back and asked him to halt.

'Can you feel their eyes on us?' he asked the dog.

'Yes. Their scent is getting stronger. It's becoming overwhelming.'

'I think they're playing with us; no doubt preparing for an ambush. We must move fast!' Viz advised, moving to the front.

GJ refocussed on being fully present in the moment, ready to leap into action and defend his companions. He stared up at the three moons, rotating at different rates overhead. To facilitate their infiltration, Viz had strategically selected this precise, protracted phase of the lunar cycle where the colours were the murkiest. They edged forwards, in near darkness, ever deeper into forest where the tree trunks were so close they could only pass in single file.

GJ's mind drifted again, trying to settle his edginess with comforting thoughts. He was missing the endlessly patient and soothing presence of Octy. The Octavian had always been kind to him, never failing to offer a generous supply of samples of whatever he was cutting up in the kitchen, cuddles or both. He wondered where he was right now, having parted with him in Zermatt when they had entered the White

Corridor. His tail started to sway happily as images of other allies filled his mind. He imagined the quiet, composed Queen Christina, wife of Kalan, and her unassuming sister, Aquilegia.

Witnessing the reunion of Ellie and Ro, and experiencing his own emotional one with Geo, had been uplifting, albeit bittersweet moments. Spiteful enemies had robbed them of lives together. In his view, the separation had been most cruel for the newborn twins of the newlyweds. Eff and Izzie had been deliberately raised apart, in highly challenging environments. Izzie was now finally living with both parents, assisting her mother, the new Praeceptorum of Rectangulum City with her many duties.

In contrast, no one on Luna Tribus was sure what had become of the strange, intense protégé of Master Sabi. GJ knew in his heart that Eff would have gone to Earth and most likely Caves Beach, making him fear for his humans.

'We need to pick up our pace,' Viz whispered to his companions.

'Yes, I fear they're closing in on us,' Kalan shared.

'More happy thoughts,' the young dog told himself. The face of Sandy flashed into his mind, the female Veterinarian who had helped save his life after his mother had died precipitously giving birth. Next came Annie, her kind nurturing mother who had adopted Geo as a puppy from a pet shop in Caves Beach. He wondered how her husband Glen, The Prof and his friend Gavin were doing; researchers whose animanaut program had involved launching animals into space in pursuit of new worlds. It was how Geo and the rats had discovered

Luna Tribus. Their arrival had triggered a cascade of events that were still playing out.

His calming reverie was broken by a cacophony of shrill cries and aggressive growls. GJ's fur stood tall. On high alert, he crouched low to the ground, with his heart racing, ready to pounce. Kalan and Viz moved closer, flanking him on either side. The magician was ready to unleash a barrage of spells and Kalan, blows from the pointy ended, thick tree branch he was holding like a vampire slayer.

'We're almost at the entrance of the secret tunnel I told you about,' Kalan shared.

'The exit point of the escape route from your sleeping chamber?' GJ checked.

'Exactly. Master Sabi won't have predicted that the least safe location for him in my palace, is in my bed!' Kalan insisted loudly, his anger overwhelming his sensibility.

'Shh!' Viz warned him.

The howling intensified. The distance between the trees grew wider making them feel more exposed. The unpleasant sound of hissing, squealing, fighting cats continued to bombard their ears.

'We have to hope that the innate arrogance of Master Sabi has rendered him sloppy with his security,' said GJ.

'Old school, bricks and mortar hidden chambers and passageways could easily be overlooked by a sophisticated magician. Hopefully it hasn't occurred to him to specifically search the palace and its grounds for such architectural gems,' Kalan responded.

'You may be right, as magic is everything to him,' said Viz.

'I'm worried about his poisonous feline devotees. One bite and we're dead!' GJ reminded them.

'I can now manage the effects of their toxic saliva,' Viz reassured him.

'I'd have preferred a vaccination,' Kalan complained.

'What is that?' GJ enquired.

'A needle to prevent a disease. They're big on it on Earth and...'

Viz interrupted, saying, 'hush! The fiendish cats are gathering momentum! I am hearing more with each step we take!'

'Let's not overread what that could mean. The explanation is probably as simple as the fact that we're getting close to your castle, where we assume they are residing,' GJ observed, attempting to reassure himself, as much as them.

'Your optimism is precious,' Viz murmured, unconvinced.

'I'd go as far as suggesting they'd have ambushed us already, if they knew we were here. I don't think they can smell us,' said GJ.

'Perhaps you're right. My pheromone concealing spell must be working.'

Appalled by the idea of his beloved palace being infested by countless cats, Kalan said, 'the vision of them breeding, fighting and marking inside my home is almost too much to bear! It's making me angry.'

'Time to take charge, boss! Find us a way in, so we can remove every last one of those stinkers, together,' GJ urged, mustering his courage.

'We can do this! Follow me and no more talking, until I tell you it's safe,' said the distressed king. They set off at a cautious, snail like pace.

'Our game is up! I saw something move in the shadows!' GJ reported, struggling to suppress a round of barking. A quick succession of blood-curdling screams erupted from a frenzied attacker, as the cat launched itself like a missile, aiming directly for Kalan's neck. With lightning-fast reflexes, GJ intercepted it, rising up to meet the foe, midair, before wrestling with it on the ground. The dog ultimately prevailed, immobilising his opponent by clamping one of his front paws firmly and precisely across its windpipe.

The humanoids stood back watching the asphyxiating assassin desperately struggle to pull free. Copious, frothy saliva poured from its contorted mouth as it perished.

'You can pull back now,' Viz told GJ, after checking it was dead.

'Yuck!' the dog complained, releasing his grip and attempting to remove a tuft of grey fur that had become rammed under his nails. He spat it out.

'That was a close call! Thank you, GJ,' said Kalan, his voice still quivering from the burst of adrenaline the attack had triggered.

'I was wrong. They *are* on to us. We should walk faster,' GJ suggested, again fighting his fear.

'Running would be better!' cried Viz, sensing a wave of cats were fast approaching.

As fast as their legs would carry them, Kalan led them out of the forest and across an open field. Long blades of untended grass offered minimal concealment. Under the awning of a double storey, circular building, they paused to catch their breath. In its base was an arched doorway protected by a wrought iron grille, fashioned from a series of parallel poles; each top was twisted into a convoluted spiral. Individual letters, in a swirling font, had been affixed in a vertical line to the adjacent wall, spelling the word 'Menagerie'.

'What is this place?' GJ enquired, as soon as he had stopped panting, sufficiently to speak.

'A contentious issue between us. We'll explain later,' said Kalan, staring at Viz. Oblivious to the comment, the magician was intently focused, scanning the area around them. His staff was pointed outwards ready to defend them.

'Hurry!' he told his brother who was reaching up on tip toes, and extending his hand towards the 'M' in the sign on the wall. Kalan's fingers reached knowingly behind the metallic letter and an ornate key fell into his palm. An overgrown stone path wound around the building to an unassuming wire-framed door, where he placed the key into the barrel of a rusty lock. With a 'click' they had access.

Kalan went inside first. The empty animal enclosure contained a tidy stack of folded blankets. He pushed them aside, revealing a cleverly concealed, sliding wooden trapdoor which he opened, revealing an entrance to a space, barely wide enough to accommodate a humanoid. The king lowered himself into the hidden chamber where he flicked a light switch, causing two lines of dim, dust covered, incandescent bulbs to illuminate a passageway. GJ athletically jumped into the opening, landing on the stone floor and skidding to a stop. Viz followed, before reaching up and pulling the hatch back into place.

No words were exchanged as they moved deeper underground. After a short distance, the path turned sharply to their right, prior to abruptly stopping at the base of a narrow, metal, spiral staircase. GJ stared up at a single thread of light bulbs that continued vertically, encircling a support pole.

'It wraps around the inside of one of the central spires of the castle. We need to travel to the top. The treads are narrow, especially as the helix tightens, so be mindful of where you place your feet,' Kalan instructed. GJ went first, his agility and fitness putting the brothers to shame. Round and round, up and up, they went. Such was the eerie absence of sound, that GJ's heavy panting seemed booming to those following him. It was a relief when the staircase opened out onto a broad landing, enabling the three infiltrators to transiently rest together on the floor.

Kalan eventually stood up. He placed a warning finger across his lips before moving towards a wall where he withdrew something concealed in a crevice between bricks. The telescoped spy device was cleverly positioned, offering a wide-angle view of the room beyond. Kalan extended it a short distance before rotating the eyepiece in order to provide a clearer image.

On the bed, where he had slumbered carefree so many moon rotations ago, someone appeared to be sleeping. Kalan increased the magnification in order to study the individual wrapped up in his soft grey linens. Their head was supported on the feathery pillow he had often dreamed about whilst trapped on Earth. He focused on their face. It was Master Sabi.

Overwhelmed with a fit of rage, he threw his weight against the barrier between them. The segment sprang forwards, allowing him to ambush his nemesis. The others burst in behind him, too slow to stop the unscripted assault. When GJ reached his side, Kalan had already picked up a stray extra pillow, applied it over his victim's face and was trying to smother him.

'Don't kill him yet! We need information!' commanded Viz, trying to stop the suffocation.

'Remember the plan! We're here to capture him alive!' GJ urged.

Kalan scowled and reluctantly released his captive. He stepped back and observed the plethoric face of the shocked, now awake magician who was coughing and spluttering. Viz and GJ, completely consumed by stopping their friend's fervent attack, failed to notice they had company. More than a dozen, seething, hissing, skinny, hairless, green-eyed cats encircled them.

'Get them!' one of them commanded, unleashing a simultaneous assault on the intruders.

The humanoids, back-to-back, defended themselves, swatting the creatures aside with powerful slaps from their tightly clenched fists. GJ attempted to follow suit. Being smaller in size, he was far less effective. Shrewdly recognising the weakest of their targets, the feline attack intensified on GJ. The fearless canine thrashed around on the ground, flinging them off his back, desperately trying to avoid being bitten by razor-sharp, pointy teeth.

Naked, Master Sabi stood up, revealing his bony frame, covered with a layer of flabby muscle and saggy skin. He grinned sardonically, enjoying the chaos as he donned one of Kalan's ruby robes retrieved from the back of a nearby chair.

'Let loose, my obedient beauties! Take them down! Pin them to the floor! Have your fun, only remember that *I* need *them* alive!'

GJ was starting to tire. He knew he was outnumbered and a change of tactic would be needed if he was to survive. With renewed energy and an intensely ferocious growl, he unexpectedly rolled towards the nearest wall, crushing at least one attacker and throwing three more off his back. He lunged at Master Sabi, wiping the smile off his overconfident face. The wiry figure fell onto the floor, winded, as he felt the impact of the adult sized Chocolate Labrador on his torso.

'Take that, you fiend!' GJ proclaimed, now resting with his full weight across his ribs and observing the unpleasant effect it was having. Master Sabi looked pale and helpless. He was gasping like a guppy out of water.

'Never mess with a Chocolate Labrador!' Kalan exclaimed.

GJ looked up, hoping his friends were holding their own. The cats had retreated towards the doorway. They were now otherwise occupied, frozen in their tracks, trembling and staring at a newly arrived player; a creature with an enormous head and thick woolly mane.

‘Come here now!’ the lion commanded. His deep authoritative voice echoed throughout the room. Obediently the cats skulked over. They sat down in a row before him and started rubbing and licking the various wounds they had received during the altercation.

‘Menagerie! Thank you!’ gushed the fast-recovering Kalan.

‘My king,’ he acknowledged, with a respectful bow of his head. Throwing formality to the wind, Kalan threw his arms around his neck, and held him like a child would their teddy bear. GJ watched on, feeling relief and astonishment in equal parts.

‘Hello, old friend,’ said Viz, politely, now smiling. Menagerie nodded politely.

‘What will you have me do with the miserable intruder who has been sleeping in your bed?’

‘I’ve got him under control,’ said GJ, as their eyes met. The dog was stunned momentarily, unable to blink.

‘Who are you?’

‘I’m GJ, the Earth Explorer and more recently explorer of other worlds,’ he replied, before returning to his work, systematically licking his captive all over, unleashing his tongue in between flying insults such as, ‘take that you varmint! That’s for keeping dogs from kipping on their master’s bed! That’s for stopping the kibble treats. That’s for using those poor bats to do your dirty work!’

Master Sabi, pinned to the carpet on his back, struggled and screamed, writhed and eventually begged for mercy. Kalan scratched his chin and said, ‘why is he so paralysed?’

'Clearly, you've never been "almost" licked to death,' Menagerie stated, with a deadpan expression. Kalan remained perplexed. 'Let me spell it out for you. The repeated merciless tongue-lashings of an expert animal licker on humanoid skin are impossible to tolerate for long. It's like being tickled to some extent. Whilst it might be pleasant in small doses, it becomes unbearable if protracted, particularly on sensitive areas of skin.'

'How do you know that?' Kalan enquired.

'I've made logical conclusions based on the intense thoughts and feelings I'm absorbing from Master Sabi.'

Viz, quick to take advantage of the moment, reached into his backpack and brought out a set of metallic rings, similar to the handcuffs that police on Earth would use to apprehend a criminal.

'This is what we came here to do,' he stated, kneeling next to GJ and snapping cold bands around each of the now exhausted magician's wrists.

'We thought it fitting that someone who has wreaked such atrocity on Earth should be brought to justice using a process similar to what would happen there,' Kalan told the lion.

'You can get off him now,' Viz told GJ. Master Sabi's eyes now stared straight ahead vacantly, confirming he was in a trance. The dog retreated, stretched and shook his fur, relieved the encounter was over.

'Does anyone have any mouthwash? I'm a bit over tasting these disgusting vermin,' he remarked dramatically, to no one in particular.

'Your restraints are very effective, brother. I imagine the police on Earth would appreciate your upgrade,' Kalan commented.

'What's so remarkable about them?' Menagerie enquired.

'I've applied a special coating to the inner lining of each cuff. As soon as there is skin contact, the powerful chemical compound is released, turning the wearer into a subdued, obedient…kitten.'

'Talking about kittens; what are we going to do with these horrible feline menaces cowering over there in the corner?' GJ requested.

Menagerie looked worried.

'You're not going to hurt them, are you? As much as they have disgraced themselves at a high level, I assure you they mean well.' The whimpering cats pleaded with their eyes at the lion, appearing vulnerable.

'You were always such a giant soft touch,' Kalan noted, shaking his head, amused.

'You raised me that way, my king.'

GJ raised his left eyebrow questioningly and said, 'how exactly do you know each other?'

'On one of our trips into the White Corridor, Viz and I found an abandoned, starving lion cub snared and injured, lying within a trap. He was trembling. We didn't know what to do.'

'It was in the early days of our reckless adventures to other worlds. He was so tiny and we were his only hope of surviving,' added Viz.

'Where exactly did you find him?' GJ pressed.

'On a world we never came to know the name of. We didn't venture very far from the wormhole and were never able to find it again,' Viz explained.

'Viz wanted to take him but knew I was against such interventions. Then in that moment, as we were leaving, I looked over my shoulder and couldn't leave him to die. Together we released him from the trap, wrapped him in my coat and brought him back here,' said Kalan.

'Then why did you fall out over Viz relocating the chimpanzees to Periculosis? Geo told me about it and we never understood what your issue was. It seemed like a giant double standard,' remarked GJ.

'That's exactly what it was,' said Kalan, looking and feeling guilty. He turned to Viz. 'I'm truly sorry, brother. I should have apologised before now. My pride has cost us precious years of knowing each other.'

'It's good of you to finally say it. On reflection, it was probably for the best that we stopped travelling; young fools that we were.' The siblings embraced, prompting the cats to respond with a string of sarcastic comments, belittling their sentiment. The lion turned and scowled at them. They ignored him initially until a deep growl caused them to stop.

'Why did you call him "Menagerie"?' asked GJ.

'That story will have to wait. It's related to the history of human animal keeping on Earth. We need to stay focused,' stated Kalan, noticing that one of the cats had stood up and was attempting to skulk away.

'Back here, now!' Menagerie commanded, causing the cat to obey.

'You seem to have quite a connection with this sorry lot, my friend. What can you tell us about them?' enquired Kalan.

'I've gotten to know some of them since they were brought here by that nasty invader.' He pointed to the motionless Master Sabi. 'This sorry lot are well down the pecking order. They're not so bright and simply follow orders. I do trust them somewhat, as they've always concealed me from their superiors. I do admit it's most likely a transactional allegiance at best.'

'How have you helped them?' Viz checked.

'The replicator device Kalan gave me is still working well. I've shared my pellets with them, as well as my enclosure. It's positively luxurious compared to where that brute of a magician expects them to reside. He relocated them from the hot planet of Ember to the bitterly cold cellars, devoid of blankets and with rationed food.'

'Surely Master Sabi knows of your existence?' queried Viz.

'If he does, he's never acted on it.'

'Perhaps he's liked keeping you on your toes and treating you as his servant, babysitting?' GJ suggested to the lion.

'That may be giving him too much credit. He's devoid of kindness,' said Viz, fleetingly remembering the torture he endured.

Triggered by sudden screaming and hissing outside the door, the cats in the room jumped up and started squealing. Their backs were arched and their eyes grew wide. The source of the outburst entered the room, causing the subservient felines to scramble to reposition themselves into a row, poised, standing upright on their back legs, like soldiers awaiting instructions.

With a confident stride, an alarmingly skinny, hairless, immaculately groomed, pale pink-coated, Sphynx cat slinked into the bedchamber. Her triangular face and disproportionately large pointed ears were striking.

'I see we have guests my darlings,' she acknowledged with a lowering of long lashes over penetrating, electric blue eyes. She strutted around the room imperiously, using the act to study her enemies. She weaved between them, provocatively rubbing her silken integument on their stationary lower limbs. She stopped at the feet of Menagerie and pouted her lips before looking up at him innocently and saying, 'I assume you are the angel; the benevolent protector who I always thought was merely a fictitious superhero of the needy dreamers among my ranks? The fact that you are real, handsome too, is an unexpected surprise,' she gushed, coyly.

Totally unfazed, the lion dropped down on the floor in an attempt to bring his gaze more in line with her own. He stared piercingly into her eyes for the longest time. Strangely, there was no blinking from either party.

'I hope this isn't going to be a "love at first sight" scenario? Surely, he can recognise how totally distasteful her tacky advances are? It's revolting to watch,' GJ whispered to Kalan.

'It's reminding me a bit of when you met Maria,' he teased. The dog reflected on how he had fallen fast for the exuberant female Golden

Labrador Retriever he had left on Earth. She had won his heart on their adventures in Cornwall. Menagerie, his penetrating stare still unbroken with the cat, interrupted their exchange.

'I can hear you two over there. Do not concern yourself. I am no fool.'

'I'd never think that of you,' replied Kalan. After a short delay he added, 'I know what you're doing. What is the verdict?'

Viz, who had been closely observing the unexpected interaction was uncommonly perplexed.

'Menagerie's gift is to be able to literally visualise the essence of any living creature. When he goes deeper, he can read their thoughts and intentions. He's been analysing this manipulative upstart and based on his distasteful expression, I don't think she's going to be his future life partner,' Kalan whispered.

'Her name is Sateen. Her heart is pure evil. She means to harm us. She is buying time with her ridiculous coquettish play until the rest of her litter and their offspring arrive. The beasts that are coming are currently being loaded with extra poison that will flow through their bites, in doses rapidly lethal to humanoids and I suspect to any creature not of their kind. As you thought GJ, even the most docile cats I have nurtured have been using me to their own ends; laughing behind my back. I knew it in my heart but didn't want to believe it. They've taken advantage of my loneliness. Sateen thinks she can take advantage of my warmheartedness and coerce me into turning against you. So ready yourselves to fight, as we have company fast approaching and I can't hold her much longer.'

'Prepare to revert to our plan!' Viz warned. In a flash, he withdrew two identical, tall thin bottles from his bag, each in the shape of a tree. He removed their caps, revealing spray nozzles, and handed one to Kalan. As they were readying their weapons, one of the cats involved in the initial fight, unexpectedly lurched forward, viciously directing her fangs at the pulsating artery in the neck of the vulnerable lion, who remained dazed after his intense encounter.

GJ pounced forward, springing into the air and intercepting the attacker. The nasty cat drew its last gasping breath shortly after he landed heavily on top of it, instantaneously crushing its skull. Shocked, Menagerie spun around. He examined the female and gently closed her eyes. His tears started to flow. She was from the clowder he had been sheltering.

'This isn't the moment to feel sad. Get angry friend! We're under attack!' GJ cried, jolting him from his emotional state.

As predicted, the room filled fast with a new wave of blood thirsty felines out for their blood.

'Go for the weak brown one first!' another of Menagerie's former associates shouted. GJ spun around and transiently felt overwhelmed, recognising that they were seriously outnumbered. The menacing figures started hurling themselves at him. Viz and Kalan extended their arms and started pumping the bottles, aerosolising their contents until a pink cloud gripped the air.

'I'm all out! I hope this works or we're doomed!' cried Kalan.

'Out of what?' Menagerie enquired, after a short coughing fit.

'Viz's special potion,' Kalan replied.

'Is everyone alright?' Viz checked. Fortunately, no one had been bitten.

'You are a legend!' GJ told him. As their vision was restored, they could see tiny, squirming kittens, the size of baby mice, strewn around the room. They started meowing helplessly.

'How adorable!' Menagerie declared.

'Don't fall for their act again,' GJ warned.

The lion padded over to him and bowed formally in front of the dog.

'From this moment, I am your humble servant. I pledge that my life is now yours, for you have selflessly saved me, oh wise one. I will protect you until either of us perishes. What did you say your name was?'

'I'm GJ. What you're promising is a bit over the top,' he replied, feeling embarrassed. Menagerie's earnest words continued to flow.

'I will never fail to listen to your counsel again. Despite my abilities, I missed the true intentions of those I nurtured. It is an empty moment when you realise that your friendships have not been real. I have been played.'

'Kindness is not a crime,' Viz reassured the despairing lion.

'I share your disappointment that individuals can be duplicitous,' said GJ.

'You have known such a character?'

'Yes.' His thoughts turned to Kalan's grandson, Eff. Whilst letting him believe he was acting for good, the young humanoid had played a complex game, with a different hand, using a different face for his nasty aunts, Master Sabi, Big Timmy, the Inflecto based resistance led by Aquilegia and Queen Christina, his parents and their allies. He sighed. 'I once assumed that everyone was authentic, sharing their thoughts, with actions consistently based on good values.'

'I feel you have much to teach me. I will never leave your side,' Menagerie affirmed.

'About this pledge thing…I don't think it's necessary. Saving you was nothing more than what my father, Geo, would have done,' GJ stated, thinking about the senior dog and hoping he was safe.

Menagerie dropped down, his eyes like saucers, and replied, 'are you talking about the great monster Geo who stirs fear in the hearts of cats?'

'Probably!' replied GJ, proudly.

Kalan and Viz burst out laughing.

'We should leave before there are more menaces to contend with,' Menagerie warned.

'I had hoped reclaiming my kingdom would feel more victorious,' Kalan told Viz, as they surveyed the catastrophic destruction of what had previously been a majestic place of unparalleled grandeur across Luna Tribus.

'At least we have achieved our first goal. We have Master Sabi. Our intelligence was good. We can rebuild,' Viz replied. His sense of relief was profound.

They inspected each room. No space was spared from acts of vandalism. The smell of urine and faeces, embedded in the slashed rugs and soft furnishings was disgusting.

'The blatant disrespect for our property is overwhelming,' noted Viz.

'Destruction of this magnitude reflects their deranged minds,' stated GJ.

'It wasn't only the cats who were deranged,' Menagerie reported.

'Really?' Viz checked.

'Master Sabi was behind a great deal of the damage. I could hear his rantings late at night as he smashed the crockery or took aim at furniture, mirrors or whatever else was in the room he fancied. He acted out his bitter jealously regarding the intellect, benevolence and determination your family possesses.'

Lost in his own thoughts, Kalan didn't respond.

'You seem troubled my king,' Menagerie noted.

'This all feels wrong. Why would this power-hungry, sophisticated magician be content to reside with such distasteful, selfish creatures in this filth? I'm also struggling to believe that we apprehended him so easily.'

'What do you think was going on here, strategically?' GJ asked the lion.

Fortunately, Menagerie's kindness had been misinterpreted as weakness. As a result, he had been privy to more than a trivial amount of information from conversations, overheard between his feline companions. It seemed that Master Sabi had devised several parallel, linked assignments, using more dominant cats like Sateen as his agents. Groups of them had been sent away on transporters to pursue secret agendas in Rectangulum City, on Earth and possibly other worlds.

'We must leave here for now, secure our prisoner and update the others,' GJ insisted. No one argued.

They headed back to their transporter. It remained hidden in thick grass on the other side of the dense overgrown forest that surrounded the palace wall. Kalan carried a basket filled with the wriggling kittens, destined for a protracted stay in the dungeon of the praeceptorum in Rectangulum City. Viz carried the still motionless Master Sabi, positioned over one shoulder like a loaded sack. It was a relief when he could be rested, flat on his back in the cargo hold.

'I've never flown before,' Menagerie shared, feeling a flutter of excitement.

'You're going to love it!' the dog insisted. Under GJ's tutorage the lion awkwardly wrapped a seat restraint around his ample torso. Viz took the controls and they ascended vertically.

The moons were reflecting vibrant shades of pure colour, allowing the full extent of the damage to be appreciated. Despite the grounds being in tatters, the walls and turrets of the now abandoned castle were intact.

'At least the main structures are still standing,' GJ remarked.

'Master Sabi did have the decency to bury the citizens he murdered,' said Menagerie,' pointing out the mass grave below. He had watched it be prepared, to dispose of the dead humanoids who had been unable to defend themselves against the merciless venomous cats.

Kalan placed a clenched fist upon his chest, peered out of the window and said, 'I vow that when I next return, it will be to reinstate the glory that is Kaleido.' As if the lands were a living entity he added, 'I'm sorry for what I have allowed to happen to you. Please forgive your unworthy king.'

GJ nuzzled close to his leg and rubbed his wet nose against his still tense hand.

'It's not all your fault, nor is it your quest alone to make things right. Enjoy this rare moment of victory, as for once we are returning to those we care for with good news.'

Kalan rubbed the ears of the warm-hearted dog, then ran his hands down his silky back. He felt better with each stroke.

'Goodbye for now,' said Viz as they zoomed upwards then forwards, hurtling towards the three slowly turning moons. With every passing lacuna they were now unexpectedly infusing the atmosphere with an ominous, deepening purple hue.

'It shouldn't be getting dark again so soon,' Kalan remarked to his brother.

Long before they approached Rectangulum City, Menagerie had sensed that something was dreadfully wrong. They descended towards the private landing platform of the praeceptorum. It was situated close to the central palace courtyard, surrounded by resplendent white and gold towers of varying heights. As they touched down, out his window Kalan spotted Tobias waiting for them. The monks humanoid face was ashen.

Chapter 2
RECTANGULUM CITY

Kalan remained silent as Viz concentrated on landing the transporter. They hovered close to the ground as he manoeuvred it sideways, before dropping down midway between a set of green flashing lights that designated the perimeter of the parking bay.

GJ pressed his face against his window.

'Tobias is out there with Aquilegia. It's very odd not to have anyone else waiting to receive us,' he told Menagerie. During the journey he had briefed his new companion on who the key players were in their team.

'Something is dreadfully wrong. It is protocol for a squadron of guards to meet every arrival to this landing zone,' Viz explained.

The hatch had barely opened when GJ leapt out, ran forward and enthusiastically greeted Tobias. He jumped up and placed both front paws onto his broad shoulders and licked his face.

'I see you're still not revealing your true self?' he whispered. The forehead of the troubled canine-hybrid monk was deeply furrowed.

'All in good time, Geo Junior. Grave events have unfolded here that do not give me hope that such a juncture is nearing.' The dog retreated and faced Aquilegia, the Officialis of Inflecto.

'My lady,' GJ nodded, trying to stay calm. He failed. Overcome with happiness at being reunited with his friends, the rambunctious young dog jumped up again, almost knocking the genteel lady over.

'Down boy!' she insisted. He dropped and sat at her feet.

'Oopsy! It's so exciting being back here with you. There's so much to tell.'

'Developments here have left little to be happy about,' she stated, as her eyes darted around, scanning the vicinity in a paranoid fashion.

'We should come on board to speak. I suspect it is safer than out here. We don't know who to trust right now,' said Tobias. The pair followed GJ back onto the ship. The Malinois monk closed the hatch behind them. The dog introduced them to Menagerie.

'Something terrible has clearly taken place. What is it?' requested Kalan.

'We were out together, away from the palace for a short period working with trusted contacts on completing the prison, when the attack happened,' Aquilegia explained.

'When we returned, we found them,' Tobias continued. He gulped.

'Who? What?' Kalan urged, imagining the worst.

'Christina, Ellie, Ro, Izzie and some of their attendants have been affected,' said Aquilegia.

'We presume that they were about to share a meal and must have been ambushed,' Tobias advised.

'Are they dead?' GJ blurted. Kalan held his breath.

'No. They appear to be victims of a dark curse. Whilst we found them first, we went on to find that the affliction involves everyone inside the palace walls,' Tobias replied.

'What is the nature of this curse?' Viz requested.

A loud cackle and the sound of hands clapping in thunderous applause interrupted their discourse. A voice from the cargo bay started jeering.

'I am so clever and you are all so frightfully moronic! A good many of those you know and love have entered a fragile stasis. I am proud to announce that I have turned them into sand sculptures.'

'It's true,' Tobias confirmed. Aquilegia recognised the voice and said, 'I see that you have been successful in capturing the coward behind this heinous development?'

'Yes, Master Sabi is on board, along with dozens of his mindless meowing minions,' GJ replied.

'You nitwits are simply too much!' Master Sabi chortled to himself.

Tobias pulled back the divider that separated them from their prisoner. The cuffed figure was now wide awake. An arrogant smirk was plastered across his face.

'You were so convinced that your pathetic plan to capture me would work, that you never stopped to think it might be *my* plan to use your feeble efforts for my own ends. It was obvious that Kalan would ultimately try to reclaim his kingdom and Viz was always against me. You fell into my hands when you put into play your ill-conceived idea to go to Kaleido and try to dispose of me. When news of it reached my ears from trusted informants in your palace, I was nothing short of thrilled.'

'What have we done?' said Kalan, holding his head in his hands.

'With you out of the picture, those remaining in Rectangulum City dropped the ball by allowing security to slip. Their focus prematurely shifted from protecting the palace towards awaiting your triumphant return. Defences were down, leaving this place completely vulnerable. As soon as you set down on Kaleido, one of my other teams came here and delivered my most complex potion ever brewed. They dosed your family, friends and loyal citizens.' He shifted his gaze to Tobias and Aquilegia and said, 'it's such a shame they missed the two of you; meddlesome supporters that you are.'

Kalan looked stricken. Tobias locked eyes with Master Sabi.

'We meet at last, nasty magician. Did you anticipate that by the time you arrived here we would have prepared a temporary prison for you?'

Master Sabi laughed, leaned forwards and said, 'I cannot be restrained. Not by you monk, not by anyone. I am the most powerful magician in existence!'

'The only accolade I'm awarding you right now is the title of biggest ego!' said Aquilegia, bravely. He glared at her.

'Before we end his boastful babbling, do you want to see if we can coax him into telling us more about what he's done and why?' Tobias asked Viz, loud enough for their captive to hear.

'He would have tried to escape already if he wasn't desperate to regale us with details of what his nasty mind has designed to hurt us,' Viz replied.

Master Sabi laughed again, more malevolently.

'Arrogant fools! You think you know me, yet you have no idea what I'm truly capable of! You think you're better than me and that will be your failing.' He paused and childishly stared at the ceiling before saying, 'I don't wish to say anything else at this time.'

'Excellent. It means we can stop listening to your whining trap express your inferiority complex,' said Tobias, with a gruff tone.

'On your feet monster!' GJ instructed, moving closer.

'I don't wish to walk at this stage either. Bring forth a carriage, animal,' he replied, sneering.

'You're talking again, oh self-entitled fly in the ointment. Hush!' Tobias scolded, waggling a finger side to side and tutting.

'You'll do as GJ told you. Get up now!' Menagerie roared, bursting forth, stopping close to the face of the prisoner, causing him to jump. 'Now who are you calling an animal?'

'You're nothing more than a pathetic baby! Like you'd ever hurt anyone? You're not so bright either. Those cats of mine played you like a fiddle.'

'How dare you insult my friend!' GJ reacted. With gnashing teeth he lunged at Master Sabi, pushing him from his sitting position, back onto the ground. He resumed licking his neck mercilessly. Unexpectedly, this time, the magician fought back, rising to his feet and forcefully throwing the dog backwards. Luckily his fall was broken by Menagerie.

'Get off me! Enough of that disgusting slobber! Having to submit to you once, was quite enough!'

'What do you mean?' cried GJ, now back on his feet.

'You genuinely believed that you could immobilise someone of my calibre by merely licking them? You are the lamest of the lame; almost not even worth expending my enormous brainpower on.' He barely drew a breath before continuing his insults. 'I'm really disappointed in you Viz. Surely after your exposure to my talent, you shouldn't have concluded that a lightweight handcuff potion was going to paralyse me? Kalan, how could you, the magnanimous king, have missed that I was such a phenomenal actor?' Before he could hurl more ridicule, Tobias came forward swiftly and with one well-formed punch planted squarely against his jaw, knocked him to the floor, unconscious.

'Now that's my brand of magic, you irritating little man!' He turned to Aquilegia and said, 'you didn't warn me he was so annoying.' She smiled. The monk picked him up. 'He's so dreadfully scrawny. I imagined he'd be bigger. Let's get out of here.'

The group disembarked in single file. Aquilegia ran ahead. They came together again outside the entrance to the sculpture garden. She was holding a magenta robe in her arms.

'This is where the main attack occurred,' Tobias warned, as he lowered their captive onto a nearby bench. With Kalan's assistance Master Sabi was firmly wrapped in the beautiful robe. Aquilegia secured it with a matching ivory-coloured sash. She pulled a drawstring around the hood after ensuring it covered his head and eyes.

'Why have you placed such a devious enemy within such a lovely cloth?' Menagerie enquired.

'It's because we are classy,' said GJ, repeating what Ellie had stated, when it was being designed.

'It's not what it appears. Every thread of the fabric is infused with the most powerful disarming potions we could concoct. While the hood covers his face, deep sleep is induced. While his body is covered, his limbs are paralysed,' Viz explained.

'The weavers and tailors finished making the robe shortly after your departure. Fortunately for us, several magicians loyal to Ellie were spared,' Tobias reported.

'Is the definitive prison ready?' Kalan checked.

'It is,' Aquilegia confirmed. He sighed in relief.

GJ, desperate for a hurry up, ran into the garden in search of a suction system to relieve his waste. Menagerie followed.

'The fountains are incredible. They look like golden trees!' He stared at his feet then added, 'the gardens of Kaleido were once even nicer as the plants were alive.' As GJ emptied his bladder, the lion admired pots of delicate, artificial flowers.

The dog's attention was drawn to a snowy white, marble table a short distance away. He padded towards it and spotted a sculpture of two humanoids sitting on a bench seat. One was leaning in towards the other. Their fingers were intertwined.

‘It’s Ellie and Ro!’ barked GJ. Aquilegia had followed and was soon at their side.

‘Stay back! They are in a precarious state.’

‘What were they doing when they were frozen?’ asked Menagerie.

‘They were ambushed in a private moment. Note that their lips are almost touching. They are trapped in the intimacy of a promised kiss. We are looking at true love,’ she uttered. Her voice broke off in distress. Menagerie nodded and said, ‘it’s the most poignant piece of art I’ve ever seen and you know how extraordinary your sister’s collection was, back on Kaleido.’

‘Was?’ Aquilegia checked.

‘I’m sorry to have to tell you that it has been vandalised,’ the lion shared.

‘They are not artworks! They are real people. They are *my* people!’ GJ exclaimed. He looked around for Kalan, desperate to share his distress with him. Nearby, he found the Kaleidan lost in his own thoughts. Menagerie sensed his despair as he stood next to another figure. It was Christina. He realised that they had been separated for longer than they had ever been together and were now, again parted.

‘I never told you enough that I loved you. I know we never experienced fireworks and rainbows, yet our feelings were true. Now what have they done to you?’ said Kalan. He studied her surfaces, careful not to get too close, fearful of displacing the grains of sand.

His eyes moved to a nearby sculpture. Planted mid step at her side was his confident and kind granddaughter, Izzie. She was as warm as

Eff had seemed cold. Tobias moved to his side and placed a comforting hand firmly on his shoulder.

'I suggest you examine them carefully, then meet us back in the foyer,' instructed Aquilegia, before retreating with Tobias to watch over Master Sabi.

When they came together, Viz said, 'it is exactly as he boasted. They have been turned into sand sculptures.'

Tobias lifted Master Sabi up again and beckoned for the others to follow him.

'There's something else you need to see.'

They followed him inside the palace, along a series of wide corridors that revealed the scope of the affliction. Many more figures, each trapped in moments of life's usual activities, were sand sculptures in various stages of drying out. Tobias led them outside through the public entrance into a forum where events were commonly held. He pointed to a pile of rubble in front of an entry gate.

GJ ran towards it. He spotted a less dissolved, gritty object within the sandy mound. Recognising it as a foot, a choking sound escaped his throat.

'This is our fault. When we returned, Aquilegia and I walked in through this doorway. This subject must have been on their way out when the curse struck,' Tobias confessed, staring at the disintegrated body. It was impossible to know their identity.

'The body broke into pieces on impact and is continuing to disintegrate. The fragments are constantly getting smaller; clumps are becoming grains; grains are dissolving into dust. I fear that eventually there will be no evidence that they ever existed,' warned Aquilegia.

'As soon as a crack appears, the process of disintegration starts to accelerate,' explained Tobias. He showed them the figure of a messenger a few metres away. Their forearm had a linear fissure that was trickling sand. The line had spread to the hand which had already fallen off. 'Only the fingers were missing when we were last here, not long before you returned.'

'Should we spray them with water to make the sand stickier?' suggested GJ.

'We can't risk washing them away,' said Aquilegia.

'This is worse than I thought, as it isn't a stable curse,' Viz commented.

'All it would take is an intruder to mess around in here and they'd be gone forever. It would be like a toddler stepping on sandcastles at the beach,' GJ shared. Then came much sniffing as he examined the piles of sand. 'How can this be? This is familiar. I'd bet my life that it's sand from Caves Beach!'

'That's what Tobias thought,' Aquilegia replied.

The monk leaned down next to GJ and said, 'I can feel a cross-examination coming on! Care to join me?'

'Time is of the essence. Let's take him to the throne room,' Viz suggested.

Fighting waves of anger, Kalan acknowledged that in his heightened state of emotion he could not be trusted to be involved. He retreated to Ellie's concealed observation area high above, where he waited with Aquilegia and Menagerie.

Tobias laid their prisoner on the cold ceramic floor in front of the dais. Viz pulled back the hood, allowing their captive to stir. After a few breaths he started to come round. His darting eyes took in his surrounds. A transient look of horror crossed his wrinkled face as he realised his limbs were paralysed. A look of recognition passed over his face.

'My dear Viz. The Quadfect potion is not very original, yet I have to agree it is effective. Perhaps you are smarter than you seem?'

'Are you sure that's all we used?'

'We?' he checked, frowning.

'Not all who claim allegiance are truly loyal. There comes a time when everyone must choose a side. Ellie and I have had some excellent help from those you once called your friends. In answer to your question. The Quadfect potion was one of the ingredients.'

He ignored the response and said, 'I'm assuming you've been reunited with your loved ones whilst I've been taking a restful nap? Where is dear Kalan? It would make me very happy to ask him what he thinks of my creations. I know how much his family love their fine art. I enjoyed beheading the sculptures his wife collected in their private garden.'

'Art appreciation is the purview of the educated,' said Viz, refusing to be baited.

Tobias was in no mood for nonsense.

'Let's cut to the chase. What do we need to do to reverse your devilish deed?'

'Why should I tell you anything? I can think of nothing better than watching you ooze helplessness. Besides, what makes you think it has a cure?'

'That's not your style old man,' Viz chipped in.

The two magicians battled verbally back and forth for the longest time, with Viz becoming no clearer in his understanding of what Master Sabi's end game was.

GJ had remained an observer. Now more frustrated than Tobias was, he said to Viz, 'may I attempt to get him to spill the beans?'

'I do need a break,' he replied.

'I'm at risk of breaking his arms so he'll never practice magic again,' declared Tobias, glaring.

'Such brutishness; the *purview* of the uneducated. You are an unsophisticated animal,' Master Sabi goaded.

'Perhaps I am,' said Tobias, flashing his teeth.

Before Master Sabi could comment, GJ started pawing and licking his face. In between giant wet licks he said, 'let's take a break from the questions so I can give you a decent grooming. You are rather stinky. Lying about like this, wrapped in that warm robe means you are generating quite a nasty stench. Let's stay on top of it. Impeccable hygiene is the *purview* of us animals.' The dog hoped he had used his new word correctly as his tongue darted up Master Sabi's flaring nostrils, then in and out of each of his hairy ear canals. 'You are so icky, so full of dust and grime. You are lucky I am here to help. You told me before that my tongue isn't a big deal for you, so let me continue. My father Geo taught me to always take pride in such activities.'

He lay down on Master Sabi's torso, adding to the discomfort being inflicted and to allow maximal direct access to his face.

'Get him off me! Pull him back! It's too much!'

GJ stopped nibbling his eyebrow. He turned his head and called out to Menagerie, requesting he join the interrogation. The lion bolted down the stairs and was soon at his side.

'Don't try to deceive us. My talented friend will know if any word that comes out of your speech hole is untrue.'

'How may I assist?' asked Menagerie.

'Change positions with me and stare into his eyes. Do what you did to that feline femme fatale. When I ask him questions, tell me if what he says is true.'

'I'm ready,' Menagerie reported, when he had locked onto his target.

'Ask him if he really finds my licking unbearable? We need to know if he's lying.' It transpired that he found lion breath as intolerably disgusting as GJ's mouthing, a revelation that Menagerie periodically used to great effect during the encounter. Unfortunately, they struggled to extract much information.

'He has the strongest mind I have ever encountered. His intentions are clearly malicious. It is frustrating that I am unable to see through the wall he has constructed. I'm sorry, it's very disappointing,' he lamented after the sleeping hood had been repositioned.

'It wasn't a waste. Don't underestimate what we have learned,' said Tobias.

Kalan and Aquilegia rejoined them.

'From what we've gleaned there is no way we could have avoided the attack,' noted Kalan. They were now aware of how the potion had been delivered. They had been incorrect in thinking it had been dispersed in the air. Julinda, sister of Sateen, had been sent to Rectangulum City with ampoules of the delayed onset potion, and successfully contaminated the water supply to the fountains.

The structures had been the pride and joy of the late Praeceptorum Mergen. He had constructed a water detoxification plant on his island, along with a pumping station and piping system that ensured fresh, drinkable water was available to those within the palace; a privilege exclusively for those in his court.

'Most importantly, you managed to extract the fact that there is an antidote,' said Aquilegia, relieved.

'He also seems to be acting alone. I had wondered if somehow, he had remained in cahoots with any, or all, of Eff, HM and the Ghosties,' stated GJ.

Menagerie roared. He leapt up and started sniffing.

'We have company!' he warned, with a deep growl.

'Of the putrid variety!' GJ clarified, after a frenzy of nose twitching.

Instinctively Tobias moved to protect their captive, locating himself at the side of the robed figure.

'Did I hear you talking about me?' came a smug voice. Slinking proudly across the room was another Sphynx cat.

'I am Julinda, the favourite of Master Sabi. Give him to me.'

GJ padded forward and defiantly said, 'he's having a power nap right now, sweetheart!'

'Don't be in a difficult mood, you dumb little doggy,' she goaded, still advancing. She surveyed the room, mentally marking off a list of those who were present. Confidently, she slinked away from GJ and stopped in front of a sand statue that he had not observed before.

'Oh goody! A new one! I see my work is continuing.'

All eyes turned to the figure. Tobias involuntary howled in distress. It was Aquilegia. She had been struck mid stride, her cape still billowing behind her. Tendrils of hair outlined her determined face.

'Has anyone else been thirsty in the last few days and been sipping from the fountain faucets? If so, you had best be finding an unoccupied surface to rest on,' the cat recommended.

'Tobias? Have you been drinking the water?' Kalan urgently enquired, looking worried. He shook his head and replied, 'I only consume what I can trust. Before he left, Octo, the Head of Octavia, presented me with my own replicator device so I never needed to drink liquid.'

'What a shame. What a fine addition you would have made to my collection,' Julinda reflected.

Unable to contain himself, Kalan lurched forward and grabbed her. His firm hands encircled her skinny neck prompting her to cough and splutter for breath. She was stronger than she appeared, courtesy of the potions her master had laced her with. As they wrestled on the ground, her glimmering necklace of gold became displaced. It was embedded with three gems, each the pure primary colours of the three moons of Luna Tribus. The cat threw herself onto the gems and swallowed them.

'Kalan! Get a grip! That's enough! We need her alive for more questioning,' Viz commanded.

'She's swallowed something. Make her spit them out,' Tobias insisted. As Kalan's fingers started to release Julinda from his iron grip, she cried in a husky voice, 'you're too late, impulsive king! The last of my potion supply is kicking in. In this concentrated form, I will perish in moments. I will tell you nothing!' True to her word, she precipitously dissolved into dust.

'Master Sabi really knows his magic! I don't know any potion that would do what we've witnessed, let alone an agent that makes a subject so loyal, they would die for its maker,' Viz commented.

'That trait may not have been entirely due to a potion. Cats can be very loyal. It's why they were such popular Earth pets,' Tobias informed him.

'The fact that Master Sabi can elicit such actions from his followers, yet use them without regard for their welfare, makes me think he's extremely powerful but he doesn't understand love,' GJ noted.

'Will that be to our advantage, wise one?' asked the lion.

'Without restraint, it will be our downfall,' Viz answered. He turned to his brother and said, 'look where your love of family has taken us? You lost control...again!'

Kalan, now recovered from the scuffle, was profoundly embarrassed. His eye caught the necklace, partially embedded in the dust.

'What do we have here?' he muttered, leaning down, picking it up then spreading it across his palm.

'Kalan! You're doing it again! Drop it at once!' Viz screamed. Shaken by the intensity of his brother's caution, he obeyed. 'You need to stop being so impulsive! It is classic for potions to be stored in body jewellery. Do you have a death wish?' As the item hit the hard floor, an object sprang from the chunky clasp.

'It's a scroll! It looks like a larger version of the ones we removed from Big's ear canals. On that occasion they were infused with a subduing potion, so we must take care,' GJ observed.

'Who's Big?' Menagerie enquired.

'Another friend we left on Earth. He's a Saint Bernard dog who was used to carry a message to us from here, to obtain our help.'

Viz crouched down and secured the scroll and necklace inside a leather pouch sourced from the pocket of his robe. He expertly avoided direct contact with any of the surfaces. He stood up and said, 'I swear Master Sabi wanted us to find it. I think it's time to pay a visit to his tower. We can avail ourselves of his resources to read what it says. Who would like to join me?'

‘Master Sabi boasted about keeping in his chamber a catalogue of every magical device and potion constituent in existence,’ Viz told Tobias, Kalan, GJ and Menagerie, as they approached. They entered cautiously, anticipating a bevy of magical boobytraps. They were not disappointed. In lesser hands than those of Viz, their approach might have resulted in various limbs or heads being dismembered.

Located in the highest room of the tallest tower in the palace complex, Master Sabi’s residence provided a magnificent view of the city and beyond. Variously sized and oriented rectangular shaped shiny gold windows, each with blue tinted glass, were embedded within the white circular walls.

They lingered, trying to locate items to help with the scroll examination. Drawing a blank, the party extended their search to other floors that housed The Academy of Magic, before returning to the study, empty handed. They sat on the floor to regroup, agitated with the lack of progress.

‘I can’t believe we haven’t found a magnifying device,’ stated Tobias, thinking how easy it would be if they were back at his monastery.

‘Hang on a minute! I’ve been so stupid. We’ve been looking in the wrong places,’ cried Viz. The monk raised an eyebrow. ‘We didn’t go to the museum in the basement. I’d forgotten that it has an “Alien Antiquities” section.’

‘I didn’t know that there was such a place. It does makes sense. We had always assumed that we weren’t the first to discover wormholes and the White Corridor,’ remarked Kalan.

‘I wonder who curated the collection?’ asked Tobias. Viz didn’t know. He left the others debating the matter.

‘It’s another mystery, like where I was born,’ said Menagerie.

When he returned, the magician was carrying a brass monocular microscope, complete with a set of intact lenses and box of glass slides. Tobias was astonished to learn that Viz and Kalan had no idea how it worked, so he offered to set it up on one of the white marble work benches in the study.

Viz moved aside racks of test tubes, rows of beakers and various sized flasks. He dwelled, studying the shelves underneath that were laden with glass jars, each filled with a coloured substance. There were different sections for solids, liquids and swirling gases. Tobias went to work readying the microscope for use.

‘I’m ready to unroll the paper,’ the monk advised. With Viz and Kalan standing close on either side, he picked up tiny forceps, procured from a box of instruments in a nearby drawer. With a steady hand and aided by drops of sterile water, he opened the scroll then sandwiched it, between two rectangular glass slides. Upon completion, he placed it on the specimen holder on the stage of the microscope and peered through its eyepiece.

‘What does it say?’ asked GJ, frustrated at not being tall enough to see what was going on.

'Darn it! There's not enough light. I've only worked with instruments that come with an electric source,' Tobias shared.

Viz moved to his side, concentrated intensely and encircled the neck of the instrument with his fingers. An intense glow lit up the area around it. Tobias thanked him and looked into the eyepiece again. His thoughts turned to The Prof, wishing he was present, with his reassuring intellect and calming brand of humour. He slowly brought the text into focus using the coarse and fine adjustment knobs. After studying the writing for a protracted period, he said, 'it's English, a common language of Earth.'

'How unoriginal to copy Eff's idea of using a scroll to communicate with us. As an aside, we were wondering if you could eventually upgrade the polyglot devices, so we can speak, read and write in any language?' remarked Kalan.

'Ellie achieved that while she was in exile. She was very generous showing me how she can gift those abilities and amazingly no longer needing to implant a device. Can I take a look at the text to confirm I have correctly managed my own upgrade? Then I can do the same for you.' Tobias stepped back so he could examine the scroll.

'Can you understand it?' asked Kalan, impatiently.

'Yes. I think it's a riddle.' He stepped back and weaved a series of complex hand and finger movements around the heads of his companions. 'Now you too have the latest version of the polyglot. Ellie would be happy if she knew about this.'

Kalan took his turn reading the message.

'What does it say?' asked GJ when he had finished. Kalan read it out slowly, as Tobias transcribed the words in a note book, removed from his robe.

'Before the moons turn pure, those turned to sand from the place of the invader must shower in the drink of stars, the vision of the devil.
Hope starts from scouring universally for a falsely purported complexly brewed medicinal where a trio of austere globules dance with organisms without chlorophyll. Find the mentees of the potion master monk. Find the masters apprentice daughter at the understated place of coffee and toffee and sit in her lazy chair and stare, or find the resplendent place of oranges and search the labyrinths if you dare.
Even then so close you will be but in an endless sea. Only the girl in love will be able to see. Find the cure but dispense it only with a dragon sword. A dose for one will be an antidote for all.'

'What's a riddle?' questioned GJ.

'It's a puzzle, or as we call it here an "aenigma"; something cryptically constructed requiring problem-solving skills to unravel it. I expect Master Sabi has taken delight in manifesting this; selecting words that deliberately hide meaning,' Viz replied.

'It's poetic with an alluring quality. I'll give him that,' noted Kalan.

'Please don't,' said Tobias, seriously.

GJ dropped down onto the cool ground under the bench. Deep in thought, he scratched at his head with his front paw.

'I wish The Prof was here,' he muttered.

'I was thinking exactly the same thing!' Kalan exclaimed.

'Me too,' Tobias confessed.

'You'd like him, Viz and Menagerie. He is a mastermind when it comes to unravelling mysteries. If we were all together back in Annie's kitchen at Caves Beach, I'm sure with his help, we could figure it out fast,' GJ insisted.

'My order would be useful in trying to decipher this too. Several of them have devoted their lives to interpreting obscure writings,' Tobias shared. Kalan agreed and said, 'instinctively, I believe the answers are back on Earth. This riddle is in English and the victims have been turned to sand, specific to Geo's place of origin.'

'We need all the help we can get. It's hard not to conclude that this is malicious retribution on those who befriended Geo. If there's one thing I know for certain, it's how malevolent the likes of Master Sabi can be. The only person I have known who can hold a grudge more than he can, was Mergen and we must not forget that he was like a son to Master Sabi.'

'This is deeply personal,' Kalan agreed.

'What exactly did Geo do to attract such hatred?' asked Menagerie. GJ beamed and replied dramatically:

'A great many things did my father do,
but all from the heart, because he was smart
and nothing I'm embarrassed to tell you.
You need to guess when…'

Tobias patted GJ's head gently and interrupted.

'I'm sorry to stop you, as it was sounding very poetic.'

'That's what I was going for. Did you like it? Perhaps I'll be the "Great bard GJ" and only talk like this going forwards?'

'What do you know of bards?' Viz checked.

'Ellie told me that poetry is popular on Luna Tribus and there was a competition every gyrus for the best bard. She used to recite common childhood rhymes to me when I was a tiny puppy.'

'Master Sabi would have been similarly raised,' remarked Kalan.

'It probably explains why he's selected this particular brand of intellectual torment,' said Tobias.

'If we conclude that the antidote isn't here in his study, I say we turn our energy to securing our prisoner definitively. He may still have other accomplices lurking, working towards freeing him,' Kalan suggested.

'We weren't sure of the best place to imprison him. Earth now seems fitting and it's likely the antidote is there,' GJ proposed.

Chapter 3
IVOR

Plans to go to Earth started forming straight away.

'We'll take the invisible force field with us and find an appropriate remote location to hide Master Sabi,' advised Viz.

'*The invisible what? It sounds a lot!*' GJ responded, using his new annoying, sing-song voice. Kalan groaned.

'The prison that Viz designed is an impenetrable, invisible space. It is compact and ready to assemble. I will carry it in my backpack,' Tobias explained.

'How will we get to Caves Beach?' asked Menagerie.

'We need to use a wormhole to enter the White Corridor then locate the functioning door to Switzerland. It means we can see Octy and he can arrange to take us home!' GJ gushed.

'The wormhole Eff used to bring us here was close to one of the guarded checkpoints near the eastern section of the outer wall,' Kalan recalled.

'We can load our prisoner into a transporter and land right next to it,' Viz proposed.

'I'm not going with you,' Kalan suddenly announced.

'Why?' asked Menagerie.

'My uncontrolled outbursts are a liability. Besides, someone needs to stay here and protect the victims from further foul play until you return, with the antidote.' No one argued with his logic.

'You will not be alone. The magician's we trust have been tasked with setting up a perimeter around the victims to help preserve them. To ensure they are protected from enemies, the unaffected guards who were off duty have also moved into the palace,' Viz reassured him.

'We should rejuvenate before setting off,' Menagerie suggested, now yawning.

'If I was petty, I'd sleep in *his* bed!' said Kalan.

'I wouldn't do that. I wasn't exaggerating when I said he was stinky,' said GJ, making the king smile.

They stretched out on the floor of the study. Viz struggled to go to sleep. He lay awake listening to the Chocolate Labrador snore, admiring his capacity to switch off. Unable to stop his racing thoughts, it was a relief, when the moons turned bright, signalling an end to the rejuvenation period. He tried not to dwell on the nagging suspicion that the moon cycle was becoming increasingly erratic.

Sleep had also eluded Tobias, who was equally troubled. His mind had stayed racing in top gear, obsessing about the meaning of the riddle. When he woke, Menagerie, well versed in using a food replicator, offered to be responsible for making food for the group, going forwards. Tobias gave him his machine to use, along with the backpack it came in. Viz lengthened the straps to encircle his chest, making it comfortable for him to carry.

'Do you think Master Sabi looked much older and thinner than when you last saw him?' Kalan asked his brother as he finished munching on his pellets.

'I hadn't thought about his haggard appearance being an ageing phenomenon,' he replied.

'I know it's hard to look good naked, but he looked terrible!' said Kalan, grimacing.

'It's a mental image I'd like to erase!' Viz chuckled.

'If it was ageing, then perhaps he has been making trips to Earth to say, hide a cure?' GJ suggested.

'Does wormhole travel cause that?' Menagerie enquired.

'We're not sure if it's travelling through a wormhole that isn't optimally functioning or a consequence of time passing at a different rate on different worlds,' offered Kalan.

'Surely a lacuna is a lacuna, regardless of where it is being measured?' the lion responded.

'That's what I used to think. Then Eff kept appearing through portals appearing disproportionately older to us each time,' Kalan explained.

'I think it arises from crossing 'dirty wormholes': those that aren't made by an expert. My research on Harlequin made me believe that you have to be highly skilled in using chromotrophin to avoid such problems,' Viz concluded.

'You are aware that is the material wormholes are made of?' Kalan checked with Menagerie.

‘I am now. What do they look like?’ questioned the lion, intrigued. GJ described the sparkling, glowing rays.

‘I think the quantity of chromotrophin applied to a portal is inversely correlated with the time delay expected from a crossing. Master Sabi insisted the Compasse and their monitored wormholes should be avoided, so we were forced to study how they worked from scratch. He arrogantly believed he could master the art and the Cornish experiments proved that he was on his way to doing so.’

‘If he is so amazing, why avoid the Compasse? Surely, he could have forced them to tell him how to make wormholes? Didn’t he get you to involuntarily tell him about them, in the first instance?’ asked GJ.

‘He’s afraid of them. They are more powerful than he will ever be. It was much easier to find a work around, than risk their wrath.’

‘Could he have been experimenting alone, without you knowing about it?’ asked Kalan.

‘It’s possible. He wasn’t around much in the collectios before you came back. If he’d appeared older, it would have been easy to conceal as robes can hide a great deal.’

‘What if the wormholes *we* use cause a time delay? We could go to the wrong time from the one where the antidote is hidden in. Alternatively, if we do find it, we could subsequently return to a Rectangulum City existing long after everyone we love have perished,’ proposed GJ, now pacing.

‘These are risks we will have to take,’ said Menagerie.

'I expect Master Sabi would be aiming to inflict maximal pain on those we care for, here and on Earth, so we need to work out how to safely travel to a time where they are still alive,' suggested Kalan.

'I agree. He'll want them to be drawn into this distressing conundrum,' added Tobias.

'I will try to ensure that any portal we enter has a similar chromotrophin density to the English ones I helped enrich,' promised Viz.

'Do you think the wormhole above our heads could be the one Master Sabi used to go to Earth?' Menagerie enquired. They simultaneously looked up to where he was pointing.

'How could we have missed that?' Viz exclaimed.

'It's been there the whole time. I didn't know what it was until GJ described a wormhole.'

They stared at it for a protracted period, wondering how it had featured in Master Sabi's plots.

'It was through one of these portals that we rescued you,' Kalan told the lion, reminiscing.

'I don't remember it. Did you go back or forwards in time when you visited my birth world?'

'As far as I know, not significantly either way. Now you mention it, I can only say that we didn't lose time here.'

'I can see why you'd like to know your roots. Perhaps you have living relatives? When this is all over, I'd like to help you find your original home. Until then, given that you insist on remaining with me, you'll have to adopt my family as your own. They're going to love meeting you,' GJ insisted.

'The prospect of going to Earth is rather exciting. I never thought I'd leave Kaleido. Life can change so fast!'

'You'll need to be mindful that where you are going is a far cry from Luna Tribus. On Earth, creatures similar to you only exist in certain rural locations or zoos,' Kalan informed the magnificent, gold maned gentle giant.

'Viz will have to keep you concealed like Ellie did for Octy,' stated GJ.

Viz, oblivious to the conversation, had fixated on studying the wormhole.

'Are you worried it might not be safe?' Tobias checked with him.

'Yes. I'd like to study it for a bit longer before we avail ourselves of it. There's also the issue of how Master Sabi used it. I've not heard of a portal that is orientated horizontally or attached to a ceiling like this one is.'

'The wormhole under the spa in Zermatt was horizontal and flat. We stepped over an edge, near the ledge, then jumped into the middle. It swallowed us up, without a fuss,' GJ told him, slipping back into rhyme. Tobias winced.

'I see. That has given me an idea,' said Viz.

'I feel totally useless right now. While you're deciding what to do, I'd like to start putting myself to work. I'm going to take a transporter to the other settlements and try to enlist some help, particularly with security,' Kalan announced.

'You're right. Word needs to reach Inflecto and Octavia about this crisis,' said Viz.

'Perhaps you could enlist the help of the healers in Pluvia Silva too?' GJ suggested.

'Who are they?' queried Menagerie.

'Geo told me of his visit there. Two sisters saved Big Timmy when he was dying from a squork bite. They may have a different perspective on how to help. Even if they can't cure the victims, they might know of novel ways to further protect those who have been enchanted.'

'It's a reasonable idea. Unus and Multis are good souls. Even if their methods aren't helpful, their presence will be good for you, Kalan,' said Viz, smiling.

'How so?' his brother enquired. He had never met a Pluvia Silvan. Their reputation of being suspicious of strangers made him hesitant to reach out to them.

'You'll see. They are kind, and if nothing else, may amuse you.'

'I forgot that you visited them and taught them how to protect themselves against squorks,' the dog stated.

'It was the least I could do, as I did foolishly invent them.'

'I forgot that,' said GJ.

'Are you sure you shouldn't stay with Kalan? He needs a friend right now,' Tobias said to Menagerie.

'I know he is sad and will get lonely. I'd stay, if it were not for my life debt to GJ, which is binding.'

'I will be fine,' Kalan reassured him. 'It's time your life became richer. Locking you up for all those years as my possession, was incredibly selfish. I'm sorry that I didn't know better at the time. My experiences after we parted have taught me the incalculable value of freedom.'

'I would not be alive if it were not for you, my king.'

'Then consider yourself my representative on this quest. Go and fight for my family.'

Viz picked out a specific jar from Master Sabi's collection. He unscrewed the lid and confirmed it was what he thought it was. It resembled a waxy lip balm.

'I'm glad I remembered this. The gelatinous yellow material in this container is one of Master Sabi's most brilliant inventions. He only shares it with his most trusted, senior allies which obviously never included me!' He scooped up some of the material on his index finger and rubbed it behind his own upper teeth. He screwed up his face.

'How does it taste?' asked GJ.

'Indescribably awful! At least it is passing quickly, as a permanent coating forms.' He waited a few more lacunae then added, 'now I can't tell that it's even there.'

'What does it do?' Tobias requested, intrigued.

'When you sweep your gums with your tongue you activate it.' He disappeared then after a short delay reappeared. 'The second sweep reverses the spell.' He repeated the process several times.

'It's very impressive. I wish we'd had it when we were creeping around Kaleido,' stated Kalan.

'Indeed! It's apparently hard to detect too. Each of you should have some and I'm going to take this jar, and whatever else might help us, with me.'

He handed the jar around so they could apply some. He found a second jar of the substance and gave it to Tobias to keep.

When Kalan returned, the others were ready to leave.

'I have more bad tidings. Inflecto had already sent their extra guards with Aquilegia, as escorts. Most of them have been impacted by the potion, as they consumed water from the fountains. I met with Octo next. As a result, Octavia has been placed on high alert, requiring all members of their garrison to step up in protection of their settlement. They are spooked, worried they could be targeted next by another one of Master Sabi's plots, yet to unfold.'

'They are right to worry. As producers of the replicator devices, they have a vital role in feeding the entire Planetary System of Luna Tribus,' Tobias remarked.

'What about Pluvia Silva?' asked GJ.

'As you predicted, they are sending a contingent to help in any way they can. I've done the numbers. All able bodies will be appreciated in the event of an attack. I'm on the verge of enlisting capable citizens,' advised Kalan.

'I cannot leave you alone in such a vulnerable situation, brother,' said Viz. He turned to Tobias and said, 'I have limited knowledge of Earth. You must lead the mission. Secure the prisoner. Find the antidote. We'll be waiting here.' Kalan looked relieved.

'Don't worry, Tobias! *You still have us and we won't cause a fuss*,' cried GJ, observing the tension in his jaw. The monk leaned down, stroked his back and said, 'then obviously, all will be well. I only ask that you stop the rhyming. For some reason I find it agitating.'

'I'm sorry,' said GJ, hanging his head.

'Don't be. It's a *me* issue.' He stared up at the wormhole. 'Given I am now in charge of the outgoing mission, I'd like to raise a nagging concern I have about using this portal.'

'I know. It could lead anywhere, including straight into a trap,' said Viz.

'Master Sabi would have predicted that we'd come here at some stage after he was captured. I'm still finding the fact he allowed that to happen rather unnerving,' said Tobias.

'Then we should go with our first plan. Can you take us to the other wormhole in your transporter?' GJ asked Kalan. The king shook his head.

'There's more bad news. I stopped there on my way to Inflecto. It's gone!'

'Then this is our only hope. At least it seems to be in perfect condition,' Viz stated.

'It feels like we are being forced to use it, which makes me more concerned,' voiced Tobias. He picked up Master Sabi and threw him over one of his broad shoulders. 'We've talked enough. More action and less worrying is needed. Make haste chaps. It's now the three of us and this bag of bones.' He extended his hand to Kalan and shook it. 'Until we meet again, friend.' He nodded at Viz. 'I feel this is far from over. See you soon.'

'At least we're heading off in style!' GJ exclaimed.

'What do you mean?' Kalan checked. Viz had discovered the likely method that Master Sabi had been using to enter his personal wormhole. GJ had watched him trial it several times and was now keen to experience it himself.

'Hit me baby!' the dog instructed, eager to keep the mood positive.

Viz sprinkled the travellers with shimmering contents from an ornate, stubby, glass pot that had been resting next to the bed of the magician. A transient shower of silver sparkles encircled them. Their feet lifted off the ground.

'This is the most blissful feeling I've ever known!' Menagerie cried, as he floated upwards.

'What a buzz! I'm going to be forever envious of seagulls after this,' GJ shared, only half-seriously. Tobias had nothing to say as he floated upwards, momentarily overcome by the serenity of the experience.

A heartbeat later and with the grace of a feather, their feet returned softly to firm ground. An unpleasant stark white light blinded them, before they were precipitously plunged into darkness. As they slipped into oblivion each registered the presence of many others and their shocked gasps. A throaty voice proclaimed, 'it is true!'

Tobias, lying face down on a hard surface started to panic as soon as he opened his eyes.

'Master Sabi! He must not escape!' he cried. He rolled over onto his back, sat bolt upright then jumped to his feet. Furiously blinking, desperate to adjust to the dim conditions, he desperately tried to locate his prisoner. GJ was awakened by his alarm and instinctively started inhaling the air.

'Is that you, GJ?' the monk asked.

'Yes. You're right to worry! I can't detect the monster!' he reported, struggling not to panic.

'There are many other strong scents here. They seem familiar. I wish I could place them,' shared Tobias, still struggling with the darkness.

GJ located the lion and pawed the still sleeping Menagerie awake.

'Where are we?' he asked sleepily, still in the twilight of a peaceful slumber.

'You are in my quarters,' came a calm, commanding, yet welcoming voice.

Not dissimilar to a dimmer switch being turned up, the light intensity smoothly increased. Standing before them was a humanoid they had never met before. His hair was straw coloured and hung to his shoulders with a hint of a careless wave. He was dressed in a simple long brown tunic, pulled in at the waist by a silken plaited red cord.

'I am The Oneidon, Leader of the Compasse. I have come to seek reason not to sentence you to eternal detention. You have been accused of conspiracy with the intent of conquering all beings, as supreme rulers of the universe.'

'Are you joking, mate?' GJ blurted. It sounded so ludicrous to the Chocolate Labrador that he entered a fit of laughter and started rolling around on the floor on his back, with flailing limbs.

'I don't even understand half of those words, let alone know what they might mean,' the lion responded.

Tobias leaned down and whispered to the still writhing dog, 'GJ, I think we're in a spot of trouble. Please get up. This is serious.' The dog retreated to the monk's side and stood still, assuming his grandest posture. After a significant pause to allow his heart rate to settle, Tobias's head tilted slightly, his eyebrows narrowed and his gaze directly met the eyes of their inquisitor.

'Sir, respectfully, who has provided sufficiently compelling evidence for you to so hastily accuse us of such serious crimes?'

The Oneidon hesitated before replying.

'That is a fair question.' Commencing with GJ, he pointed to each of his captives in turn, as he summarised his understanding of their intentions.

'You are the son of the Earth dog known as "Geo the Space Explorer", who arrived on Luna Tribus in a rocket ship with two lower beings called rats. You corrupted, then stole Elektra Heredis from Rectangulum City. You are Menagerie, a mind reader, stolen from Earth to use as a weapon by the now overthrown King of Kaleido. Last and by no means least, you are Tobias, a human thug and bounty hunter, who gains inherent pleasure from playing a support role in executing disruptive plots.'

'Then you are ill informed on all accounts,' Tobias replied.

'Where do you get your information?' GJ added, desperately trying not to resume chuckling. Without trepidation he wandered close to The Oneidon and started sniffing, then licking his leg. He looked up and said, 'you smell and taste familiar.'

'What are you doing dog?' the leader demanded, momentarily thrown off guard.

'Evaluating *you*. It's only fair.'

'GJ, perhaps The Oneidon isn't in the mood for being studied?' said Tobias.

'Yes, we're supposed to be having an important talk,' The Oneidon reiterated. Tobias got the fleeting impression he too was trying not to laugh.

'Sorry, back to that,' GJ acknowledged. He looked up at The Oneidon. 'Someone has clearly been lying to you. Was it our prisoner Master Sabi, the old skinny man wrapped up like a mummy? If so, I bet he didn't tell you that we were on our way back to Earth to imprison him, as he's actually the one wreaking havoc. The truth is that he has turned the residents of Rectangulum City, including the new praeceptorum, our friend Ellie, into statues made of sand from my home. Do you know Caves Beach?'

Menagerie joined the conversation, saying, 'we need to urgently find the antidote, most likely hidden on Earth. The magician is taunting us with a perplexing riddle. It holds the key to saving everyone before they are doomed forever.'

'Show him the riddle, Tobias,' GJ urged.

'I have a transcribed copy, obtained after examining the original scroll which required a microscope to read it. It's located within the pocket of my robe,' Tobias advised. The Oneidon, although hard to read, was listening intently and becoming increasingly interested. He leaned forward and was about to remove the item when Menagerie stepped between them and said, 'are you sure he can be trusted? What if he destroys it?'

'Do not fear, I have memorised every word,' Tobias responded calmly. The Oneidon, taken aback by the lion's protectiveness, was permitted to withdraw the document which he unfolded and digested without difficulty.

'You haven't answered my question. Who has provided the false information about us?' requested Tobias, politely.

The Oneidon flicked his hands in an intricate series of circles above his head, triggering previously dark areas around them to now have light. The illusion of having been confined within a small area was over. They stood in a vast cavern, the limits of which were still unclear, as shadow and light danced at the peripheries.

'I thought we detected others,' GJ commented to Tobias as each took in the scene.

They were surrounded by a silent ring of observers, all sharing the same manner of dress.

'These are the Compasse Monitors,' The Oneidon explained. He approached the nearest individual and said, 'bring forth our other guest.' A smug looking Master Sabi was led into the gathering. His confining robe had been removed and the officer escorting him was carrying it over his arm.

'My liege,' he said, in a sickly-sweet voice.

'You have done well bringing them to me,' said The Oneidon.

'Surely you aren't going to believe his rubbish? I may have to bite him! In fact, that's exactly what I am going to do!' warned GJ, becoming enraged. Before anyone could intervene, he threw himself at the magician and started thrashing about, with his sharp incisors firmly embedded in his left leg.

'Get off me, filthy dog!' his victim protested. He was too afraid to unleash a spell.

'I've seen enough. Please reapply the robe, Tobias. GJ will be getting tired jaws,' The Oneidon instructed. The prisoner was covered once more. GJ started turning around in circles, dramatically spitting on the ground.

'That was disgusting! Why do I keep getting mouthfuls of badly tasting losers?' he protested.

'You could have just licked him. I've heard it's poorly tolerated when used excessively,' The Oneidon stated, neutrally. Then locking eyes with Tobias, he added quietly, 'you'd agree with me, wouldn't you, my Malinois brother?' A deep understanding passed between them. 'You have returned home,' he whispered. He started making intricate hand movements. All evidence of darkness dissolved. In its place, a golden incandescent light revealed a space of gargantuan proportions. The walls were glistening, not from precious jewels or burning torches. Countless pairs of twinkling, excited green eyes belonging to a sea of hooded figures, were poised for information regarding the rumour that had spread like wildfire amongst their order.

'Hail Tobias! Our brother has returned home!' The Oneidon shouted. Following their masters lead, each of his hybrid pack transfigured to their true morphological state, revealing dark fur, long snouts and twitching pointy ears.

Tobias was completely overwhelmed. His humanoid facial features melted away. He had no words. Nor was it a time for silence. Tobias stood up to his full height and howled, a powerful expression of release and power. The room answered, echoing his call.

Tobias struggled to comprehend that the moment his entire order had been waiting for, had finally arrived. The perilous situation on Luna Tribus that had brought him there, made it impossible to feel the exultation he had dreamt of. With the pressing need to find the antidote weighing heavily on his mind, the monk was reluctant to delay returning to Earth. GJ convinced him to linger for a short while.

'We could use the help of the Compasse and you owe it to your order to find out what you can,' he had insisted.

The Oneidon seamlessly grasped Tobias's competing priorities. He applied no pressure, eager to build a relationship and accordingly offered his full assistance.

'You two need to talk. I need to eat. What do you do for nutrition around here?' asked GJ, when hunger eventually got the better of him.

'Apologies for not offering sustenance sooner. We consume a specific plant called "alga". It is delicious and meets our every need,' said The Oneidon. He signalled for quantities to be brought, then led them to his office to wait for it to arrive. Master Sabi was left behind, entrusted to the watch of a trio of burly monks.

'I hope it tastes better than replicator pellets that claim to do the same thing,' GJ whispered to Menagerie.

'Tell me about your order,' The Oneidon began, as soon as they were seated. Tobias provided an eloquent summary of how things had evolved on Earth: the structure of the order, their integration into the local, rural Belgian society with a successful, self-funding business enterprise, the development of technology and the never forgotten, overarching pursuit of finding a way to return home. Another monk entered and unobtrusively placed a tray on the desk, containing bowls of alga for each of them.

'Thank you, Florian,' he told his second in charge. He left. The Oneidon handed them out and demonstrated how the dish was best consumed. He leaned over and noisily sucked the green, soup-like contents into his mouth. GJ copied.

'It's very moreish. Astonishing! How can it taste like bacon?' asked the Chocolate Labrador.

'I'm glad you like it. It is rather excellent,' their host agreed.

'How did we end up on Earth, devoid of any memory of our origins and no way to return?' Tobias enquired, as soon as he had drained his bowl.

'We can only draw information from the recorded history, as told by our scribes. There is a detailed account that tells of your disappearance at a juncture immediately prior to Harlequin undergoing its cyclical explosion. The miners were in their ships retreating back to Ivor when it happened.'

'Ivor? Is that what you call this place?' interrupted GJ.

'Yes, this is the central hub of our home, beyond which we have an extended and well-maintained system of illuminance scaffolds that constitute the wormhole network; more commonly known as the White Corridor.'

'You are the true wormholes makers!' Menagerie said excitedly.

He nodded, smiled enigmatically and said, 'let me show you, our operations.'

He led them back to the area they had first entered, known as 'The Cathedral', before traversing a series of smaller, yet still vast spaces.

'Each of these areas serves a different practical function for the sizeable community that live here,' he explained, eventually reaching the most distant of them. 'The room beyond that door is where the wormholes are made.' A monitor stood either side, guarding it. An ivory scabbard housing a short, broad bladed dagger, was attached to the drawstring securing their robes at tapered waists. The Oneidon instructed the pair to move away from the entrance, permitting their passage.

'Are you aware that wormholes are created from chromotrophin?'

'Yes,' replied the guests.

'This is where we store it. Whilst chromotrophin is a descriptive, more scientific term for it, the Compasse name is "vitae".'

'Meaning life,' mouthed Tobias.

The area looked similar to the barrel storage chamber where the Head of the Order of the Malinois had overseen the brewing of beer. Innumerable cylindrical metal vessels lay on their side, stacked in layers extending high above their heads.

'The miners load the fresh harvest into these vats which are transported here for storage. We drain quantities of the vitae as we require it, using the taps on the end.' He carefully turned the handle of one of the barrels, allowed a portion of glistening, crystalline material to fall into his palm. He handed it around for their inspection before retrieving it and placing it inside a pocket within his robe. With the tips of his hairy, extended fingers, the Oneidon tapped on a series of vessels, producing resonant, hollow notes.

‘As you can hear, we are getting low on supply. The end of this cycle is nearing. During harvest these are densely packed.’

‘Are you saying that our order were miners?’ Tobias checked.

‘Yes. It is an important role. Let me tell you more about Harlequin and what we hypothesise happened.’ They departed and headed back towards his office. ‘The planet is highly volatile due to its natural, cyclical rhythm of disintegration and renewal. After the vitae is harvested, the planet must be transiently abandoned before it explodes. After it spontaneously blows apart, the residual fragments are strongly attracted back to each other. Over time, they progressively bind together and the land mass reforms. As the core reestablishes itself, a new supply of vitae starts to form deep within its crust. It can then be mined, permitting new scaffolds and wormholes to be created here. Until then, this store becomes even more precious as it is the only way we can safely maintain the portals that allow movement between worlds.’

‘Is that why you have the corridor monitors?’ asked GJ.

‘Precisely. Our role is to facilitate safe travel, vital for innovation and growth of sentient races. Our order are the devoted creators and protectors of a system that joins so many souls. Passage across poorly functioning wormholes cannot be permitted. It means at this part of the cycle, crossings are highly controlled.’

‘Our friends Kalan and Viz told us that when they were young, they never sensed any monitor presence. Has something changed?’ asked Tobias.

'Yes and no. Our brothers have always patrolled the corridors. They are faultlessly unobtrusive, unless there is a safety issue necessitating intervention. We have been watching your prisoner, Master Sabi, for a long time, suspecting he had a dark agenda. As proof was obtained, we have struggled to push back against his expanding pool of agents. As a consequence, there has never been as many monitors.'

'What agenda? What is his ultimate goal?' GJ pressed.

'Initially, we thought he was acting for the praeceptorum. We established that the scorned leader, Mergen, was trying to prevent a repeat episode after the cascade of events triggered by the arrival of the dog, Geo. Losing control of his daughter Elektra had a profound effect on the narcissistic ruler. He wanted to make sure his planet had impenetrable walls. To that end, he sought to control all methods of passage to and from The Planetary System of Luna Tribus.'

'That's how you got dragged into this!' said Tobias.

'Yes. After Mergen's death, Master Sabi's personal ambitions of power escalated. He wants to take over our role and ultimately eliminate us. He has played a long game, attempting to gain my trust, whilst duplicitously acting against me.'

Chapter 4
WORMHOLES

GJ described to The Oneidon the wormhole locator device Kalan had come to possess that was once Master Sabi's.

'We think he used it to locate his first wormhole on Luna Tribus. Viz, our friend who was forced to help him study wormholes, didn't seem to know ruggleworms were living inside it and vital for its functionality.'

'Yes, we have studied the tiny creatures. They remain somewhat of an enigma to us. We don't know where they originated. We do know that they are a natural predator of wormholes, attracted insatiably to vitae but not reliant on it for their nutrition. When they first appeared, it took some time to work out that they were the reason wormholes were decaying at an alarming rate. In contrast, we know a great deal about the shells you have described. They are native to a planet called Spiral Seas.' His rugged facial features softened as he described the warm breezes and gentle waters of the place. It was clearly special to him.

'It sounds like our Caves Beach. We have the same shells there!' GJ interjected.

'I know. I'm getting to that.'

'Sorry!'

The Oneidon smiled and continued.

'The residents of the small, water covered planet grow shells to protect their helical bodies. When my predecessor was visiting there, he told them about the problem The Compasse were facing with the vitae. They counselled him that some defenceless creatures, like themselves, find solace in having a protective home to retreat into. So rather than exterminating the ruggleworms, they suggested he might confine them, by drawing them inside abandoned shells that they readily donated for that purpose. It was highly effective. They were subsequently relocated far away from here, housed within their new homes where they could no longer be a threat.'

'On Earth? At Caves Beach perchance?' GJ asked, with a knowing smile.

'Yes. For the longest time there have been no ruggleworms in Ivor. I assumed they became inseparable from their shells and harmless to your world.'

'That seems to be largely the case. They have contributed to making the landscape and identity of Caves Beach so beautiful and unique,' reported Tobias.

'They feed on plankton and when their life span ends, the shells are washed up on the sandy shore where they are admired and sometimes even taken, treated as treasures,' explained GJ, repeating what he had learned from his humans.

'How would Master Sabi have obtained a shell with ruggleworms that were alive?' Menagerie wondered.

'I have no idea. I was not aware that this had occurred. It sounds like he didn't appreciate the true value of what he had come to possess. Fortunately, we've found no evidence of ruggleworms destroying wormholes since his obsession with The White Corridor began.'

'Someone must have given the device to him,' Tobias insisted.

'You're right. I shall have to ponder that,' said The Oneidon, frowning.

'Why do time differences sometimes arise when individuals travel across wormholes?' asked GJ.

'We know the optimal concentration and volume of vitae needed to make any delay minimal. We have a consistent formula, known only to our master crafters. Time passes in every location at a constant rate. If you go somewhere else, the same amount of time should be lost where you came from. We do not permit travel across a wormhole that is not maintained to our rigorous standards.'

'Master Sabi and his posse have been using dirty wormholes. Geo must have done the same, as twenty years had passed when it seemed like mere months to him when he escaped back to Earth with Ellie, Ro and the rats,' GJ reported.

'We must have missed their passage. Do you know where they entered the White Corridor when they left Luna Tribus?'

'Periculosis.'

'That area was once densely populated with wormholes. We'd presumed they had disappeared altogether on the Luna Tribus side, as the doors were barely glowing on the White Corridor side. As a result, long ago we stopped frequent patrolling near there.'

'Do you know where Eff, Geo and the others with them went once they recently entered the White Corridor?' asked GJ.

'No. I was not aware of that either. As I told you, our patrols have been rather stretched lately.'

'You looked troubled, Tobias,' said The Oneidon, having noticed ugly furrows appear on his brow.

'Please do not take offence. I am working up to asking you what I think is the major unanswered cause of concern for me,' he replied.

'There must be no discomfort between us, brother. Share your worries.'

'I'll ask him for you,' said GJ. 'What we wish to know, is where you really stand with Master Sabi. You allowed him to have a private wormhole in his study that leads straight to Ivor. You may have even made it exclusively for him. Despite those facts you want us to think you are on our side. Seriously? What are you playing at?'

'You must have been complicit in allowing him to create a facility on Harlequin to study chromotrophin,' Tobias added.

'It does sounds terrible when you put it like that,' The Oneidon responded, wincing.

'Then how is it?' Tobias pressed.

'I felt it was strategic to keep my enemy close. Through supporting him in a way we had total control of, I believed that we could learn the true limits of his power and gain insights into his future plans. When you arrived through the portal having imprisoned him, we needed to confirm our own assessment of you. We have reliable intelligence throughout our network. As the recent events on Luna Tribus, and his capture on Kaleido became known to us, we knew it was time to end our relationship with Master Sabi. It was only about how and when.'

When they were again seated in his office, The Oneidon said, 'I am dwelling on the mystery of the wormhole locator device and how Master Sabi might have acquired it. Are you familiar with the term "eidolon"?'

Menagerie started to tremble and said, 'I'm sure I've never heard that term before, yet hearing it is like having dread poured into my core.'

'Your fear is warranted. Some of our order respond to the name in the same way you have,' acknowledged The Oneidon.

'I have never heard the term,' Tobias admitted. GJ concurred.

'It came to our brothers during Transcendence.'

'What is that?' asked GJ.

'Tobias, are you aware that some of us can have visions of the future when we enter deep contemplation together?'

'Is it like meditation? We are well versed in that,' he responded.

'It's a higher level of joined consciousness, that isn't achievable by all. It starts with loud howling.'

'Then, no,' Tobias responded, fascinated. His thoughts turned to his brothers back on Earth. 'My order will have much to learn. I can't tell you how much it will mean to them to have the opportunity to return to their true home. Many of them have never faltered in believing that their phase on Earth is merely transitory.'

'All who wish to visit or join us will be welcome.'

'Back to the eidolon thing. What are you talking about?' asked GJ.

'An eidolon is an apparition, a phantom if you will, lacking in a concrete form but capable of entering the body of any living individual and taking over their soul and actions,' The Oneidon replied, in a hushed tone.

'Where do they come from?' asked Menagerie.

'We don't know. It is suspected that without their subject being aware, an eidolon has for reasons that are unclear, periodically manipulated the actions of Master Sabi and possibly others you know.'

'An eidolon might be the entity who gave the wormhole locator device to Master Sabi, allowing him to enter the White Corridor and trigger in him a new found obsession for control,' suggested GJ. The Oneidon nodded.

Tobias let out an extended, whistling sigh.

'There is a more pressing problem I have alluded to, relevant to your quest,' The Oneidon stated.

'You're running out of vitae,' noted Tobias.

'Indeed. The wormholes to Earth that you seek are in desperate need of repair. There is insufficient vitae to bring any of them up to rigorous safety standards.'

'We noticed that Master Sabi is showing signs of accelerated ageing. He must have been travelling to Earth using dirty wormholes. Perhaps we need to use one of them?' GJ suggested.

'I cannot allow that.'

'What about one of the wormholes to Cornwall that he created?' asked Tobias.

'As way of correction, he didn't make them from scratch. There have always been wormholes concentrated in that area of Earth. For ego purposes, he led his co-conspirators into thinking he'd done all the hard work, when he merely serviced a small number of them with the vitae he had stolen. We made sure it was only a small amount of poor quality. We also know that his results weren't as good as he led others to believe. The level of enrichment was marginal. Normal levels of expected natural decay would have rendered them unsafe by now.'

'Do you have any idea which doors he's been using to go to Earth?' asked Menagerie.

'I wish I did. I fear the antidote you seek is hidden in an unknown place and time. The likelihood is that he has been returning from a future Earth, far from the one you left in Zermatt.'

They met again after a short rejuvenation break.

'I'd like to interrogate Master Sabi and try to establish precisely which wormhole he has been using to travel to Earth. At least that way we can get to his last exit point,' Tobias told The Oneidon. The older Compasse smiled mischievously.

'Good minds think alike. During your rest period my brothers have taken the liberty of doing that very thing. He insists he has been traveling back and forth directly to Caves Beach. Unfortunately, despite our most compelling efforts we could not extract the Earth year he last left behind. He had the audacity to brag about having successfully mastered minimising time delays and tried to negotiate freedom by giving us his superior specifications for vitae enrichment!'

'I don't trust anything he says!' cried Menagerie.

'Actually, I believe him, as he will want to cause as much distress to you as he can. It would be surprising if you weren't needing to return to a time where at least some of your trusted companions were still alive to share your pain,' The Oneidon insisted.

'That's what we thought,' said Tobias.

'It's hopeless! Even if we went there and found the antidote, we would have to return using a dirty wormhole that could bring us back here too late to help the afflicted,' Menagerie concluded.

'That is true. Fortunately, I have another solution for you,' said The Oneidon, enigmatically.

'That's a relief!' GJ exclaimed.

'Then I'd like to get going. We have people to save and I yearn to bring my order the answers we have been seeking,' said Tobias. He stood up and asked for their prisoner to be returned.

'He could remain here,' offered The Oneidon.

‘I trust he would be secure here, yet my instincts tell me that his role in this quagmire is far from over. I’d like another opportunity to try to extract information from him. Sticking with our plan to imprison him on Earth feels right,’ Tobias replied.

‘As you wish.’

A monitor arrived shortly thereafter and handed over the unconscious, tightly wrapped Master Sabi. Once again Tobias positioned him over his shoulder.

‘I’d like another crack at him too!’ insisted GJ, raising his paws ready to fight.

The Oneidon smiled and led them back to the vitae storage vault. At the back of the space was a simple door they had failed to notice on their first visit. He opened it and led them beyond.

‘This is a protected section of the White Corridor that is not connected to the greater network. The portals beyond are my own creations.’ He stopped outside a door marked with the symbol of a bird. ‘Before I became The Oneidon, I travelled extensively, first working as an enthusiastic mapper of doors and worlds. I think you’ll agree with my belief that few truly yearn to explore; fewer still have the necessary adaptability, tolerance of discomfort and ability to plan in the moment. I believe I was born for it!’

‘He sounds like you,’ GJ commented. The two hybrids smiled at each other knowingly, their prominent canine teeth revealed in a moment of connection, beyond mere kinship.

‘I thought your name was Oneidon?’ Menagerie checked.

'No. The Oneidon is the name of the role, which I adopted.'

'You must have seen a great many things,' said Tobias, in awe. He nodded.

'It was a significant reason why my predecessor selected me to replace him. I have accordingly been to Earth on many occasions. Most regrettably, I never detected evidence of your existence there.'

'It was not our time,' Tobias replied.

'It will be soon. Listen carefully as I explain some peculiarities about this particular wormhole. To become The Oneidon, the candidate must have the ability to perform every role of our order at an exceedingly high level. This includes monitoring, mapping, scribing, mining and building. All of these require a high level of spirituality, community commitment and advanced magical ability. It is magic that is ultimately needed to make a wormhole. Despite his considerable talents, Master Sabi has failed to appreciate this key element of the process.'

'How is magic needed?' asked Tobias, intrigued.

'To cause the pieces of vitae to adhere to each other as one. Back to this place. We are standing in the "Testing Hall". At my testing I was required to showcase what I had learned to date by manifesting a unique creation. This is the wormhole you will use to continue your journey. Part of what makes it special is that you will arrive at your destination utilising transport the likes of which you have never experienced.' Menagerie looked worried. 'Do not worry lion. All will become clear and it will be a wondrous experience.' He stroked his mane, causing him to relax.

'We must tether your prisoner to your body, Tobias.' The Oneidon conjured a length of strong plaited cord and tied it around the pair. It pulled in firmly on its own accord. 'This is where we must part for now. The Compasse will continue to ponder the riddle and bring word if there are any breakthroughs.' He handed Tobias a heavily frayed piece of paper. 'Each of you need to hold on to this piece of yellow parchment. Do not let go of it.'

'What is it?' asked GJ.

'Your favourite line it seems! You are so curious; impatient too.'

'Sorry,' he replied, feeling bad.

'Don't be. Tempered by caution they are excellent traits.' The dog smiled and repeated his question. 'My creation will take you to the time on Earth that you require. Your need is evaluated through her analysis of your touch.'

'Her?' the dog checked.

'Yes.'

'This is unfathomable,' Tobias responded, struggling to suppress disbelief.

'Which part?'

'The ability of your creation to take us to our required moment in time, a juncture that *we* can't even pinpoint,' Tobias replied.

'This is where you must take a leap beyond science, to faith in a higher being with infinite powers. The Compasse are connected to such an entity, some of us more than others. As The Oneidon, I have the ability to convene with them directly.'

'A god?' the bewildered monk uttered.

'That is a construct you know from your life on Earth. There are other named deities worshipped on other worlds. We are the intermediary between this ultimate creator and every being linked by portals to the White Corridor.'

'I have so much to learn,' said Tobias, feeling overcome.

'That time is not now. Return to me when your quest has been completed.' He redirected the conversation to the paper. 'When you wish to travel between separate locations on Earth, unfold the paper and tell her that place. You may also request to return here at any time. If you need my help, simply tap the page and call for me.' He opened the door.

'See you soon, Oneid…'

GJ's last word was broken by a sudden rush of air. He was falling. Icy gusts made his floppy ears vibrate wildly. In the battering breeze Tobias struggled to open his eyes. He squinted at Menagerie. Flakes of snow were forming a thick blanket across his coat. The object they were still each gripping, started to wobble. Now in freefall, the trio were consumed by fear as it started to pull away. The lion lost grip completely as the paper started to fold itself in half. As it folded in half again, it flapped precipitously, causing GJ and Tobias to also lose their hold.

GJ, with both ears now plastered to his head, managed to watch the paper transform itself in a series of choreographed, precise movements into an enormous, stunning paper crane. In a heartbeat it came to life. Pale yellow turned to scarlet. She started to flap her wings then entered a deep dive, gracefully scooping up the three falling figures.

Once on board, each grasped her feathers. As she slowed, they adjusted themselves, enabling a more comfortable flight, seated upright on her downy back. She turned her head around and briefly glanced over her shoulder to ensure they were recovering from the unexpected ordeal. Lashes resembling soft brushes rimmed sapphire eyes which were dotted with tiny ice crystals. She flickered her lids to maintain her sight, before flying lower. After masterfully manoeuvring her wings against the strong currents, she gently landed between snow covered trees, the tallest and straightest that GJ had ever seen.

'I am Orizuru. Please disembark whilst I rest momentarily. We will then continue,' she advised. The passengers jumped down, sinking into a collection of freshly fallen, powdery snow. A strong breeze blew accumulated white clumps off branches above their heads. One of them hit GJ's brow, causing him to jump.

'Where are we?' asked Tobias.

'This is Jigokudani Yaen-koen in Japan. We are high up in the mountains. This is a special place; Master Oneidon's special place.'

'It feels very peaceful here,' Menagerie commented.

A glimmer of dawn was rising between the wavering branches in the distance. GJ wandered a short distance in search of a private place to go hurry up, the term he used for a wee. He found an appealing area where he could take aim directly on a tree trunk. It felt remarkably good to return to his preferred method of eliminating water. The suction tube system on Luna Tribus had been intrusive. As he was finishing, he felt his hackles rise, causing him to spin around.

A group of pink-faced monkeys, with thick shaggy coats, were watching him intently. The realisation that they had been spotted by the dog, triggered deafening screeches.

'Hey you guys, how about chilling? Can't a dog do his business without an audience?'

'What are you doing here in our territory?' the largest of his observers demanded.

'Taking a leak, as you have witnessed,' replied GJ, trying to appear relaxed. He was now surrounded by countless, agitated monkeys. 'You probably wouldn't believe me if I told you the whole truth,' he added.

'Try us!' demanded an even larger male who was now standing behind him, accompanied by increasing numbers of new arrivals to the scene.

'Alright then. My name is GJ. I have arrived here through a wormhole riding on the back of a paper crane who magically came to life. My companions and I are on an urgent mission to find an antidote to cure our friends who have been turned into sand sculptures. We are transporting the evil prisoner who committed the atrocity.'

'Back off!' commanded the latest arrival, a massive monkey that bounded through the crowd. 'He is no threat if he is an ally of Oneidon.' A wave of muttering of the Compasse leader's name filled the air. 'I am Onsen, friend of our mutual friend.' He bowed and the rest of the gathering followed. 'Come with us to our home. You can warm yourself there and tell us of Oneidon.'

'Oneidon forget us,' an almost equally sized female called out.

'Oneidon never forget us, Nagano,' Onsen reprimanded her.

'The Oneidon is well. He has been busy. Did you know he is now Head of the Compasse?'

'I told you Nagano. Oneidon not come visit, as busy.'

'Thank you for your offer of hospitality. First, I need to go and get my friends. They are waiting for me further back in the woods,' GJ explained.

When he rejoined Tobias and Menagerie, Orizuru was nowhere to be seen. The lion updated him that shortly after his departure, she had reverted to being the sheet of paper.

GJ introduced Onsen and said, 'they seem to know The Oneidon. I think we should follow them.'

They set off along a rough path following a procession of monkeys. Twists and turns took them progressively higher into snow-capped mountains. Tobias eventually called for a rest. He was starting to struggle to keep up. In the harsh conditions, the burden of the added weight of his passenger was becoming excessive. After his breathing normalised, they set off again, crossing a narrow man-made bridge enabling passage over a chasm, with fast running rapids in its base.

On the other side, another set of seemingly endless, steep steps opened out onto a landing. Tobias was panting heavily as they stepped inside a vast sheltered area where a semicircular wall of jutting snow-covered rocks was framed by white tipped evergreens.

The view was stunning. In the distance, like swarming bees, countless monkeys swung between tree branches. The fast-rising sun was causing multiple rainbows to form within fine mist over natural hot spa baths. The rocky pools had been filled with bubbling water emerging from depths well below the surface. Pairs and groups of primates were soaking and grooming in many of them.

'Would you like to soak as we talk?' Onsen asked his guests.

'That would be fantastic,' said GJ. The leader of the troop signalled for the largest of the pools to be vacated. The dog dipped a paw into the water then without hesitation dived in. The displaced water splashed widely, covering Menagerie and countless nosey spectators. Several monkey babies squealed in delight. Overheating quickly in the hot environment, GJ emerged, creating a further round of drenching as he vigorously shook his coat.

Tobias untied Master Sabi and left him under the diligent watch of Menagerie, who remained at the water's edge having declined the offer to bathe. The exhausted monk removed his robe, tunic and trousers and lowered himself into the water. Every muscle in his body seemed to be aching. As his core temperature rose, so did his energy level.

GJ wandered around talking to the local inhabitants before entering a cooler adjacent pool where he stood almost fully submerged, with only his head peering across at his friends.

'Tell us of The Oneidon,' Onsen asked Tobias once he had allowed him time to rest. The hybrid responded, drawing from the minimal information he had gained since meeting him. It became apparent that the Head of the Compasse had once been a frequent visitor to the macaques.

'We called him "The Storyteller". He would often come and bathe with us and tell tales of far-off places,' Onsen told them.

'Can you tell us stories like he did?' a young monkey enquired.

'I can,' GJ intervened. He progressed to regaling them with details of the riddle and their quest to find an antidote for their loved ones back on Luna Tribus. They gasped when he pointed to the bound figure, and explained his villainous role.

'What year is it?' Tobias eventually enquired.

'2006,' replied Onsen, causing GJ to become uncommonly desolate.

'What's wrong?' Menagerie checked.

'It means we've been away for a very long time. We're going to need to brace for significant changes,' GJ warned.

'If The Oneidon is correct, then we have been delivered to *when* we need to be. It is a good start,' said Tobias.

'Our next step is to travel to *where* we need to be. We should get moving,' suggested Menagerie.

'Thank you, Onsen. This has been a welcome extravagance. Your hospitality has been most appreciated,' said Tobias, as he donned his robe, feeling rejuvenated.

'Please return when you have been victorious. Until then, we wish you well in securing your prisoner. Australia is an apt location,' Onsen remarked.

'Why do you say that?' asked Tobias.

'Your criminal is going to a destination with a long tradition for managing outlaws,' stated Onsen.

'Really?' Menagerie checked, turning to GJ. 'From your description, I have only imagined the beauty of Earth, with clear turquoise waters and pale powdery beaches.'

'There is a colony of our kin in the southern state of Tasmania. They are held by humans within an enclosure located within a park. It's in a town called Launceston. Have you heard of it?' Onsen enquired.

'No,' said Tobias.

'We imagine it to be a prison, although the tourists think that the residents are happy. We've been led to believe they have unlimited food,' Nagano explained.

'It is an area for prisons. There is another place called Port Arthur where the most dangerous inmates across the lands were once incarcerated. Some went mad, and many perished there,' Onsen added.

'You seem very well informed. How do you know this?' asked GJ, impressed.

'From the endless murmurings of the multitude of visitors who come here. They call us the "Snow Monkeys". We are very special to the humans who come far and wide to watch us bathe. They stare at us for long periods and chatter away about other places they have previously seen our kind. In return, we love to hear their conversations. Oneidon gave us the ability to understand any language they speak.'

'How did he do that?' asked Menagerie.

'Magic of course! I thought you knew him?' said Nagano, suspiciously.

'Don't be rude,' Onsen scolded. 'They can understand us, so Oneidon must have given them that gift too.'

'So much for Viz and Kalan inventing the polyglot!' GJ murmured to Tobias.

'Indeed!' he replied.

'You must leave now. The crowds will be here soon,' Onsen warned. They walked away and found a dry, open space to prepare to leave.

'I meant to say, do you remember that conversation long ago when Ro tried to convince you that your ability to transfigure was a form of magic?' asked GJ. Tobias groaned. 'I can't wait to tell him about your Compasse brothers. He was right. With some mentoring, you are most likely a powerful magician too!'

'We'll see. Enough of that nonsense.'

'Mark my words!' GJ told Menagerie.

Tobias held out the enchanted parchment and again, each held on to a corner.

'Please take us to Caves Beach,' Tobias stated clearly. Orizuru reappeared. Moments later they were boarding the crane.

Her passengers waved to the monkeys as she soared up into the clear blue sky before accelerating. They moved at such a frenetic speed that it was impossible to make out any scenery.

'I'm starving again!' GJ announced, gripped by pangs of hunger.

'I could replicate some food,' Menagerie offered.

'Too late. We seem to be descending,' Tobias noted.

The familiar coastline of Caves Beach came into view. The sun was shining. The cloudless skyline appeared to merge with the azure sea. It was dotted with elongated tanker ships on their way to the nearby container port in the City of Newcastle.

'I see it! We're home! I do hope Annie has been baking!' GJ exclaimed.

'Please set us down as close as possible to the main cave,' Tobias whispered into Orizuru's ear.

'Time to make ourselves invisible. Who knows what awaits,' GJ told the lion.

Orizuru landed in the sand dunes behind a stretch of beach devoid of humans, half way between the caves and site of the caravan park.

'Welcome to Earth,' GJ told Menagerie. They jumped off her back, landing in soft warm sand. After bidding her thanks, Tobias watched the crane transfigure back into the sheet of parchment. He concentrated, this time sensing the energy of The Oneidon as she completed the routine. The notion that he could compel energy to flow through his body, vital for a magician, was nothing short of astonishing.

Unable to control his excitement, GJ ran off. He sprinted up the beach a short way before turning towards the ocean and plunging into the lapping water. After jumping over a series of gentle crests and swimming out towards the horizon, he turned around and rode a curling wave expertly into shore. He bounded a short distance towards drier sand before regaining situational awareness and returning to his friends.

'Sorry about that,' the dog said, sheepishly. They headed towards the caves.

'The tide is too high for us to use the lower entrance,' Tobias reported after inspecting the area. They retreated back up the beach where GJ stumbled on an abandoned Turban shell. He pawed it along the sand, playing with it like a basketball being dribbled on a court. Menagerie found another one and studied it.

'Anyone home?' he enquired, as he tapped at the patterned, apple sized object, thinking about ruggleworms.

'What are those people doing?' Tobias asked GJ. The dog stared in the direction he was pointing. In the distance, further up the beach, well beyond the empty surf life saving club, he had noticed two figures in the water. They were negotiating peaking waves on surfboards. Like marionettes, they were attached to wires that were connected to coloured kites high above their heads, the likes of which neither had seen before. The brisk winds were making the material billow, pulling them along at high speed, like sails on a boat.

'I have no idea. It looks like they're having fun!' GJ observed.

'Before we try to use the cliff top entrance to The Prof's facility, let's go and see what's going on at the caravan park,' Tobias suggested.

'I'd like a closer look at those kite things on the way,' said GJ.

He raced ahead again a short distance before stopping in his tracks to sniff the air. Tobias and Menagerie joined him, a trio of sensitive noses analysing the breeze.

'I can smell many new things. What's spooked you?' Menagerie enquired.

'I think I know. I recognise a signature. It's Eff, isn't it?' Tobias checked with GJ.

'Yes. There's also another bewildering presence. It's familiar, yet distinctly different to what I know,' GJ stated.

'We need to move closer. I'm grateful we are invisible,' remarked Tobias, as he adjusted Master Sabi, again tightly strapped to his back.

The male kite surfer rode his board expertly into the shore and stopped to rest in the shallows. Deeply tanned and muscular with tangled shoulder length white blonde hair, Eff's appearance was a stark contrast to the weedy individual they recalled, whose allegiance they were both still questioning. His female associate was gliding parallel along the coast, her long golden hair flowing behind her.

'Hello Eff,' Tobias said politely, interrupting the sun baking figure.

'My goodness!' cried Eff, jumping up, shocked.

'Sorry to startle you.'

'Tobias, GJ, I can't believe it's you! Who is with you?'

'You can see me?' queried Menagerie.

'Yes.'

'He's a gifted magician. That's why he can see through our concealment,' GJ explained. Menagerie introduced himself.

'You should stay invisible as you will definitely appear out of place around here,' suggested Eff. He narrowed his eyes, blocking out the sun sufficiently to take in the robed figure Tobias was hauling. 'Who are you carrying? Are they in need of assistance?' His voice was calmer, softer, more expressive than Tobias recalled.

'We have an old friend of yours with us. More on that later.'

'Kate! Kate!' the son of Ellie and Ro shouted to his surfing companion. Responding to his call, she negotiated the currents in order to glide onto the beach. She expertly landed in the edge nearby, before jumping off her board. Still holding her green and yellow kite overhead, she walked towards them, wearing red and white striped board shorts and a flattering, pale blue bikini top.

'This is Kate. She is Sandy's daughter,' Eff told them.

'We have been gone a long time!' Tobias lamented.

'Who are you talking to?' asked Kate.

'We have unexpected visitors. Tobias has returned with GJ and a new friend, a lion called Menagerie.'

The young woman smiled. Her unmistakable resemblance to her mother left no doubts that what he had said was true. She seemed completely unfazed, responding exactly how her grandmother Annie might have.

'This is so exciting! You have obviously come a long way. You must be starving!' she gushed. 'Where are you? Come closer, so I can give each of you a hug.'

'I think it would be better to do that up at the house,' Eff sensibly suggested.

'Be a dear and pack up our kites,' Kate said to him, as she pulled a t-shirt over her head. It had been wrapped in a fluffy candy pink towel located a few paces away. He nodded. She kissed his cheek and said, 'I'll see you at home soon.'

She led them up the beach, then along the path GJ knew well. The dog paused and gasped as they passed over the sand dunes.

'Tobias, can you believe it? It's completely different.'

Beyond a grass fringed bitumen surfaced car park, not a caravan was in sight. In its place was a housing development, with single and double level residences, sprawled across the sloping hillside. It was reminiscent of a fishing village, with a wetland pond stretched out in front. A bar, café, restaurant and function centre had been erected off to one side.

'The Prof generously paid for our house to be built. It has the best sea view,' Kate explained, as they followed a boardwalk towards a nearby house, the largest on the site.

'Mum! Mum! It's happening!' she called out, as she alighted a short flight of stairs onto its front wooden deck. Kate slid a glass door aside and ushered the new arrivals inside. Sandy, sprawled on a plush couch in the loungeroom beyond, looked up over silver rimmed glasses from the book she was reading. Her long hair had been cut into a short bob and was steaked with grey. Her figure was fuller.

Tobias reappeared first, cueing the dog to follow.

'GJ, Tobias, I can't believe it's you!' she exclaimed, jumping up and embracing each in turn.

'Hello Sandy. We have another friend with us too,' the monk explained. Now hidden from prying eyes, GJ instructed Menagerie that it was safe to reappear. The two women jumped as the lion came into view.

Chapter 5
CAVES BEACH

Sandy led them upstairs to the kitchen. In the style of her mother, she insisted on immediately preparing vast quantities of food.

'It will be a big change from replicator offerings,' Kate mused.

'It sure will!' GJ replied.

'Have the machines been upgraded? I've only ever seen Uncle Octy's and that was very cool!'

Menagerie removed the device from his backpack and gave it to her to peruse, while Tobias laid the robed figure on the polished wooden floor.

'Does your friend need help?' asked Sandy, alarmed.

'No, and he's not our friend. I'll explain everything soon. What we urgently need to know is whether Eff can be trusted,' Tobias responded.

'Of course! He's Ro and Ellie's boy and has become a son to me since he washed up on the shore that terrible day, two years ago.'

'What happened?' GJ interrupted, sensing her distress.

'It was one of the worst days of my life. Geo died in my arms.' Tears flowed. She turned and busied herself, filling a shiny kettle with tap water and placing it upon the stove. Kate wrapped an arm around her mother's shoulders.

'Do you want me to tell them the rest, mum?'

'I will,' a familiar voice insisted.

An albino rat shuffled in, prompting GJ to bound towards him. He skidded on polished floor boards, almost bowling him over. He was less skinny than the dog remembered him to be. Snuggles pulled GJ's ear playfully and said, 'it's good to see you, kiddo.'

'I'm sorry to interrupt this reunion. We need to talk quickly. What happened after we parted?' Tobias asked him.

'Why the hurry?' Snuggles replied.

'Eff will be here soon. Back on Luna Tribus, despite believing he was working with us, he acted independently, disappearing with atrocious company whose eyes were set on conquering Earth. Now he's the first individual we meet upon our return. What are we to think?' said Tobias.

Snuggles nodded.

'It was Geo's idea to try to permanently eliminate any ongoing threat from Ellie's family. He too was unsure of Eff's ultimate intentions, so when we were together in the White Corridor, he convinced him to use a wormhole he knew would open under the sea. He intentionally tried to drown them all, expecting we would perish too.'

'How brave!' cried Menagerie. GJ introduced his new friend.

'You're very woolly,' the rat responded.

'Keep going Snuggles,' Tobias urged.

'We were ready to die as heroes; old men that we already were.'

GJ looked sad and said, 'Geo would have done anything for Earth and he must have sensed what atrocities those horrible individuals could get up to here.'

Sandy, having recovered her composure, joined in.

'Only the rats, Eff and Smiley survived. They were washed up on the beach half-drowned. Geo took his last breaths after the rising tide, aided by the dolphins, brought him as close to home as they could deliver him.'

Sadness gripped the room as each remembered the special dog.

'It's possible that some of the cats survived too. One of the Ghosties was never seen again either,' Snuggles corrected.

'Where is Big Timmy now? Is he still alive?' GJ checked. Snuggles smiled and replied, 'he's got his hands full these days as you will no doubt soon see. He's living up at the caves. Smiley and Sir Geo help him and Becky out, as much as they can.'

'Who's Becky? Sir Geo?' asked GJ.

The sliding door downstairs opened and then closed again. Eff appeared up the stairs.

'We've been hearing about the day you arrived here, Eff,' Tobias explained, eager to hear more.

'These amazing women saved my life,' he stated humbly.

Kate looked lovingly into his eyes. Eff placed an arm protectively around each woman and gave them a tight squeeze. It was clear that they had become a close-knit family.

‘We were asking if you were trustworthy. You left Luna Tribus without confiding in us about your plan. From our point of view, it looked like you were on the side of your grandmother and aunts,’ GJ stated, boldly.

‘I can see how that would have looked. I’m sorry. I only ever wanted to restore my mother to her rightful position as praeceptorum. It was better that you didn’t know what I was planning. Did it work?’

‘Yes, although there have been grave developments we will discuss in due course,’ said Tobias. Eff’s eyes hovered over the prisoner.

‘I assume that will include you telling us why you have arrived here with Master Sabi in a complex, magically induced, subdued state?’

‘It will. Given you don’t seem to have strayed far, we must give you the benefit of the doubt,’ the monk replied.

‘Rest assured, I am only guilty of being a naïve fool. As ill-conceived as it might sound now, I had no idea what would happen once I lured my aunts and grandmother into the White Corridor away from Rectangulum City.’

‘Unleashing them on Caves Beach could have had dreadful consequences for Earth. We are fortunate Geo took matters into his own hands,’ said GJ.

‘As I’ve said on many occasions to Kate, Sandy and the others who survived that day, I am sorry about what happened and grateful to him for his sacrifice. I have embraced the precious second chance he gave me to have a good life. The past two years have been wondrous.’

'We all deserve a chance to be happy. The bottom line is we'd trust Eff with our lives,' said Sandy, desperate to take the heat off him.

'You always did,' murmured Tobias, with a wink. She blushed.

'A great deal has happened since those days when we first met,' the older woman insisted.

'I've heard all the stories and we always felt there would be more adventures to come. This is a momentous day!' cried Kate.

The mood lightened. They sat down to talk at the dining table. Sandy toasted a batch of crumpets and served them with organic salted butter and homemade strawberry conserve. Menagerie said very little, trying to piece together how the new information fitted with the stories of the past he had recently heard from GJ. Sandy noticed that he had jam smeared across his whiskered chin. She politely handed him a tea towel hoping he'd take the hint to wipe it off. Realising that he was completely oblivious to the issue, she moved to his side.

'Would it be acceptable if I wiped the sticky material off your mane?' He nodded. As she leaned across to remove the material, their eyes locked. Despite not meaning to look into her soul and read her thoughts, he saw Sandy as a young girl at the Parkes radio telescope, meeting and forming an instantaneous heavy crush on a young Eff. The cryptic remarks of Tobias, now made sense.

Thank you,' he responded. She sat down again.

'Your words are troubling Tobias; your sudden appearance even more so. How are my family? What is going on?' Eff enquired, draining his coffee mug.

'They are in danger. Master Sabi has unleashed his fury upon us all.' He explained the situation. There were gasps. 'We need your help if there is any chance of saving them.'

'It is imperative that we imprison him properly as soon as possible,' said Eff, leaving his seat to more closely examine the robed figure.

'We should move somewhere more private. As Snuggles mentioned, the cats that came through the wormhole survived their near drowning. They have most likely bred, as nasty tabbies have recently been terrorising the rat and mice population. Life has taught me that you can't be too careful when discussing anything to do with our unusual past,' Sandy counselled.

'Can you clarify for me which bodies you actually recovered?' GJ requested, in a loud whisper.

'My grandmother Lisa and Aunt Felicity are buried in the graveyard at Skydog. Geo is there too. The Prof thought it was the right thing to do,' Eff replied.

'We never found the body of Madeleine and assume she was taken by the sea,' Snuggles concluded.

Sandy reopened the kitchen meeting room in the research facility inside the caves. It had not been used in many years. Master Sabi was laid out in a corner, still completely covered in the robe. With Kate's help, the women set to work making a batch of traditional beef Cornish pasties. They used a recipe shared between generations, acquired during

Annie's visit to Cornwall. As they ate, the riddle became the focus of conversation. Tobias expressed a desire to communicate with his order.

'We'll have to feed him soon,' Sandy remarked, looking concerned.

'Not too soon. I can't bear the thought of having to lick him again so we can obtain any level of acceptable co-operation,' said GJ.

'We can't focus on unravelling the riddle until he is safely secured,' stated Eff. Before this could be discussed further, they were interrupted by the arrival of a mischief of rats.

'You've returned!' Big Timmy shrieked as he ran towards GJ. 'I'd have come sooner except we were out foraging.'

'It's uncle GJ! Woweee!' buzzed a baby rat.

'What was it like having Papa Timmy raise you?' squealed another excited voice.

'Uncle GJ, you are such a Geo; so big and brown!' another squeaked.

'They are very cute!' the Chocolate Labrador reacted, filled with joy. He started rolling around the floor with the band of tiny offspring, allowing them to climb all over him.

'When will Becky be home?' Snuggles enquired.

'I'm not sure. Word of your return has been sent. Smiley went to retrieve her and he'll be desperate to get back here to see you. Wait until you meet my Becky. She's quite a force of nature. The real family type if you get what I mean.' He laughed as he pointed to the large number of various aged children, they had been responsible for producing.

'You fathered a huge family yourself tiger!' Snuggles teased, delivering a light punch to one of GJ's legs. The dog was dumbstruck.

'Is Maria still alive?' GJ asked eventually, recalling the captivating Golden Labrador Retriever he had fallen for when he had travelled to England. She had been his first love.

'I'm sorry GJ,' Sandy interjected. She stroked his back and said, 'she died not long after her litter was delivered.'

'Like my mum did,' he reflected.

'I know,' said the vet, remembering that moment.

'She never forgot you and it was her dying wish that every one of her offspring have a name connected to you,' Snuggles added, kindly.

'That's why all Chocolate Labradors are now referred to as "Geo's",' a tiny rat explained.

'Wait until you go to see The Prof. He's kept detailed family tree information on your whole lineage,' Big Timmy added.

'How many are there?' asked GJ, bewildered.

'Maria delivered a large mixed litter of golden, black and a single brown puppy. More descendants have followed after some of these partnered with other Labradors who were still living at Skydog,' Sandy clarified.

'I can't wait for you to meet some of them!' Kate exclaimed.

Smiley bounded through the door. He appeared unchanged from when GJ had first made his acquaintance in Cornwall. The English Staffy's sky-blue fur, stocky build and toothy grin were unforgettable. They sniffed each other enthusiastically. GJ inherently trusted him, having witnessed his bravery in freeing a large number of helpless victims he had been forced to capture.

'Do you trust Eff?' GJ unobtrusively enquired, as soon as an opportunity presented itself.

'I guess so. I think he's found himself. His unrequited love for Kate has had a profound effect on his character. I don't think he was ever really in anyone's camp but his own and now he lives only for her.' GJ looked perplexed and said, 'what do you mean by unrequited?'

'They haven't mated.'

'Ohhhh.'

'How is it that you haven't aged?' GJ asked, rapidly changing the subject.

'It's thanks to Eff's magical skills in potion making. As you can see, Big Timmy and Snuggles are also beneficiaries. His backpack was well stocked with supplies when he came here and he seems to have continued his development as a magician. He's always evaluating new and unusual substances for potion making.'

Their conversation was interrupted by the noisy arrival of a plump grey rat wearing a checkered apron.

'Sweet chops, what have I missed sweet chops?' the rat directed at Big Timmy. She darted around the room, taking in the new arrivals and hopping on the spot, shifting form one foot to the other. 'It is true! Woo Hoo!'

'GJ, Tobias, new friend Menagerie, this is my Becky,' said the pudgy rat.

She ran towards them. To their surprise, the rotund female was like an athlete. She effortlessly ran up one of GJ's front paws, only stopping after having expertly positioned herself, nuzzled into his neck close to his left ear. 'It's such an honour to meet you sweetie. I only wish I'd known your papa. I never thought I'd get to meet *you*.' Next, she pounced powerfully upwards, landing on Tobias's shoulder. She pawed at his bulging biceps muscle and said, 'now you are very handsome; strong too, like my Timmy. The stories of you manhandling your enemies now make sense.'

One of Tobias's eyebrows raised with bemusement. He smiled at Big Timmy and asked what stories he had been telling.

'What's a good story without a few tall enhancements?' he replied.

Becky jumped down onto the lino covered floor and approached Menagerie. He good naturedly submitted to a systematic examination of his head, neck and torso courtesy of her twitching nose and tickling whiskers.

'Now you are *really* interesting!' she blurted.

'I've told you before, it's impolite to explore a newcomer so extensively,' Big Timmy reprimanded. Becky looked forlorn.

'I'm sorry,' she told the lion, genuinely remorseful. He smiled. 'You are so irresistibly smelly, like nothing I've encountered around these parts.'

'Where are you from?' Big Timmy enquired.

'I'm not sure.'

'You look a bit like an African lion, although your markings are not the same. They're not Asian either,' concluded Big Timmy, in an authoritative voice.

'You seem very well versed in lions,' noted Menagerie.

'Yes, it's because we are addicted to television. My Tim Tims adores documentaries. The Prof left us his set. It's in his office,' Becky explained. Menagerie took a giant sigh breath, inadvertently inhaling dust from the musty air, stirred up by the scurrying rats. It triggered a roaring sneeze that echoed round the room.

'Uncle Snuggles, I need to go hurry up,' a terrified voice whispered. A tiny baby rat nuzzled close to his elder. 'Uncle Snuggles, I'm sorry; I just have!' he cried. It reminded GJ of when he was an infant, struggling to master control of his bladder. The skinny rat hugged him close and said, 'don't worry. I'm certain he means us no ill. Our friends would never knowingly usher harm into our safe place.'

Menagerie, upset that he had caused another creature distress, dropped down, leaning on his front paws. Another one of the baby rats scurried forward and said, 'don't be sad. I will be your friend. Let's go bed time together.' He touched his tiny paw onto the lions and proceeded to curl up, using it as a pillow. The lion smiled and invited the other youngsters to do the same. He was soon surrounded by them.

'Finally, some decent help with childcare!' Becky cried.

'What has happened to Octy?' GJ enquired, changing topics.

'He lives in Zermatt, running the White Dryas Inn. He visits when he can. Beauty brings him. I have already contacted him and he should be here tomorrow. You should have seen his antennae. They became frenzied when I told him you had arrived,' Sandy remarked.

Tobias looked perplexed and asked how she could know such detail. She handed him her smart phone and tried to explain how video-telephony worked.

'May I use it to call my monastery?'

'Of course.' She helped him make the call and suggested he move to The Prof's study for some privacy.

'I'll come with you and bring back his beloved blackboard and some chalk. I'm certain that's what he'd want to do, now we've eaten. Then the riddle can be transcribed so we can study it together,' said Sandy. Eff went to help her.

While they were gone GJ updated the others regarding the terrible events on Luna Tribus.

'I can't believe that's Master Sabi lying over there!' Big Timmy reacted, as he examined the robed figure. Snuggles started poking him.

'What are we supposed to do with this villain?' he checked.

'We need to help Tobias find a safe place to exile him,' GJ explained.

When Sandy and Tobias had returned, focus shifted to trying to decipher the riddle. Stumped in their attempts to analyse it, talk turned to the ups and downs of life on Earth during the past 26 years. Sandy shared her personal story. The carefree young woman that GJ remembered, had gone on to become a responsible head of her own family. She had married a fellow veterinarian, named Michael Jones, who had helped her continue to advocate for the gradual return of domestic pets into human homes. The Pet Extinction Act had eventually been overturned, presumably as those unaffected by Master Sabi's potion came of age.

Sandy and Michael had been happy together and brought two children into the world. Kate snuggled next to her mum and proudly explained that she had inherited the family skill in the kitchen and had graduated from Hospitality School. She was now working at the recently revamped resort restaurant right next to their home. It was built on the very spot where she had played as a child.

'Wait till you meet Mikey. He's going to go nuts!' Kate said effusively. Her younger brother was living away, studying animal conservation at a university in Tasmania. 'It's summer break right now. He's gone to stay with Uncle Octy so he could go snowboarding. He'll be arriving with him.'

'Where is your dad?' GJ enquired.

'He died from malignant melanoma when we were small,' she replied, clamming up.

'What's that?' he asked, trying to understand everything fully.

Sandy explained, with tears welling in her eyes, how what had begun as a tiny dark skin lesion on his back had spread relentlessly throughout Michael's body.

'It was untreatable from diagnosis. The children had barely gone to primary school when it happened.'

'I am so sorry,' said Tobias.

Granny Annie, as they fondly called their grandmother, had helped pull Sandy from her melancholy and raise two beautiful spirited individuals.

'Where are Annie and Glen now?' Tobias checked. Both women were now too upset to continue, so Eff took over, after again placing an arm protectively around each of them.

'Glen had a lethal heart attack shortly after Geo died and Annie hasn't been the same since. The doctors think she has a condition called Dementia.'

'All the oldies are living out at Skydog now,' said Kate, rejoining the conversation. 'The Prof is faring the best, although he's not great either; riddled by severe arthritis. Poor Uncle Gavin has had to give up working the winery in the Hunter Valley, as his back has been playing up.'

'He fulfilled his dream! That's fantastic! Tobias exclaimed, smiling.

'Yes. Some good did come from the individual I now find myself surreally staring at on the floor,' stated Sandy.

'The vineyard is still running successfully as he trained a wonderful young winemaker. He is continuing to make wines under Gavin's label. It breaks his heart that he's too infirm to go there,' Sandy reported.

'As soon as Octy gets here, I think we should get Beauty to take us to Skydog. We urgently need to get The Prof's opinion on the riddle and where he thinks we should hide the prisoner,' GJ concluded.

The cave facility was home to everyone that night. GJ woke early, pressed by the need for a hurry up. He padded past the series of occupied rooms, feeling comforted by the quiet snores and rummaging sounds of those still slumbering. Up the stairs and out onto the cliffs he went where a gentle breeze was blowing salty air off the ocean. He inhaled deeply and grinned before running along the winding path he knew so well, heading down to the main cave.

Disappointingly, he found the tide too high to enter it. As he finished sprinkling a clump of washed-up seaweed on the nearby sand, he sensed that he was no longer alone. He had failed to notice that a quad bike had materialised on the beach. It was carrying a young man and brown dog and heading towards him.

'Hey GJ, it's me!' cried the invisible Octy, startling him. The excited dog turned around so rapidly that his head bumped into his own tail. They sat down together on the cool sand, enjoying the gentle waves lapping around them. 'I never doubted that one day you'd return even though the wormhole at the White Dryas disappeared as soon as you stepped through it.'

'There's so much for us to catch up on,' said GJ. Before he could complete another sentence, a Chocolate Labrador, even larger than GJ himself, lunged forward and started zooming around the pair.

'Go easy, Sir G,' another voice chipped in. A young male human with eyes like the ocean and long, pale blonde dread locks that reached below his shoulders, was watching them.

'GJ, this is Sir Geo. He's your grandson. This is Mikey, Sandy's son,' the Octavian explained. GJ was only half listening. Powerfully drawn to the other dog, he ran to greet him. After polite sniffing of each other's butts, they set about wrestling, before running together at high speed across the nearby sand dunes. Mikey called them back. They complied. Panting, each dug a hole in the moist sand before flumping down next to each other with their underbellies pressed against the cooling water.

Their natural affinity was striking, as was the bewildering effects of the magic that had caused GJ to mature faster than normal, then cease ageing altogether. As a consequence, Sir Geo appeared significantly older, with a greying muzzle his elder had not yet developed.

'Octy, who did you say this was? What are those things on his head? Is he one of your relatives?' GJ eventually asked, as his excitement settled and he took in Mikey's appearance.

'You must have missed me tell you. This is Mikey, Sandy's son,' he repeated. Mikey squatted and held out one of his locks for GJ to inspect, and said, 'these are called dreadlocks. It's a personal styling choice, although I admit Uncle Octy inspired me to wear my hair like his.'

'It suits you,' GJ responded.

'Are the others awake?' asked Octy.

'No one else was up when I passed their rooms. We're all staying at The Prof's old place.'

'I noticed the tide was high as we approached. It's on its way out now, so why don't you two go ahead and find Sandy. I'll shelter Beauty, who wishes to change into the submarine and float inside. I'll join you as soon as I can,' Octy advised. Mikey nodded and walked towards the cliff path, flanked by two enthusiastic brown dogs.

They headed straight for the kitchen, drawn to the tantalising aromas of warmly buttered toast topped with thickly spread, crunchy peanut butter. Mikey snuck up behind his mother and wrapped his towering muscular frame around her; squeezing her like a teddy bear. Her radiant smile faded quickly as she noticed his hair.

'What have you done to yourself, child? First you shock me by growing your hair such that you need to wrap it in a pony tail like your sister and now this.'

'Long hair is normal for a Luna Triban male and I like it. Ask Eff,' he retorted.

'I think its uber cool, big bro,' Kate interjected, having appeared at the door. Not far behind her was Eff. He nodded to Mikey, whose previously relaxed jaw tightened; his eyes squinted in disapproval. Recovering his manners, he moved across and shook Eff's extended hand. He had taught him this custom.

Sandy set out large bowls of food for the ravenous dogs. Octy appeared next.

'I see nothing has changed here. I bet you haven't had any breakfast yourself yet,' Octy scolded, embracing the woman he had watched grow up. He picked up a pile of serving plates, set them out on the bench and started arranging pieces of the toast on them. 'This is a table your mum would be proud of,' he nodded approvingly. 'How is she?'

'Not good,' Sandy replied, finally sitting down to eat.

Tobias arrived next, hauling their prisoner. He lowered him onto the floor, once again in the corner. He looked exhausted, having failed to drop his guard throughout the night. Octy greeted him warmly.

'I heard we have a liability on this mission. Are you getting tired of carting him around?'

'Tired is an understatement,' he replied. As Octy prepared him a cup of extra strong coffee, waves of rats joined them, their noisy chatter filling the room.

'You're very good with children,' GJ told the Octavian. He had watched him sip his tea while eight baby rats each used one of his velvety, buzzing antennae as climbing poles.

'Menagerie is the new favourite,' Becky announced, regaling the newcomers with events of the night before.

'You can never have enough love,' the orange skinned, Octavian remarked, smiling at the lion.

When everyone had finished their breakfast, Mikey asked when they were leaving for Skydog.

'I'd like to go now, if that's possible,' Tobias replied.

'Me too. From what I've been told, things need to move fast,' Octy responded. 'Who else is coming with us?'

'I wish I could go. Unfortunately, I have to head to work soon. I've only recently taken on a new senior role at the resort so it would be irresponsible for me to leave right now. Besides someone needs to take care of matters here,' Kate insisted. Big Timmy and Snuggles argued over which of them should remain behind, not only to keep her company but to help care for the vast number of rats who had come to depend on the brothers. In the end, Snuggles insisted that Big Timmy and Becky should be granted a pass to go on an adventure together.

'Kate prefers me anyway!' the skinnier rat teased.

'That is very generous of you, Snugs. Make sure you don't let him overeat, Kate. He's supposed to be on a diet,' Becky nagged. She poked his small paunch with a pointy digit and said, 'you're getting a belly to rival my big guy.'

'I'll help with the clean up, then we'll hit the road,' Octy told Sandy.

'I can prepare Beauty to leave and meet you up top in the carpark,' Mikey suggested. He had been obsessed with Octy and the magical transporter ever since he was a toddler. To their amazement, she now responded to both of their voices. Beauty had also started acting on their descriptions regarding how to transform herself into many more interesting forms of transportation.

Sandy sat in the front of Beauty, with Mikey in the driver's position of a mini bus. GJ, Sir Geo, Big Timmy and Becky squeezed onto a bench seat at the back. Tobias laid Master Sabi on the floor in front of the dogs and rats who offered to keep a watchful eye on him. Relieved, the exhausted monk stretched out on his own wide seat, using the window ledge as a pillow and almost immediately started napping. Menagerie and Octy occupied separate seats near the front.

'Where's Eff and Smiley?' Mikey queried impatiently, keen to get going.

'They're not coming with us darling,' Sandy replied.

'Why not?'

'Eff's staying behind to help Kate and Snuggles and as you know, Smiley always goes where Eff does.'

'I can't believe I'm saying it but I'm actually wishing Eff was with us!' Mikey blurted.

'Why is that?' Menagerie enquired, with interest.

'It's best to be keeping your friends close and your enemies even closer. I don't trust him.'

'That's because he fancies your sister,' Sandy teased. Failing to see the funny side of this, he became defensive.

'That's not the only reason. Geo never trusted him. He died trying to drown him. You can't see it, can you mum? You're biased!'

'Let's not have this argument every time you come home. It's futile.'

'Don't worry, Mikey,' Big Timmy shouted from the back having overheard their heated exchange. The driver looked over his shoulder and said, 'why?'

'Smiley will be spying on them. He does it constantly and the next few days will be no exception,' Becky announced.

At that moment Eff unexpectedly poked his head into the window on Sandy's side, causing them to stop speaking. Mikey's cheeks turned red. He forced a smile.

'I came to say goodbye and to wish you well.'

Sandy felt embarrassed, hoping he hadn't overheard the conversation.

'That's err, very kind of you, mate,' Mikey replied.

'Safe travels and don't worry! I'll make sure Smiley see's everything we do,' Eff replied, stepping away, smirking.

Three grey haired figures swayed back and forth on matching antique, wooden rocking chairs. They were out of sequence, as Annie kept nodding off and barely moving. The Prof and Gavin, filled with anticipation, couldn't wait for Beauty to arrive. Gavin chatted incessantly, reliving legendary tales of 'Geo the Space Explorer' as they fondly called the most extraordinary past chapters of their lives.

The Prof smiled and said, 'I think we're in for another round!' He felt a rising sense of anticipation, the likes of which he hadn't experienced in years. He rose less nimbly to his feet than he would have liked, eager to greet Beauty as she drove into view. He stretched out his spindly arms and cracked his swollen knuckles.

'Must you do that dear,' Annie protested. 'I've told you before it will give you arthritis.' He stared down at his outstretched hands; deformed and claw like from the ravages of Rheumatoid Disease. Despite his body failing him, he didn't feel old. Still as sharp as a tack, his mind was more willing than the rest of him.

'You are right dear one, I'll try to stop it. Arthritis would be terrible.'

He felt profoundly sad watching the kindest woman he had ever known slipping away, her memory failing to recall obvious things such as his severe disease.

'They're here, Annie!' announced Gavin.

'Who is here?' she asked vacantly. He told her for at least the tenth time.

'Come back here and give your aged friend a hand getting up,' Gavin shouted after The Prof. It was too late as he had already disappeared.

Sandy disembarked from the van and made a beeline to her mother's side, stopping only long enough to give The Prof a peck on his cheek. She kissed the top of Annie's head then gave Gavin a giant hug.

'How are you mum?' she enquired. The old lady appeared perplexed, unable to recall who was speaking to her so familiarly.

'She's getting worse,' Gavin stated.

'How can you tell?'

'Some days she doesn't recognise me either.'

Like an overstimulated puppy, GJ bounded up the stairs, jumped up on Annie's knee and started licking her face. Big Timmy and Becky watched from the side, curious to observe how she would react.

'That's lovely. Enough now. Drop down Geo,' she replied, responding with a firm tone.

'It's me, GJ,' he corrected.

'Geo, be a dear and go and find Big Timmy and Snuggles. It's time for dinner. Tell them I have cooked peas,' she said flatly. 'Where's my apron?' She stood up and walked inside, prompting everyone to follow her into the kitchen. Sandy and Octy remained close by, supervising her actions.

'It's only in here that the person we knew still seems to exist,' said Octy. The dog looked sad. 'Why don't you go and see where the others are GJ?' he recommended. He left in search of Sir Geo.

'I'll help you mum, as we've got guests. Tobias has come to see us,' Sandy explained, donning an apron and helping Annie tie hers in place. She was a moving target, as the old lady was already opening the refrigerator and taking out random items. Big Timmy and Becky winked at Sandy encouragingly.

'Do you think she'll remember how to use the replicator?' the female rat whispered to her partner.

'Yes, as she always loved using it so much,' Big Timmy replied.

'Don't worry. As soon as we mention it, she'll start going on about it seeming like cheating,' said Octy. He placed a basket of pre-prepared food onto the table which Sandy had helped him make for their lunch.

'Set the table, Octy. Get the nice lady with you to help,' Annie commanded. Sandy looked upset. Pushing back tears, she said, 'it hurts that she always remembers you but not me.'

'I'm sorry,' said Octy. Tobias placed his package on the floor. He sat down on a stool. Sandy brought him a glass of water. The Prof sat down next to him, eager to hear more about how they had come to this moment.

On his way inside, Mikey paused to assist Gavin transfer from his rocking chair to wheel chair. He watched him wince in pain several times.

'You're not good are you, buddy?' Mikey remarked. Sir Geo licked the older man's hand as a distraction from his discomfort.

'I miss my vines and miss making wine.'

'I didn't know that you were a bard?' said GJ. Gavin smiled after a pause, realising he was responding to his accidental prior choice of words.

'No GJ. I'm a vet by trade and a winemaker at heart.'

'Uncle Gavin, I can only imagine how badly you must miss it. Those summers I spent helping you harvest the Chardonnay were unbelievable. You do know that I nearly studied Oenology at university?'

'No!'

'In the end, it was the animals that called me.'

In a rare moment of happiness, Gavin smiled and said, 'I can understand that. Never forget that the richest lives come in chapters. It will be waiting for you, as I've willed the estate to you and your sister. Strangely, I've always imagined you making the wine and Kate running a successful restaurant there one day. Enough about me. Let's go inside. I want to hear what's going on.'

'Why hasn't Eff fixed your pain with one of his potions?' GJ asked Gavin, suspiciously.

'On multiple occasions he's tried and failed.'

As he rolled forwards, he felt something woolly brush against his arm. He looked around for a source.

'That's strange. I felt something woolly touch me,' noted Gavin.

'Are you with us, Menagerie?' Mikey checked. The lion appeared.

'Sorry. I didn't realise I was invisible. I must have accidentally tongued my gums.'

Mikey introduced him.

'How did you come to be here?' Gavin enquired, his startle quickly turning to delight.

'I am repaying a life debt to GJ!' he announced, dramatically, before describing how in Kalan's bedroom on Kaleido, he had almost had his throat ripped out. Gavin's eyes twinkled with excitement.

'I can't wait to hear more!'

'Ellie, Ro, Izzie, Aquilegia, Christina and many other innocents are in danger. We have Master Sabi with us, who needs to be imprisoned,' summarised the lion. Not for a second did Gavin question the accuracy of the information.

'Mikey, as a small fry you were always whining that you wanted a chance to be a part of something important. I can't even guess how many times you convinced The Prof to regale you with his stories. It looks like you may get your wish.'

'We need all the help we can get!' GJ insisted.

'I know he's committed many crimes, yet I do bear gratitude towards Master Sabi. The best thing he did was acquire the vineyard in the Hunter Valley. Without it, I might never have been a winemaker.'

'I don't understand,' said Menagerie.

'The first time Master Sabi came to Earth he was pursuing Ellie and needed a base to enact his wicked pet extinction plan using the bats. He chose an old winery,' said Gavin.

'Didn't I tell you that?' GJ checked with the lion.

'A memory is stirring. There's been a lot to process.'

'The brand "Geo Wines" has become synonymous with excellence in Hunter, old vine, Australian Shiraz,' said Mikey.

'Of which we'll be cracking a few of my best tonight, dear boy! We're going to need to get some Sparkling Shiraz chilling pronto. Tobias needs to try my best vintage! To the cellar gentlemen!' Gavin cried, rolling forward in his wheelchair. Mikey struggled to share his enthusiasm.

'Perhaps you should keep it to the one bottle? We need to have clear heads. Wait until you hear what we're facing.'

Chapter 6
SKYDOG

Mikey accompanied Gavin to the basement. He explained to Menagerie that it had previously been a flourishing haven for pets rescued during the now abolished Pet Extinction Policy. The dark space had been replaced by countless shelves of bottles.

'This is where Ellie and Gavin saved my life!' GJ told Menagerie. He retold the tale of the night he was born. Geo had often regaled him with it as a bedtime story. They retrieved two bottles and went back to rejoin the others.

Gavin almost rolled over Master Sabi's legs as he entered the kitchen. He insisted that Sandy plunge one of best sparkling red wines from his museum collection, into an ice bucket.

They proceeded to eat and drink, perched variously on chairs at the table or sitting on the floor. GJ briefed Gavin and The Prof on events since they had parted, including their insights into wormholes, The Compasse, ruggleworms and the mysterious eidolon. Annie drifted off to sleep in her chair by the stove. Octy recognised the disabling fatigue that the silent Tobias was experiencing and took The Prof aside to discuss his concerns.

'I'm worried about him. The burden of ensuring Master Sabi is kept secure is massive. That's before we get to the enormity of the recent realisation that he is Compasse himself. The duty to his order is at odds with his quest to save our friends back on Luna Tribus. He desperately needs our help.'

'Then we need to focus. Mikey, could you please bring my blackboard from the study?' asked The Prof.

He did as he had been asked, returning promptly and setting it up in the corner of the kitchen. Knowing that due to his arthritis, the professor was unable to write, he borrowed Tobias's copy of the riddle and started transcribing it. When he had finished, he looked to The Prof to take charge.

'It seems that haste is needed. Our friends are in peril. We need to secure this villain and find a hidden antidote to this curse. Let's start with a systematic analysis of the riddle. Please read it slowly to us, Mikey.'

The monk yawned, feeling even more tired since he had eaten. He wondered if the small glass of excellent Sparkling Shiraz he had imbibed had been a mistake. His eyelids grew heavy.

Time passed with only the sound of a ticking clock.

Now bored, with no new insights to offer, GJ asked Sir Geo where he usually lived.

'I was raised by Master Octy in Switzerland. One day I hope to travel to Octavia to see his home,' he replied. Their chatter was soon interrupted by The Prof.

'There's something that's been worrying me since you arrived back. It's about Eff. The story you have told us about events before your return, are at odds with the version he gave us,' The Prof said to GJ.

Sandy was immediately defensive.

'It's natural for individuals to see things a bit differently,' she proclaimed.

'Please don't get defensive, mum. We are all aware of how you get when it comes to Eff. This is a conversation we need to have,' said Mikey. She looked at him sternly but stopped speaking.

'What are you talking about Prof?' asked GJ.

'My understanding is, that from his perspective, he was your comrade and sacrificed himself to save his family on Luna Tribus.'

GJ stretched and scratched his right ear in thought, then said, 'he never told us what he was going to do after we parted on Phalago.'

'You see mum, you and Kate are always overly trusting of him. Mr pretty eyes never fools me!' Mikey retorted, waving his clenched fist in anger.

'He did say that he wanted his mother to be the praeceptorum rather than himself,' GJ added, trying to keep a balanced view.

Eager to defuse the tension, The Prof intervened.

'In his defence, the lad hasn't done anything to incriminate himself since he came here. I rather like him. He's super smart and not overly arrogant. Let's agree that the jury is still out. We've more important matters to discuss and we could use his help.'

Mikey sat down, trying to calm himself. He stared at Master Sabi. After a short delay, he said, 'you are right, Prof. We should be studying this psycho-bag's words and working on plans for his prison.'

'My vision isn't as good as it used to be. Can you read out what you have written, again?' The Prof requested. He closed his eyes, listening intently to each word. When Mikey finished there was silence.

'I will need a while to crystallise my thoughts,' said The Prof when he opened them.

'I'd like to say something,' Menagerie politely requested.

'Of course. What is it?' asked Gavin.

'Did you realise that your residence is under a dark enchantment?'

'What do you mean?' he replied, stunned.

'Someone has infested your home with vehicles causing a potent ill-health potion to infuse into the air. Every time someone enters your doors, their life force is subtly being sapped away. I felt it as soon as I entered. The source has now become clear to me. I can smell it.' The lion padded towards the refrigerator and removed an object that was holding a shopping list to the door. He passed the circular metallic item around the group for them to inspect.

'All I see is a simple fridge magnet,' said Mikey.

'It's more than it seems. It's an emanator!'

'You can't be serious?' Gavin reacted.

'Did you put that object there? I certainly didn't,' said The Prof.

'I don't know where it came from. Who would target our home so malevolently?' asked Gavin.

'Eff is very skilled at magic, especially potions,' Mikey started.

'Hey! That's not fair. Let's not jump to conclusions,' Sandy responded.

‘Let’s not start that debate up again,’ said The Prof, firmly.

‘The Ghosties were also expert potion users. Only one of their bodies was ever found,’ Big Timmy reminded.

‘Now that I think about it, it is a strange coincidence the way all three of you developed rapidly accelerating human diseases around the same time,’ Mikey noted.

‘I don’t believe in coincidence,’ Tobias acknowledged.

‘What exactly is an emanator?’ asked Sir Geo.

‘They are reservoirs for potions. Each is designed to slowly, continuously and endlessly aerosolise their contents,’ Menagerie explained.

‘Kind of like how an air freshener works,’ Gavin mused.

‘How do you know about them?’ GJ enquired.

‘It’s what Master Sabi used to control the cats at Kalan’s palace. He had dozens of them positioned throughout the palace. He filled them with a loyalty potion.’

‘Why weren’t you affected?’ asked Mikey.

‘I am naturally resistant to potions. My saliva contains a very powerful chemical that can neutralise most toxins. Would you like me to do that to this one?’

‘Definitely! We’d be very grateful,’ The Prof replied

‘Please hand it back to me.’ He took the object and started licking it.

‘How did you come to learn you had this ability?’ Sir Geo asked, in awe.

'I don't know. It's an intrinsic part of who I am; like seeing the essence of others and being able to read minds.'

The Prof looked particularly impressed and invigorated with hope.

'What useful skills you have, dear lion. Do you think the effects of this particular potion might be reversible?'

'I cannot say.'

The Prof looked across at Gavin, observing that his oldest friend's eyes had filled with tears. He glanced at Annie who was oblivious to what was unfolding. A rivulet of saliva was indignantly running from the corner of her lip and dripping onto the shoulder of her floral dress.

'Thank you, Menagerie. You have done us a great service,' said Gavin. He reached out and stroked his mane.

'I would like to search your home and remove the other offending agents.'

'You think there are more?' Tobias checked.

'Yes. I can sense there are numerous others.'

GJ, Sir Geo, Big Timmy and Becky followed him around as he explained what they were sniffing for. When the briefing was over, they disappeared with him, in order to hunt more down. When they returned, Sandy and Octy had prepared a large tray of freshly baked oat treats, made the old-fashioned way using Annie's famous recipe.

'We found these!' Menagerie reported, spreading their booty out on the floor.

'We should destroy them,' Gavin insisted.

‘I’ve neutralised the contents. It could be dangerous for us to try to interfere with the delivery systems,’ Menagerie warned.

‘What about storing them in an airtight container?’ Sandy suggested, sensibly.

‘Do you have such a thing?’ he checked. She sourced a voluminous plastic lunchbox from a cupboard.

‘We can take them back to Caves Beach with us and seek Eff’s advice,’ Tobias suggested.

Before Mikey could sound any objection, The Prof agreed, citing that such a plan would offer the dual benefits of watching his reaction to them finding the devices, while potentially tapping into his significant magical knowledge and skill.

‘I’m sorry to keep coming back to it, but we really must secure Master Sabi somewhere definitive. He will be withering without food and water and we cannot allow him to perish,’ Tobias explained.

You’re right,’ said Sandy.

‘Where and what did you have in mind when you discussed bringing him here with Kalan and Viz?’ The Prof enquired.

‘We intuitively felt that he should be held far from the place he calls home and his remaining loyal confederates. Earth is the place we know best and where we have the most support. Beyond that we wanted your opinion on where we should erect the prison of his exile,’ Tobias explained.

‘I hope you haven’t overestimated my wisdom,’ replied The Prof.

‘Where would you suggest we place it?’ asked GJ.

'Before I can make any sensible suggestions, I'd like more information. What else can you tell me about this prison?'

'Viz has sent us with a compact, portable, impenetrable, invisible containment facility. It needs to be carefully placed so no one stumbles across it. It will assemble itself once we activate it,' said GJ.

'It requires someone to be responsible for checking regularly on the prisoner; at minimum several times a day. He will be provided with a replicator device so he has adequate nutrition,' Menagerie added.

'That's a big ask, particularly given the astonishing longevity of a Luna Triban,' said Gavin, anxiously rubbing the snowy whiskers on his chin.

'Maybe you could consider an idea I picked up on the way here,' said GJ.

'Do tell,' said Mikey, intrigued.

'Some snow monkeys told us about a place in Tasmania that is famous for keeping prisoners, called Port Arthur.' Mikey burst out laughing.

'I know the place you are referring to. What a hoot! I work there!'

'Not coincidence again!' Tobias exclaimed.

'I didn't realise you were a prison guard? I thought you were a student?' queried GJ.

'I have a part time job as a night guide at the Historic Port Arthur Convict prison. We run ghost tours almost every night of the year and I always close up at the end. Actually, I can imagine the very spot to locate his prison, high above the ancient penitentiary building. Any murmurings from this villain will only add to the spooky atmosphere where paranormal sensing is a common occurrence.'

Sandy looked at her son with pride and said, 'our Mikey puts on quite a show for the thrill seekers.'

'We visited him last year. He made a whole class of teenage girls on a high school camp, freak out. They loved him!' Octy shared.

'The situation was aided by you breathing on their necks, acting as an invisible presence,' Sandy reminded the Octavian. Mikey laughed and said, 'Uncle Octy is the best!'

'How are you managing to work at this place in Port Arthur when you are at university?' Tobias enquired.

'I'm doing my Master's degree by research. I'm helping investigate a species called *Sarcophilus harrisii*, commonly known as the Tasmanian Devil. It's a feisty proud race only found naturally in Tasmania. Their mere existence has become threatened by an affliction called "Facial Tumour disease".' Mikey shared with the others what he had learned about the fatal transmissible cancer that caused hideous painful tumours to form on the faces, necks and sometimes bodies of the animals. 'It's wiping them out by the droves. Thanks to the polyglot translator device that Uncle Octy gave me when I was born, I've been able to talk to many of them about it. Regrettably, the cause remains elusive.'

'It's not a bad idea. Are you volunteering to become a real prison warden?' The Prof asked him.

'I guess I am; at least for a while.'

'This is an important mission. I will come and help you,' said Sir Geo.

'Perhaps at some stage Menagerie could join you too? He might be able to help you figure out if your research subjects are succumbing to an unnatural process,' GJ suggested.

'Has Eff been involved?' asked the lion. Mikey shook his head, shamefaced and said, 'perhaps in the future.'

'Tell me more about the situation?' asked the eager to please lion.

'It could well be a potion,' Menagerie concluded, when he had finished. 'I'd be happy to help in due course. Right now, I need to stay with GJ. I assume you'll want to go hunting for the antidote?' he asked the dog.

'You've got it.'

'It's a huge responsibility you'd be taking on, son,' Sandy acknowledged. 'Master Sabi is an extremely dangerous enemy.'

'I'm ready mum. I've spent my whole life waiting to be part of a bigger calling. It's in my blood.'

No one had a better idea.

Tobias yawned and said, 'thank you, Mikey. Tomorrow, we will travel to Tasmania and secure Master Sabi in his new residence.'

To relieve her anxiety over her son's decision, Sandy started collecting up the dirty dishes. They weren't very soiled, as Becky and Big Timmy had already attended to removing all the crumbs, performing the 'prewash service', as they fondly called it.

'Now that has been agreed upon, let us go back to the riddle,' suggested The Prof.

‘How about some more Sparkling Shiraz?’ suggested Gavin, having drained his glass. He looked more relaxed than The Prof had seen him in years. There were no takers.

Despite their best efforts, the group remained lost for a place to start searching for the antidote.

‘I need to sleep on it,’ said The Prof, yawning.

‘We’re not as young as we used to be. Darn it! We need rest. I don’t have an all-nighter in me anymore,’ Gavin complained, rubbing his gritty eyes.

Big Timmy and Becky, aided by the contentment of overfilled bellies, were also struggling to keep their eyes open. They took their leave. Sandy gently shook her mother and led her to her bedroom. The two ageing men followed her lead, with The Prof wheeling Gavin. Untouched by fatigue, Menagerie and Octy remained as company for Tobias.

‘I’m not ready to call it a night either. I’ve never felt so awake,’ Mikey told the monk, who was in the process of consuming another coffee so his guard duty could continue. The two dogs curled up on the floor at is feet, like croissants.

‘Tell me more about the venue we will be turning into a prison?’

‘Men and women convicted of crimes in England were transported to Port Arthur because it was located in an isolated part of Australia. Harsh physical and mental punishments were inflicted in the cold and desolate prison you will soon see,’ Mikey told them, drawing on his tour guide spiel.

By the time the sun was starting to rise, detailed plans for setting up the prison and how it would be operated, had formed. When GJ woke a short time later for a hurry-up, he found Tobias, still in the kitchen, sitting upright, leaning against the wall next to Master Sabi. His canine eyes were staring vacantly at the cupboards in the distance.

'I should watch him for a while so he can have a proper sleep,' Mikey suggested, also stirring. He had fallen asleep at the table resting his head on his arms. Sir Geo stretched and gently pawed the monk awake, causing his humanoid facial appearance to return. 'You should go to bed. We've got this.'

'The monster is my burden until he rests in a definitive prison,' Tobias replied.

'We all have to pee. At least go for a walk outside and stretch your legs,' said GJ, sensibly.

He nodded and temporarily departed. Upon his return, Tobias sat on a bench, frowning.

'What is troubling you the most, this fine morning?' the perky Chocolate Labrador enquired.

'I failed to confide in my order the revelations about our heritage. They are selflessly working on the riddle rather than celebrating.'

'That time will come soon. I think they'll forgive you for taking a few more days, after so long without answers. Besides won't you need to be able to stay with them and lead them through the inevitable, stressful events that the new knowledge will set in motion?' said GJ.

'Why haven't you told them?' asked Mikey. He had been captivated to learn about his past.

'The truth is that I don't feel ready to return to my role as head of the order until the riddle can be solved. Things have changed for me. I feel part of another calling too.'

'You have found another family in us,' said GJ.

'I have.'

'Do you think you could focus on both tasks once Master Sabi is secured and you've had some sleep?' asked Menagerie, also awake.

'Perhaps. I do have an excellent second in charge who has done a fantastic job leading our order. He understands how important our quest is. My brothers are praying for our success as we speak. They're committed to trying to decipher the riddle too.'

'We're fortunate to have their support,' said Octy. He had appeared and started quietly pottering around in the background, starting to prepare breakfast.

'I fear for those we have left trapped in that motionless, fragile state,' said Tobias.

'They didn't deserve that,' another voice chimed in. The Prof had joined them. 'Nor did we deserve to have fallen under the ill effects of a potion. Our home should be our safe place. What has happened here is a complete violation. Let's take our breakfast to my study. I'm eager to share with you what I think of the riddle.'

'You seem full of energy this morning,' noted Octy.

'I feel like my brain has woken up,' he replied.

'I'll bring a basket of warm buttery croissants to you as soon as they are out of the oven. I was inspired to make them by the appearance of GJ and Sir Geo curled up on the rug.'

Debate was already underway as to the meaning of a few select words on the blackboard when he brought a tea and coffee tray to the study. An hour later, he returned and called for a pause while the flaky pastries were distributed on napkins.

'These are fantastic, Uncle Octy,' uttered Mikey, in a garbled voice, having overstuffed his mouth.

More were handed out as others woke and were drawn to the wafting smell. As a special treat, Sandy gave one each to GJ, Sir Geo and a third to Big Timmy and Becky, for sharing.

'You'll have to tell me your recipe,' said Sandy.

'I'd be honoured. The cook at the White Dyas Inn showed me how to make them,' Octy replied, chuffed.

'Allow me to share what we've been talking about,' said The Prof, when he had finished eating.

On the chalkboard where Mikey had transcribed the riddle, multiple annotations had been added in pink chalk, in The Prof's distinctive swirling handwriting.

'I've broken it down into sections,' he explained, as he stood and pointed to the board.

'You haven't been able to write in months!' Gavin interrupted.

'I'm feeling terrific. Have you tried to walk this morning?'

Gavin hesitated, before attempting to stand up from his wheelchair. He stretched his arms above his head then started marching on the spot.

'My back is feeling the best it has been in years!' He sat down again, not wanting to push himself too far, too fast.

The Prof moved to the board and started reading, his eyesight no longer an issue.

'Before the moons turn pure, those turned to sand from the place of the invader must shower in the drink of stars, the vision of the devil.'

He turned and faced his audience. 'I think the invader refers to Geo, as his arrival on Luna Tribus was a catalyst of major change in the trajectory of the planetary system. I'm convinced that turning the victims to sand from Caves Beach is a personal and ironic act of revenge against Geo and his allies, including us. I've also concluded that the antidote must be sprayed on the affected individuals, like a shower raining down on them. It must be a liquid formulation as the word "drink" is used to describe it. I'm not sure about the last part.'

Tired, he sat down to rest. He asked Mikey to read the next sentence.

'Hope starts from scouring universally for a falsely purported complexly brewed medicinal where a trio of austere globules dance with organisms without chlorophyll.'

The Prof cracked his knuckles, which were significantly less swollen and said, 'this next part is about the chemistry of the antidote. I think it must already exist by the way it is described. Earth history is full of stories of substances that have been promoted as cures for human ailments. False claims are rare, now that there are stricter regulations. It's logical to conclude the substance must be old. Such historic medicines were classically peddled by charismatic charlatans for profit at country shows and marketed in dubious newspapers. I'm thinking the elixir must have three chemical components and another substance not from plants; as they have the pigment chlorophyll in their leaves, for photosynthesis.'

GJ looked perplexed and said, 'photo what?'

'Photosynthesis. Think of it as the process of how leaves take up carbon dioxide and make oxygen. It's the reason we can breathe,' Mikey explained. He continued with the next sentence in the riddle.

'Find the mentees of the potion master monk. Find the masters apprentice daughter at the understated place of coffee and toffee and sit in her lazy chair and stare, or find the resplendent place of oranges and search the labyrinths if you dare.'

'I think this is about who made the medicinal,' advised The Prof. Tobias agreed and said, 'the monk part of the riddle has always jumped out at me. As you know, my order is famous for making beer. There are many religious groups that sustain themselves through sales of their "special products" as well as enjoying a drop or two of liquor themselves. Some monks we know make superlative altar wines from grapes and others distil complex spirits to facilitate formal worship of their god. It's been going on for centuries. Could this mean we are looking for such an establishment?'

'Exactly what I was about to say,' The Prof admitted. 'This could also be a stab at you Tobias, acknowledging the powerful role he anticipated you would have in these rapidly unfolding events.'

'That is disturbing, yet I fear you may be correct,' the troubled Malinois monk responded, frowning.

'We need to start analysing religious orders. Your brothers would be best suited to this task,' said GJ.

'I'll contact them right away.'

'First, let me finish sharing the rest of my preliminary analysis and then I propose we form a specific strategy and allocate tasks,' The Prof recommended. Mikey again read aloud.

'Even then so close you will be but in an endless sea. Only the girl in love will be able to see. Find the cure but dispense it only with a dragon sword. A dose for one will be an antidote for all.'

'This section suggests that wherever Master Sabi has hidden the antidote, there will be lots of other items the same to choose from, as in batches. I'm imagining bottles in some kind of warehouse where liquids are packaged and stored. In this place there must be a girl we need to find to help us pick out the correct bottle. This young female and perhaps the bottle too, must be under some sort of spell. The final line suggests that once one victim is treated, the rest will automatically be freed as well.'

'Is it wrong for me to get excited about the possibility of using a sword to deliver the substance?' blurted Mikey, grinning. He underlined the word 'sword' several times.

Sandy laughed and said, 'I'm picturing you wielding some kind of hand-forged weapon, appearing like a Samurai warrior with a long blade!'

'There's no denying the fact we will be needing to acquire such a weapon! Why not a katana? I've always loved them,' Mikey admitted.

'Do not worry about us having a sword in our possession as we keep many in the armoury at the back of our monastery. All monks of our order are routinely trained in weapons of all kinds,' Tobias said flatly.

'Do you have something called a dragon sword per chance?' asked The Prof.

'Not that I'm aware of.'

'Could you teach me to sword fight?' asked Mikey, his eyes wide with excitement.

'In due course, should that be your wish. Your selfless commitment to acting as warden should be rewarded. If that is your desire then I will make it so.'

'My head is swimming with everything that's being contemplated,' Sandy confessed to Octy, as they disappeared to tidy up the kitchen.

'This feels like the old days, Sandy my darling! Glen would have loved being part of this,' Annie interrupted, suddenly striding towards the sink, to assist. She started to run hot water and said, 'we need to get on to some urgent baking. Mikey will need some serious inventory so he is well fed while he watches over the varmint! Octy, please prepare to make a list.'

Sandy dropped one of the coffee cups onto the floor. Fortunately, it only chipped.

'I can't believe you've stopped curing your own pork slabs my daughter! Mikey inherited his love of bacon from that father of his, so it is fitting that he heads off with some bacon and egg rolls. Did I teach you nothing?' she teased, giving her wide-eyed daughter a hug.

'Mum, are you OK?'

'I've never felt better. It's like I forgot who I was for a while. Now pick up a tea towel please.'

'It's wonderful that you are back!' Octy gushed. All of his antennae were buzzing with delight.

When they returned to the study with lunch, the fine tuning of the plan to establish Master Sabi in his definitive location in Port Arthur was reaching completion. Big Timmy and Becky had insisted they were going to stay with Mikey, allowing Tobias to continue searching for the antidote.

'Master Octy, I've volunteered to go too. I'm sorry that I haven't checked with you?' said Sir Geo, feeling bad. He stared lovingly up at the Octavian who had raised him from a puppy.

'I'm very proud of you for stepping up to the task. It is the honourable thing to do. Mikey cannot provide continuous watch on his own,' Octy replied.

'I cannot let you two do it,' Mikey directed at the rodent couple. They were taken aback. 'I really need the pair of you, along with Snuggles, to keep an eye on Eff. Sir Geo and I will be fine.'

'Eff does trust me. I'm most likely to pick up something suspicious, if it arose,' Big Timmy agreed. Becky jumped up and down on the spot and cried, 'you've given me an idea!' She pulled her partner aside and whispered into his ear.

'You're a genius dear lady!' Big Timmy applauded. He turned back to Mikey and announced proudly that they were volunteering their twins, Floorplank and Honey, to go with him in their place, to act as additional, reliable prison guards.

'They are highly intelligent, are always going on about wanting to be like their great Pa Timmy and go on an adventure. This is their moment!' Becky insisted.

'Can you swing by Caves Beach and pick them up on the way to Tasmania?' Big Timmy asked Tobias. He frowned and replied, 'they can join Mikey in due course. Without further delay, we need to get the prison established. As soon as it is completed, I plan to depart for Europe to meet briefly with my order. I promise I'll return to Caves Beach and hopefully bring more answers with me. The rats can then accompany me to Tasmania.'

'We have a pressing problem!' Menagerie interrupted. All eyes turned to the lion. 'Look around us! More emanators have appeared while we've been talking.' He picked one off the blackboard and tasted it. 'It's full of the same poison.' He prised another from the door to the study. GJ, with Sir Geo right behind him, ran out of the room, in search of others. They returned to report that more were appearing.

'How can there be more?' asked The Prof, fighting panic.

'They are forming in front of our eyes! There's a new one on the curtains, and now one on your lamp!' exclaimed Sandy, pointing.

'Malum!' cried Octy, using the Luna Triban expletive he hadn't used in years.

The walls of the room were slowly filling with exponentially more disks.

'It feels like we've triggered a horrible boobytrap!' The Prof remarked. He raised his hands and showed them to his companions. 'My dreadful arthritis is coming back! My fingers are swelling up and starting to deform again.'

'There can be no doubt that Menagerie has clearly diagnosed the source of our afflictions,' said Gavin, feeling his pain return.

'We need to evacuate. Everyone needs to get out of this house, right now!' Mikey insisted.

Tobias was yawning again and required Mikey to get him moving. He set him to work hauling Master Sabi to Beauty. Menagerie and the dogs helped The Prof wheel out Gavin, who was now doubled over by severe back spasms. Sandy and Octy went to the kitchen and found Annie staring into space. Innumerable disks covered the walls. She started wailing as they led her outside.

'Get this thief away from me! I won't let you steal the silver!' she screamed at her daughter.

They reconvened on the driveway where Beauty was parked.

'Someone is hell bent on causing us harm,' The Prof concluded, distressed.

'When exactly did you notice that the health of the three of you was starting to degenerate?' GJ enquired.

Gavin scratched his head then replied, 'I thought I'd injured my back during that final cracker of a harvest. It wasn't long after Geo was washed up on the beach. Annie seemed to be fading already, although she was never the same after Glen died. Grief does that to a person.'

'I'd stake my boogie board this is the work of Eff! There's no one else on this planet with this sort of capability,' Mikey insisted.

'Irrespective of who did this to my home, the fact is that we have triggered a crisis. What are we to do?' The Prof lamented. Helpless, they watched shiny disks multiply and spread themselves across the windows and outside walls. Gavin sighed deeply and said, 'it's easy. We need to go and stay at Caves Beach until we can work out how to eradicate this plague.'

'I shudder to think what a poor state we'd be in if we'd remained inside,' said Mikey.

'Probably dead!' Becky cried.

'There are plenty of your old belongings at the cave facility. We love it when our nest is full!' Big Timmy stated, desperately trying to remain upbeat.

'At least there aren't any animals still living in there now,' said Sandy, motioning to the house where even more emanators had appeared. The wooden walls were almost completely covered and they were spreading onto the roof.

‘I’m glad we moved the last pot of Fangybots last summer,’ Gavin added.

‘Where are they now?’ GJ enquired.

‘Sandy gave them to Eff to remind him of home. He keeps them in one of the rooms he remodelled especially for them in the caves. Fortunately, it’s well soundproofed,’ Big Timmy shared.

‘I’m hoping he might be able to stop this affliction. I know he’d like the chance to be useful,’ Sandy suggested.

‘I take back what I said. Eff may not be as honourable as you think he is but he wouldn’t do something this terrible to us,’ admitted Mikey. His mother smiled.

Tobias looked at the troubled group needing relocation. It was starting to rain.

‘I fear this is the point that we need to divide into two. Mikey, Sir Geo, should come with me to Tasmania, while Octy takes everyone else to Caves Beach.’

‘Don’t you need Beauty to take you there?’ Octy checked.

‘I have my own transport,’ Tobias announced. He removed Orizuru from his backpack. With Mikey’s help, Master Sabi was secured on his back. He instructed his group to touch the paper. The others watched in awe as a dazzling crane appeared.

Chapter 7
CHATSWOOD

Eff, Kate and Smiley were not at home when Beauty returned to Caves Beach. Snuggles advised they had gone out for a picnic. Floorplank and Honey were overjoyed to learn that they had been selected as prison wardens to represent their rodent family and travel to Port Arthur. Eager to demonstrate their usefulness, the inseparable siblings volunteered to retrieve the couple. GJ followed them outside, then along the grassy top of the cliffs towards the nearby Wallarah National Park.

'Why are you called Floorplank?' asked GJ.

'Not long after we were born, we nearly died,' Floorplank started to explain.

'We were very naughty and snuck outside when we shouldn't have,' said Honey, twitching her whiskers mischievously.

'As we were happily nibbling on a piece of bread, minding out own business, a surf lifesaver spotted us. He picked up a plank of wood and started trying to squash us with it!'

Honey started to giggle raucously and said, 'he kept missing, as we were way too fast for him! He got very frustrated and called his girlfriend over to help.'

'*Honey*, come here,' he kept saying to her. '*Honey*, you take the left side and herd them towards me. I'm get them with the *floor plank*,' Floorplank explained.

'Uncle Snuggles was taking a power nap at the time, when he was supposed to have been watching over us babies. Drawn to the shouting, he raced out to investigate. All he remembers hearing was the human male repeatedly scream out "floorplank" and "honey".'

They continued walking, venturing up a hill towards the overgrown remote track that led to Pinney Beach, their destination. Honey started to moan dramatically.

'My legs are getting too tired to walk! I'm exhausted Uncle GJ.'

Not to be outdone, Floorplank planted his ample rear on the ground at her side. With a touch of hysteria, he proclaimed, 'I simply can't go on.' GJ stopped and smiled, weighing up the situation.

'Really? I thought you two were superheroes? Aren't you going to be prison wardens to an evil magician from another world?' Floorplank, closely followed by his sister, immediately jumped up off the ground.

'You've got a point. I'm feeling better after the teensy rest stop,' said Floorplank, backtracking.

'Perhaps you could ignore what we foolishly did and gallantly offer to give us a carry?' Honey requested cheekily, flashing a dazzling smile.

'Uncle Snuggles is always going on about how amazing it was to ride on Geo's back,' Floorplank admitted.

GJ shook his head in disgust and said, 'you should have simply asked me. That would have been way classier.' He crouched down. 'Go on then! Jump up on my back and hold on to my neck fur, tightly.' The big dog shivered slightly under the tickling sensation of their scratchy paws running up his tail. He sniffed the air and said, 'off we go. I think I've detected a hint of Smiley. Yes, hold on kids, we're going to fly!' He picked up his pace, accelerating into an athletic run. His passengers giggled with the exhilaration.

GJ was panting when he stopped at a lookout. It was situated on a cliff edge, high above a secluded, rocky cove forged by the wind and sea that constantly battered the particular stretch of rocky coastline.

'I think I can see them,' GJ remarked. Far away on the distant wall of the inlet was a prominent section where nature had etched a number of distinctive hollows. They were smaller than the magnificent ones that had given Caves Beach its name, yet were nonetheless sufficiently large for a private picnic to be held; shelters from the scorching sun or frequent rain.

'You're right, GJ. I too can see Eff and Kate although I can't see Smiley,' Honey noted.

'It's because I'm here!' the stocky Blue Staffy announced, bursting in from behind them. There was much sniffing and chasing of each other's tails as the two dogs were reunited.

'How did you know we were here?' Floorplank enquired.

'You are very pungent. Thank goodness you are back! It's been terrible here! Things are progressing fast.' He pointed to the couple in the distance, now moulded together in a romantic embrace. 'They've been inseparable. It started as soon as you left for Skydog. I knew they'd been sneaking around for months, yet to my consternation, as soon as Sandy left, they entered a new, accelerated phase of their relationship.'

'Ooh yuk!' Honey reacted.

'I see what you mean,' said GJ, watching them.

'I think they are rubbing noses!' observed Floorplank.

'Are they smooching?' GJ asked his companions.

'I think so!' cried Honey.

'Mikey thinks Eff is a bad egg. What do you think?' GJ asked Smiley.

'I've been studying his every move for a very long time. I do think his feelings for Kate are real and sincere. I haven't seen anything to the contrary. He's never done anything vaguely troubling here. If I didn't know the background history, I'd think he was a good guy.'

'There's more to him than meets the eye. If Geo was worried about his intentions, then we should too,' the Chocolate Labrador argued. 'Is there anything he's doing that Kate and Sandy aren't aware of?'

'He works on his magic every night after he retreats to his rooms in the cave facility. He never talks about it. I have seen strange luminescent flashes of light coming from underneath his door. I've often detected unusual scents. I've heard him chant.'

'All the rats are aware of the strange things he does,' Honey admitted.

'Some of the smells that waft from his quarters are delicious,' stated Floorplank.

'I bet he's not baking biscuits!' GJ commented suspiciously.

'How was the trip to Skydog?' asked Smiley, eager to change the subject.

GJ was filling him in regarding the developments at Skydog, when Floorplank interrupted.

'Talking about flashes of light; there's something in his hand that's gleaming right now!'

'It's a ring!' GJ cried.

'I bet he's proposing marriage. I saw it on the television! Next, they'll be mating!' Floorplank insisted. The dismayed party took off, racing as fast as their legs could carry them, determined to interrupt the lingering kiss of the newly engaged couple.

GJ nudged Kate's inner thigh with his snout, causing her to pull away from her beau.

'What a surprise. It's GJ, Smiley and some ratty friends. Hello Floorplank, hello Honey,' said Kate, blushing.

'How wonderful,' responded Eff, with an obviously frustrated tone.

'We have important news. You need to return with us straight away!' GJ commanded.

'We have important news too. You are the first to hear it. Moments ago, Eff asked me to marry him and I have accepted.' She held up her left hand, revealing an emerald studded ring.

Later that night, three generations of women sat together in the kitchen.

'Your ring is very beautiful daughter,' Sandy blubbered, as her baby girl shared the details of her proposal.

'Are you sure he's the right one for you?' Annie asked gently. The scrambling of her mind had cleared again.

'I have no doubts about his love for me, Granny Annie. I have loved him from the first second I saw him,' Kate replied.

'Eff is not a human. What if you can't have children?' she enquired.

'I'm not worried about that.'

'May I see the ring?' the old woman requested. She moved closer. Annie's eyes narrowed as she studied it through her bifocals, holding her granddaughter's smooth hands in her wrinkled ones. 'I know this ring. It was Ellie's. It was the same ring that kept her skin pale.'

'Are you sure?' Kate checked.

'I have no doubt. I spent many hours sitting with Ellie as she contemplated whether she should continue to wear it. She was worried that Ro wouldn't love her if she was magenta coloured.'

GJ had been half listening, napping on a rug near the stove.

'Did you know that in the end she chose magenta and looks very beautiful that way?' he informed the women.

'I didn't know that. Good for her,' replied Annie.

'It explains why Ellie doesn't have the ring anymore,' said Sandy.

'How come Eff came to have it?' GJ checked.

'I'm sure he will tell us more about the history of the ring if we ask him. He had barely placed it on my finger when you burst in on us, GJ,' Kate replied, defensively.

‘I agree darling. I’m thrilled for you, although it seems a bit crazy. As you know, I had a bit of a crush on him myself when I was around your age. Now *you* are going to marry him,’ Sandy admitted, awkwardly.

‘We all know the story mum. It’s not like you dated him.’

‘I’m only bringing it up as a way of saying that I’ve always believed in him sweetheart and I always will. I hope he makes you as happy as your father did me,’ Sandy added.

‘Who wouldn’t want to marry such a handsome dish?’ Annie teased.

‘He’s also clever, kind, strong, funny, handsome, oh did I say handsome? Yes, I did, oops!’ Kate cried, dreamily.

‘I think I might need to throw up,’ GJ reacted, pretending to gag. ‘Actually, I think I’m tasting vomit in my mouth!’

‘We must prioritise organising an engagement party for our girl,’ Annie stated, ignoring GJ. Sandy stood up and said, ‘I’ll go and find Octy and start making it happen before we are parted again.’

‘Where are we going? When?’ asked GJ, jumping up.

‘I don’t know. I have a strong hunch that it won’t be long until Tobias returns. An intensive search for the antidote will begin and that will be consuming,’ warned Annie.

Sandy sighed and said to Kate, ‘it’s such a shame that your brother won’t be here for the celebration.’

‘Perhaps not. He’s really not a fan of your fiancée,’ GJ intervened. No one disagreed.

‘I’m so happy you are back, Granny Annie. I’ve missed you so much,’ Kate exclaimed, giving the old lady an enormous hug.

'I've missed you too. There's no one who can hold a function like you can, mum,' stated Sandy.

'I've missed me!' Annie replied, beaming. She kissed Kate on her cheek and said, 'Glen would have been so happy to see you married. Your dad would too and Geo of course. Without them, you'd never have met Eff.'

'We've lost so many we love,' Sandy sighed.

'We can't lose Ro and Ellie!' GJ asserted.

'I'd love them to be at our wedding. It would mean everything to Eff if his parents were there; his sister Izzie too. It would be a beautiful new beginning for his family,' Kate mused.

'I know that time is of the essence, so at some level it feels wrong to have a party while the lives of so many are hanging in the balance; yet I feel we must squeeze a celebration in, during the next few days,' Sandy insisted.

'It's not every day that your granddaughter gets engaged!' Annie insisted, supportively.

'You stay here, Sandy. The least I can do is go and fetch Octy for you,' said GJ, trying to sound more supportive than he felt.

Octy was unsurprised by the news. When he entered the kitchen, Kate jumped up from the table and danced around him like an over excited child on Christmas morning.

'Uncle Octy! I need your help! I need Beauty's help.'

'I remember when Eff's parents got engaged. Your parents too. How lucky am I to be involved in your special moment?' he told her. Despite his own lingering concerns about Eff, he had never doubted the depth of the young humanoid's devotion to Kate.

They sat together and worked on a plan to make the besotted woman's vision for the engagement party she had fantasised about, come to fruition. When they had finished, he said, 'it's going to be fabulous young Kate. Now off you go and find Eff and bring him to me so we can start making things happen.'

'Don't you love the exuberance of youth?' said Annie when the besotted young woman had departed.

'Their happiness is pure. A human and humanoid getting married is unique. I feel we are about to witness something epic! I need to go and speak to The Prof and Gavin about a few ideas of my own,' Octy replied. 'How about coming with me and showing some Chocolate Labrador enthusiasm?' he suggested to GJ.

'The food will be memorable,' promised Sandy.

'Perhaps it's time I gave Eff a chance?' said the dog.

'I feel certain it's what Geo would have done,' Annie counselled.

GJ stood up and moved closer to her and said, 'that's' not the only reason I'm feeling flat. The idea of having a party knowing our friends are fragile sand sculptures doesn't sit right with me. I've seen them. It was horrible.'

'I understand,' she responded. No one spoke. After a deep sigh he said, 'the bottom line is that until Tobias returns, we have a window to celebrate the nuptials. Kate and Eff are our family too. Ellie and Ro would want us to make the most of this time and support their son and his gorgeous wife-to-be.'

'The way I see it, we should take this opportunity to celebrate their happiness. Their love is rare and true. What is going on at the palace in Rectangulum City makes me even more convinced we should live every day like it is our last,' said Octy.

Kate declared that the dress standard for the engagement party should be formal. The Prof offered to buy clothing for Eff, Gavin, Octy and himself. He showed the humans the kind of outfits he had in mind on an internet website. His heart was set on commissioning bespoke three-piece suits, enlisting the expertise of a Savile Row tailor in Mayfair, London. Gavin pointed out that despite Beauty's help in transporting them to the location, one afternoon would be insufficient time for the necessary consultation and fittings to be completed.

'I've got this,' said Eff. With some complex incantations and finger movements, he replaced their simple attire of shorts and shirts with the same perfectly cut, stylish outfits they had been ogling together. Gavin's jaw dropped.

'I adore these threads! Good call Prof! We're all sorted now,' the future groom told the incredulous older males. With another series of hand flicks, their old clothes returned. 'I'll dress us again, when I get back from Sydney. I have to go there now and run a few errands with Octy. I'll make sure he looks good too.'

Eff had been bemused when his betrothed had unexpectedly asked for his help in 'pulling a few strings', as she called his magical abilities. In the carpark on the cliff top, the Octavian was waiting in the front of Beauty, transfigured as a non-descript white sedan car. He was busy reading over the list Kate had provided; actions necessary to ensure the venue she had selected was ready to accommodate her vision.

They returned in time to collect the partygoers. Sandy insisted that her daughter wear the same dress she had worn at her own engagement party. With a few minor alterations they modernised the simple, poppy red, cocktail dress. Annie removed from storage the dress she had worn to her own Las Vegas wedding to Glen. It was still a perfect fit. She joined her daughter and granddaughter, holding a number of bow ties that her wedding party had worn.

'Glen would have loved to see these worn again,' she told Kate. Together they attached them to GJ, Menagerie, Smiley, Snuggles and Big Timmy. Sandy retrieved a roll of red ribbon from her sewing box and helped Becky, Honey and Floorplank tie a matching bow onto their tails.

'It's time to get on the road,' Octy advised, having been given the task of escorting the attendees to the carpark where Eff was waiting with Beauty. She was now once again the grand, ebony limousine that had been part of the Las Vegas chapter of the family's history.

'Excellent choice!' said Annie, after sinking into a soft leather seat at the back, in between The Prof and Gavin.

Beauty recognised her voice and said, 'I feel honoured to be taking you out on this happy occasion.' She started to play soft, tinkling piano music in the background.

'Chopin was my touch!' The Prof told his friends.

'It's very stylish,' Kate responded, now snuggled up next to her fiancée, surrounded by representatives of the rat family she had grown up with. To avoid drawing attention, Octy seated himself behind the wheel, with GJ sprawled out at his side.

Kate asked Beauty to travel at conventional speeds so they could enjoy the trip. As they travelled along the Pacific Highway towards Sydney, chatter was incessant. Less than two hours later, they pulled up in the north shore suburb of Chatswood outside an unassuming Vietnamese restaurant called 'Pho'.

It felt right for Kate that they were celebrating the special event in a multicultural hotspot. She explained that the suburb was one of her favourite places to visit in the city. Before exiting the vehicle, she added, 'many people who live around here have made Australia their new home, having migrated from places far away; predominantly all over Asia. Their presence has added to the richness of our country.'

'Why did you select this particular restaurant?' asked Gavin.

'We didn't have time to travel to the actual Vietnam tonight which is my favourite place in South East Asia. Instead, for the next few hours, we will imagine that we are arriving in Ho Chi Minh City to share a magnificent banquet! I hope you like this place as much as I do.'

'I love Vietnamese food!' The Prof proclaimed.

'Thank you for making this possible, my darling Eff. One day I want to show the real Vietnam to you,' she whispered into his ear, after wrapping her arms around his neck.

'I'd like that,' he murmured.

'Where is this Vietnam place that you speak of?' GJ enquired.

'It's a ten-hour flight northwest of here on a normal plane. I went there backpacking after I finished high school, prior to starting at the hospitality college. It remains the most extraordinary place I've ever been. The people were beyond kind, the food which we will be tasting tonight, was indescribably flavoursome and the scenery distinctive and pretty.'

The Prof frowned, thinking about the Vietnam War and the many souls, including Australians, who had lost their lives or experienced trauma, from the protracted conflict. He forced himself to focus on the present.

'It does smell intoxicating,' GJ acknowledged, wildly sniffing the air. Drool started to appear in the corners of his mouth.

Kate and Eff went inside first, to liaise with the manager. The others started unloading boxes onto the pavement, ready to be carried indoors.

'A little help please!' Big Timmy called out. He was trying to drag a long, boxed item from under one of the seats towards the open door of the limousine. GJ came to assist. He pulled it down the aisle then pushed it out onto the ground with his nose. The contingent of rats, with Menagerie assisting them, went to work moving it inside.

'Take care with that! I'm told it is vital,' warned Octy.

'Where do you want them to put it Prof?' asked Snuggles, who had adopted a purely supervisory role.

'Bring it over here, please.'

The box was dragged across the empty restaurant to a table where he and Gavin were painstakingly assembling what could only be described as a sculpture. One at a time, the veterinarian unloaded from a dusty crate, a collection of matching, old fashioned, bowl-shaped goblets. He used a white linen cloth to individually polish the glasses before carefully handing each one over to his companion. The Prof, concentrating heavily, placed each item with great precision.

'You're making a tapering tower from the glasses!' Menagerie commented in awe, as the structure started to take form.

'Indeed, I am! It's a conical design called a "champagne tower" and it's all thanks to you, dear lion. It feels so good to have my hands back.'

'Where did you get those lovely glasses?' GJ enquired.

'They are Italian; from Venice to be precise. I had them made especially to celebrate the launch of my first vintage,' Gavin explained proudly.

'Now that was a great trip! I remember it well,' Octy reminisced, admiring the collection.

'They are very elegant,' Menagerie observed, admiring the gleaming transparent bowls of glass; each rim had been hand painted with a scarlet-coloured band. The Prof completed the fifth and final level of his sculpture with a single glass balanced in the middle of the four that formed the layer below.

'Eff, Octy, can you please bring in the bottles from Beauty's boot? The ones in those silver buckets please,' Gavin requested. Four, three litre capacity jeroboams, partially submerged in a slurry of ice cubes, were carried inside. They were set down on the floor adjacent to the tower. A smaller bottle, cradled inside its own shiny bucket, was placed out of sight underneath the table.

'I'm glad you decided to store the big bottles in the caves,' The Prof told Gavin.

'Me too. I hate to think what is happening at Skydog,' he replied.

'Could we have the special item now?' The Prof said to Snuggles. With Big Timmy's help, the brothers dragged the long cardboard box to his feet.

'What's inside?' asked GJ, now sniffing it.

'It's a surprise,' The Prof insisted.

In the other corner of the restaurant, Sandy and Annie had been occupied, assisting two wait staff set the tables for the guests. Shortly after their arrival, Kate had disappeared into the kitchen to liaise with the cook about the final menu. Eff unpacked a box of Turban shells; each filled with a tea candle. He scattered them around the establishment. When they were burning brightly, he used a dimmer switch to turn down the overhead lights.

'What a perfect touch! The main cave was decorated with the same lights the night your parents got engaged,' The Prof told him.

'That's what Sandy told me. I wish I could have known them better,' he replied, looking forlorn.

'Don't give up hope. I feel this chapter is far from over,' Octy reassured him.

The sombre moment was broken by the booming tones of Becky. She was leading a complex discussion with the other rats on the virtues of Vietnamese food. She reprimanded Big Timmy for drooling over a colourful menu, featuring photographs of each dish.

'I wonder what "Cha gio" and "Pho bo dac biet" would taste like?' Floorplank asked Honey, struggling to pronounce the words.

'I bet it's like chicken. Doesn't everything taste like that?' Snuggles suggested, pretending to be serious.

'Kate has briefed me extensively and I assure you it's more nuanced than that,' Becky defended.

Eff laughed, watching the hungry animals and listening to their amusing appraisal of the extensive, exotic offerings. Floorplank looked up to find him observing them and said, 'how did you make this scenario possible?' He had astutely noticed that they were the only customers present. The staff were interacting with the eclectic guests, including the various animals, as if they had known them forever.

'I love this place! A human apologised for asking me to move aside so he could place some condiments on the table I was blocking. It's a far cry from being chased with a floor plank!' Honey told him. Without a hint of arrogance he replied, 'it wasn't a big deal. I came here with Octy as soon as Kate asked me to and doused the staff with an uncomplicated influencing potion. They are doing exactly as I requested, which is to make us all feel welcome for our exclusive event.'

GJ eyed the young man suspiciously, listening to his every word. He desperately wanted to believe that he was well intentioned but he was still plagued by doubt. He rounded up Menagerie, Smiley and Octy and asked them to join him outside.

'What's wrong? Are you unwell?' asked Octy.

'I've had a terrible thought I needed to share. What if Eff has used some sort of love potion to influence Kate and make her fall for him?'

'Why would he do that?' asked Octy, unconvinced.

'I don't know. I suppose it doesn't make sense.'

'Stop worrying, GJ. I think he really has changed. Caves Beach and the humans have a way of making you see what really matters in life,' Octy said, reassuringly.

'I agree with Octy. It's been the same for me. I was previously appallingly uptight. It's extraordinary I never developed a stomach ulcer,' added Smiley.

'Menagerie, could you look inside Eff's mind and see if he is pure of heart?' GJ requested.

'I could. The question is, would that be an appropriate thing for tonight?' the lion replied, frowning.

'I guess it would set the record straight once and for all. Eff isn't stupid. He's fully aware that doubts exist about his character,' Octy suggested.

‘I think we should leave it alone. This should be a happy night. Let’s go inside before we are missed,’ Smiley recommended.

When they returned to the restaurant, Eff and Kate were standing with The Prof next to the resplendent sculpture of glasses.

‘Sorry, we needed a hurry up,’ GJ apologised, feeling guilty for holding up the commencement of the program.

The Prof started his speech.

‘There are some things on Earth that are “magic” of a simple kind. This is one of them. My dear friend Gavin has created a special “potion” that is not the product of a spell. Before me is what happens when you combine nature with science, creativity, art and love. Behold! Gavin has gifted to the happy couple tonight this fountain of his finest sparkling wine!’ He turned and signalled him to lift the first jeroboam and start pouring the sparkling wine contents into the top glass of the tower. As it overflowed, gold liquid started to drizzle onto the layers below, then down to progressively lower lying glasses as these filled. Tiny beads of escaping air formed a fine mist that exuded from the cascading liquid. It was captivating to watch.

As The Prof picked up the second bottle and continued to focus, meticulously pouring, Gavin explained that he had created the concoction exclusively from small batches of grapes tended by his own hands. He had made them into separate still wines, then blended and left them to ferment; this process releasing the bubbles and distinct complex yeast, perfume and honey flavours that he hoped they would find exquisite to taste.

‘I’ve always loved this potion. It is the ultimate drink of celebration!’ The Prof gushed.

‘I wonder if it has become popular in Octavia?’ GJ said to Octy.

‘Why do you say that?’

‘I thought The Prof sent a bottle of French Champagne, fruit cake with cheese and a note, in the rocket that took Geo, Snuggles and Big Timmy on their historic expedition to Luna Tribus?’

‘The bottle was never opened,’ said Octy.

‘Really?’ GJ checked.

‘What became of it?’ asked Eff, intrigued.

‘We gifted it to Ellie and Ro as a wedding present,’ Snuggles clarified.

‘It was in one of their backpacks when we returned to Caves Beach the first time,’ Big Timmy added.

‘What happened to it after that?’ asked Eff, drawn to the conversation. Before anyone could answer, Gavin was asking for their attention again.

‘It is time for us to make a toast to the happy couple and wish them good health,’ said Gavin, cueing his co-conspirator to spring into action. From under the table, The Prof retrieved the smaller bottle of wine, together with a stainless-steel silver sword. The metal weapon shimmered as he demonstrated how to wield it by dramatically slicing the air in a series of bold, figure of eight actions.

Eff looked puzzled as to its relevance. It was unlike the sharp, plain combat weapons he was familiar with. This shiny piece had a prominent flat blade and rounded spine. Expertly, with dramatic flair,

The Prof raised the weapon high into the air above his head. With his other hand, he firmly held the bottle in a tilted position, slightly head up, with the end pointing towards the nearby wall. In a confident, strong single slash, the rounded edge of his blade powerfully grazed the side of the bottle before slicing its end, complete with the cork, cleanly away from its body.

Gavin promptly brought forward two extra glasses and captured the effervescing contents that now flowed, barely spilling a drop. He handed one to Kate, the other to Eff. The Prof smiled at them and said, 'sip from each other's glass then make a wish. It will come true.'

'Let me guide you,' said Gavin, with sentimental tears forming, as he basked in their happiness. Under instruction, the couple's arms carefully crossed over each other's, taking care not to spill the bubbling contents of their delicate goblets. Gracefully, they leaned forward and drank from the glass being presented. After swallowing a mouthful of the delicious fluid, their eyes locked momentarily, drinking in each other, lost in their own private world. The depth of their feeling for each other was visibly raw and intense.

'That bottle was extra special and one that I did not make,' explained Gavin, smiling. The Prof took over.

'It was the exact bottle GJ mentioned that Ellie and Ro returned to me; the one that was launched into space with Geo and the rats. Eff, your parents wanted me to have it, despite it having been gifted to them as a wedding present. It is therefore fitting that it should be shared by you two!'

The couple were rendered speechless.

'Now it is our moment to partake of another wonderful vintage…mine,' said Gavin, chuckling. 'It's time for the rest of us to toast the happy couple!' He started handing out glasses from the top layers of the fountain.

'A sip only!' insisted Sandy, ever the Veterinarian, when GJ and Menagerie asked for a glass to share. The Prof placed it on a chair in front of them, at nose height. Gavin crouched down and placed another onto the ground, so the mature rats could sample it, before standing tall and stretching, grateful to be free of back pain. He raised his own glass high into the air and said, 'to Kate and Eff! To true love! To the family we choose for ourselves!' The audience echoed his words before proceeding to sample their own drink. Cheers erupted. After a lingering kiss to seal their memory of the moment, the couple stepped apart and the formalities were concluded.

'Please be seated. Dinner is ready!' the restaurant owner announced, having watched the toast, waiting for the right interval to make his announcement.

'That move you performed with the sword was totally awesome!' GJ gushed to The Prof a short time later.

'Where did you learn how to do it?' Menagerie questioned.

'France. When Gavin decided he wanted to specialise in making fine sparkling wines, we travelled together to the famous Champagne region. He studied the art with the very best of mentors. I kept him company and learned a few tricks myself.'

'The sword is specific to the pastime you witnessed. It is called a Champagne Sabre. "Sabrage" is the art of wielding it to open Champagne bottles. It dates back to the times of the French Revolution and a famous conqueror called Napoleon Bonaparte. Members of his army would use swords to open bottles of champagne during their victory parties,' Gavin explained.

'Napoleon was known to have coined an insightful quotation about the drink. He said, "in victory one deserves it; in defeat one needs it!" It's why sparkling wine is a drink of celebration at events such as tonight,' said The Prof.

'Hopefully we will only ever experience this drink at happy moments. We *are* going to be victorious in finding the antidote!' Kate insisted

Eff was totally captivated by what he had witnessed. He asked the Prof to teach him how to perform sabrage.

'I will do that. Wouldn't it be wonderful if you could use the technique to open the bottle you will share with your parents and sister at your wedding? When the time comes, I will lend you the sword. Correction, I will gift it to you,' he replied effusively.

The party sat down at the closely arranged tables. Share platters of exotic food were distributed and voraciously consumed. Glasses were slowly drained. In the act of swallowing his last mouthful,' The Prof almost choked.

'What is it?' Gavin pressed, slapping him on the back.

'I think I know what the antidote is! It's Champagne!'

'Really?' Kate queried.

‘It would fit with the riddle. Think about it. Champagne was once called the “devil’s drink” because the first bottles used to house it were made too thinly. They would sometimes explode under the pressure of the forming bubbles and the glass shards would kill the remueur. People concluded it was the work of the devil!’

‘The rem who?’ asked GJ.

‘The remueur is the person who works in the chalky underground caves where it is made, performing a process called “remuage” or “riddling”. They painstakingly turn and downwards tilt the bottles with the aim of slowly shifting the yeast sediment to the neck, while the wine is maturing. These days machines are mostly used to do this,’ said Gavin. He paused briefly in thought then went on, now with bursting excitement. ‘You’re right Prof! The famous Monk Dom Perignon, who is attributed to inventing Champagne, was supposed to have said “I’m drinking the stars!” when he described it.’

‘It was falsely marketed as a medicinal. The doctors of Reims once claimed it was a cure for many ailments, including the parasitic infection malaria!’ The Prof recalled. He pulled out his copy of the riddle.

‘Master Sabi would have known that it is your favourite drink, Prof. The fact Gavin specialised in production of sparkling wines made with the same technique would have been easy to discover,’ said Sandy.

‘This is the breakthrough we needed! I feel we must prematurely end our party, darling,’ Kate told Eff. He nodded.

‘Without tonight we might never have had this realisation,’ GJ observed.

‘Surely there is time for a few more nibbles?’ cried a chorus of pleading voices from the separate, low table that had been designated for the family of rats.

‘We’ve not been allowed to try that bubble stuff so we can’t go home yet!’ pleaded Floorplank.

‘Before we go, as compensation, I need to consume my body weight in noodles!’ Honey insisted.

Chapter 8
BELGIUM

Eff cleared his throat nervously and stood up. He intertwined his fingers in Kate's and panned around the room.

'I'd like to say something before we call it a night. It is very awkward, yet it needs to be said. There are some of you with nagging doubts about the purity of my intentions. Even tonight, I overheard some of you discussing this.' The relevant individuals hung their heads. 'I can understand your concerns, particularly those of GJ, Snuggles and Timothy. You lived through the events that unfolded with my mentor, Master Sabi, my grandmother and aunts, prior to me being washed up in the paradise, which is now my home. Geo was so convinced that I was a traitor, that he lured me through a deadly underwater wormhole. He sacrificed himself, hoping that I would drown with the rest of my relatives.'

The evening turned sombre. Kate stood up next to him and placed a supportive arm around his shoulder and said, 'you are right, my darling. We need to extinguish once and for all, any ill feelings.' There was a long awkward silence. Eff broke it by turning his attention to the lion.

'Menagerie, I'm wondering if you could help us?'

'How may I serve?'

'Earlier tonight, I heard GJ suggest that you might be able to delve inside my head and discover my true nature. Would you do that for me? Would you do it now?'

GJ felt embarrassed at having been overheard. He was also impressed with the acuity of Eff's hearing.

'I am your servant. Please crouch down on the floor in front of me,' he instructed.

Kate sat down cross-legged next to the pair, captivated. Two sets of eyes locked and blinking ceased. No one spoke. Anticipation gripped the room. Menagerie was the first to drop his gaze. He stood up and shook his mane before casting his verdict.

'He is pure of heart!'

'I have always known this,' Kate murmured in his ear. Sandy similarly smiled at her future son-in-law, experiencing relief and vindication in equal measures.

Each of those in attendance took a turn, variously offering apologies, affirmations of friendship and words of support to Eff. Big Timmy hovered, embarrassed by the lack of faith he knew he had always harboured deep within him.

'I watched you grow from a baby. Shame on me for ever doubting you,' he said honestly. Eff asked him to jump on his shoulder so they could exchange some private words.

'Timothy, I am not angry at you, as I have often doubted myself. My heart was thumping in the seconds before I stared into the eyes of the lion. To be raised by selfish individuals who denied me the sincere love of parents does something to a child. I knew it had previously made me want to trust no one and be a total island. What I didn't know, was whether it had left a permanent dark imprint upon me.'

'Geo's final act inadvertently gave you freedom; the chance to be the person you were meant to be, free of their control and expectations. You are truly the child of the couple who now need your help,' the rat responded. 'As an aside, going forwards, please call me Big Timmy.'

'I will,' said Eff. He turned to the shame faced Chocolate Labrador.

'GJ; Kate and I want to help you find the antidote and to be with you when it is administered.'

'I am sorry for being so stubbornly biased. You will be most welcome at my side wherever the riddle takes Menagerie and I.'

Sandy stood next to her mother. Worry lines indented her forehead. Annie patted her daughter's hand and said, 'you've got to let her go. Everyone should have at least one thrilling adventure in their lifetime and Kate's future is now with Eff. She needs to be at his side and know who he is. She needs to know his roots. I feel our girl is destined to be the first of us to see Luna Tribus.'

Kate raised an eyebrow having sensed they were talking about her. She moved to their side and said, 'don't worry. As soon as we are successful, I'll come back and together we'll plan the most wonderful wedding that Caves Beach has ever seen!'

'When the time comes, I'm coming with you to Rectangulum City. I thought I was on the way out and my biggest regret was not having ventured further within The White Corridor when I had the chance.

This feels like a second chance to experience Luna Tribus!' The Prof exclaimed.

Octy declared he was not returning to Zermatt the next day as originally planned and would also go with them in pursuit of the antidote.

'What will you do, Gavin?' GJ requested.

'I'm not sure,' he said honestly.

'I suggest we sit down again, briefly. I have arranged for dessert to come now, starting with a serving for my most important ratty guests,' Kate interrupted. She asked the five rodents to jump onto the table in front of her. A waiter set down an enormous share bowl of 'Che Thai'. 'This is for you. Show me your best nibbles, slurps and chews...swim in it if you like.'

The squealing rats ran towards the milky fruit cocktail, making an enormous mess as they flicked their heads around, sampling the coconut cream, pieces of lychee, jackfruit and chewy jellies. Individual serves of the same dish were handed out to the other guests. Floorplank made a bold move, diving head first into the mix, burying his head. Honey laughed so hard she lost balance and toppled in, quickly resurfacing and flicking her fur, showering Kate with sticky fluid. A lump of cream hit Big Timmy in the face.

Standing at the side of the dish, chomping on a lychee, the patriarch of the family crossed his arms, appearing unimpressed. The sheepish culprit waited for his wrath. Instead, Big Timmy scooped up a handful of cream and threw it at the younger rat.

‘Food fight!’ Snuggles announced.

‘You’re incorrigible!’ Becky retorted from the other side of the bowl, prompting the instigator to procure a fistful of red jelly and fling it at her, triggering a chase.

Gavin retreated out of firing range. He started collecting up his special glasses and packed away the sabre. With Octy’s help they were loaded into Beauty.

‘Time to go,’ Eff announced. With a subtle flickering of his fingers, all traces of mess were gone. The Prof paid for dinner in cash, as the guests piled into the limousine.

‘Thank you,’ the magician told the restaurant manager and his staff. He was almost to the door when he doubled back and added, ‘we were the most unremarkable individuals you have ever catered for.’

They were soon back on the freeway, heading north out of Sydney.

‘We need to urgently contact Tobias and update him with our new analysis,’ GJ told The Prof, as Beauty picked up speed. He nodded.

‘I wonder how Mikey is getting on with his new role as prison warden?’ Annie mused. Gavin was sitting between Sandy and her mother. He linked arms with them and said, ‘I may not be ready to leave Earth but I am up for an adventure. How about the three of us go and see our boy? One of my unfulfilled life goals is to buy a campervan and take it on the road. Are you with me?’

Annie shook her head half-heartedly and replied, ‘there’s no road to Tasmania you crazy man. Have you forgotten that it’s the island state?’

'There is a massive ferry that regularly transports people and vehicles, even enormous trucks, across the Bass Strait. I've read that it has a restaurant and cabins you can bunk in for the night, as the crew sail you across.'

'Why do you know so much about Tasmania?' Sandy enquired.

'Back in the day, there was a growing industry of winemakers who like me, focused on making sparkling wines using traditional French methods of production. I met a few at wine competitions. It was a lost opportunity to have never taken them up on the invitation to visit their estates and see their set ups.'

'It's a great idea. I am very worried about Mikey. I'm sure he can use our help,' said Sandy.

'Honey and I have been wondering when and how we were going to get to our new post,' Floorplank chimed in. The sibling rats had been scurrying around listening into various conversations, as they were accustomed to doing.

'Who's going to look after our Caves Beach residences if we go on the road?' Sandy fretted.

'Me, of course!' Becky boomed. She ran and bounced off Sandy's leg before jumping onto her shoulder. 'I don't have lofty aspirations. Reliable Becky is going to stay home with my big ratty family and take care of everything!'

Overhearing her speak, Big Timmy scurried across the headrest and jumped onto Sandy's other shoulder.

'Becky is very capable. You shouldn't worry for a moment. You should definitely go and be with Mikey. Besides, it is probably best to break the news regarding his sister's engagement in person.'

Annie leaned over and called for Becky to cross onto her arm. She lifted her close to her face and said, 'never doubt the supreme importance of what you have offered to do. Keeping the home fires burning is vital. Family and home are what we are fighting for.'

Having grown close to the family of rats, Smiley felt torn regarding what he should do.

'I think I'll remain with Becky.'

'Good for you,' said Kate.

'We are used to you constantly spying on us. How will we cope without you?' teased Eff.

'You've been saved from needing earplugs. I need to warn you that I'm quite a chatterbox. It's taken great restraint to keep quiet all these months, while I was stalking you.' The magician laughed.

There was minimal traffic. Beauty cruised along the road, resisting the urge to go faster, given the likelihood of her passengers soon being separated.

'Tell me about your sister?' Kate unexpectedly asked her fiancée. Aided by the comfort of full bellies, the rest of the occupants had been lulled into a peaceful silence. Several of them were napping. Eff shrugged his shoulders.

'I hardly know her. My mother raised her with Geo in their own prison on Phalago. I have only met her the one time when GJ, my father and the others led us there on the rescue mission.'

'What did she seem like? Do you think she will like me?'

He chuckled and stroked her silky hair tenderly before replying, 'of course she will. Who wouldn't adore you?'

'I can tell you more about Izzie,' GJ offered. He stood up and walked up the aisle to their side.

'Ro said he thought she was like her mother; headstrong and beautiful, with a strong moral compass.'

'What's a moral compass?' Menagerie enquired, now also awake.

'It means her decisions are always true to good values. Things like honesty, family, hard work, protecting the weak and fighting for what is right,' explained Eff.

'Izzie was lucky to have been raised under such an influence,' the lion replied.

'You were lucky too, with Kalan finding you as a cub and raising you in his palace,' GJ reminded him.

'You had us of course,' Big Timmy and Snuggles told GJ, now also joining in. Eff looked sad.

'Hey, break out of that self-pity, lad!' Big Timmy told him. He nibbled his leg playfully and said, 'you were the luckiest of them all. You were raised by me!' Their laughter woke Octy. Eff grimaced, struggling to see the funny side of the banter.

'Jealousy is only harmful if it is unacknowledged and disingenuously acted upon. Healing can come from talking about such feelings,' Octy pronounced in a quiet voice. Eff sighed deeply.

'I'm not jealous of Izzie. I feel robbed, angry that my sister and I have been deprived of knowing each other. I desperately want to know her one day.'

'What did you remember liking about her the most when you met her?' Kate enquired. Eff closed his eyes in thought. When he opened them, he said, 'her natural warmth and belief in us as siblings. She felt we had a connection that was special.'

'You are twins. That is *very* special,' remarked Kate.

The Prof opened his eyes and stretched.

'I feel better after a power nap. I must have been more tired than I thought, as it has just come to me that we don't need to wait to get home to call Tobias. We can do it now.' He reached into his pocket and removed his smart phone. He pressed it to his ear and waited for a response.

The call ended in The Prof agreeing that a contingent would join the monk in Belgium as soon as possible. They planned to meet there before moving closer to the Champagne region of France, where the riddle was steering them.

'Things sound frantic there. His order has taken the bombshell news about their origins in ways he never anticipated,' said The Prof.

'Why don't you drop us off and go straight to him tonight?' Gavin suggested.

‘It sounds like he could use a friend right now,’ remarked Sandy.

‘When will you realistically be able to leave for Tasmania to be with Mikey?’ Kate asked Gavin.

‘There’s a caravan dealership in Newcastle. We can be on our way in a few days.’

‘I can’t wait to go to Belgium! I only need a few minutes to pack some things. Can we swing by the beach house?’ she then asked Octy.

‘Sure. We’ll come and get you when we’re ready to go,’ he replied.

After dropping off the women, Beauty pulled into the carpark at the top of the cliffs.

‘I think you should take the sabre with you as a good omen, Prof,’ Gavin insisted.

‘That’s very kind although I fear it isn’t the sabre we will ultimately require. I have never heard of a dragon sword. What if it is hidden on another world where such mythical creatures reside?’ Gavin sighed and said, ‘take it anyway.’ He left it lying on the seat. They exited, each carrying a box of glasses back towards the underground cave facility. Becky hugged Big Timmy. Peering over his shoulder on tiptoes, she said dramatically to Snuggles, ‘try not to get him killed!’ She started blubbering. Too emotional to continue speaking, she scurried off with Floorplank and Honey.

‘I’d like a moment to make some adjustments to Beauty,’ Eff told Octy. He moved to the front seat next him, leaving GJ and Menagerie waiting in the back. Almost immediately they fell asleep.

With a slight 'jolt' Beauty's wheels touched the firmly packed soil of the airstrip located a few miles from the Malinois Monastery. Tobias was waiting, his van parked in a thicket adjacent to the runway. He was accompanied by two other monks who greeted them formally and insisted on carrying some of their bags.

'This is Flanders, my oldest confidante. He is in charge of our order when I am not in residence. Matteo is the third in command. Much has happened here since my return and revelations.'

'I helped look after your father when he was recovering here,' Flanders informed Eff, as they approached the van. There was plenty of room for Kate, Eff, Octy, GJ, Menagerie, Big Timmy and Snuggles in the back. Flanders steered the vehicle towards the monastery as Matteo, at his side, made polite conversation with the guests. Beauty, having transformed into a simple car, followed closely behind. The Prof and Tobias rode in the front, desperate for a few moments to talk freely.

'You look exceedingly well. What is different?' Tobias asked The Prof.

'My arthritis has resolved. It is nothing short of miraculous!' He described how it had come about.

'How worrying,' Tobias responded, with a grave expression. He shivered as a sudden chill spread up and down his spine.

'While we are alone, I wanted to tell you something else that I know will trouble you. Eff and Kate are now engaged to be married.' Tobias shook his head and grimaced.

'In another development, Menagerie evaluated his soul at their celebratory party. I'm pleased to report that I think we can trust Eff,' shared The Prof.

'I trust Menagerie. This is excellent news. I fear we'll need his help in these dark times. Having the assistance of someone as powerful as Eff is a massive asset.' The Prof nodded and added, 'notwithstanding the fact Kate deserves to be with someone who is fundamentally good.'

'They appear happy together.'

'It's impossible not to feel optimistic about the future when you watch how they look at each other. Events at their engagement party were pivotal in helping decipher the riddle.'

The van stopped and they got out. It was Kate's first trip to Europe and her excitement was palpable. Awestruck, she stood still, taking in the magnificent gilded portico at the front of the ancient ivy-cloaked, stone building that was Tobias's home. He led his guests into the main hall where they were confronted by a frenzied chaotic scene. A sea of monks, many of whom had assumed their natural canine facial morphology, scurried across the open space hauling bulging satchels on their backs.

'What is going on here?' The Prof enquired.

'They're madly packing to go home, and I mean madly,' Flanders answered.

'It's the moment we've been praying for since our descendants settled here,' Matteo added, enthusiastically. Tobias frowned and whispered to The Prof, 'I'll brief you in my quarters. Much has occurred in the short interval since we spoke on the phone.' He led them away from the chaos down a hall towards his personal quarters.

'Flanders, please join us. Matteo, could I ask that you check that everything we discussed is being attended to?' The rotund Matteo nodded and hurried away.

They entered a high-ceilinged space with a single, oval, stained-glass window. Golden light bathed the room. GJ sneezed, having sniffed the floor too deeply and inhaled a breath full of thick dust. The fine grey material coating everything in the room, reflected the fact it had been left undisturbed in its owner's absence.

'We should sit around the fire. It's chilly in here, a significant change from Caves Beach,' said Tobias. Eff wrapped his arm around the shoulder of his petite fiancée. He closed his eyes and released a warming spell.

'I love it when you do things like that!' she gushed. Tobias smiled to himself as he used an iron poker to stoke a log of burning wood. The crackling warmth was welcomed by the other travellers who were wearing thin garments, unsuitable for winter in the Northern Hemisphere. Flanders left to retrieve warm robes for them to wrap around themselves. He handed them out, prior to departing a second time to procure a large pot of hot tea.

When they were seated, staring into the flames, The Prof said, 'you should go first. What's been going on here, Tobias?'

'I called my brothers together as soon as I returned. Sharing what I had discovered about our history caused nothing short of pandemonium. The news about our Compasse heritage was polarising. Many are filled with joy and want to immediately join their ancestral descendants in Ivor. Fear regarding what may be waiting within the walls of the White Corridor has consumed others. Another subset of naysayers are urging for caution, advocating that only a few monks should be permitted to travel ahead to define the risks for the others. In contrast, a few have absolutely no inclination to leave Earth, content with their lives here. They are trying to focus on their regular duties as if nothing has happened.'

'How are you managing this?' The Prof asked, intrigued.

'It's been challenging, to say the least. Earlier today, I announced that after I find the antidote, I will personally lead a contingent of volunteers to Ivor. Those you saw running around when we traversed the great hall were those I approved as the first travellers. Matteo is one of them. Flanders has declared that he wishes to stay and run the monastery which has brought calm to those who see their future here.' He turned to his brother and said, 'your calmness in the face of uncertainty will be invaluable when we eventually leave.'

'All will be as it is meant to,' he replied.

'You sound like The Oneidon. He said something similar to us,' said GJ.

'It is as it should be,' stated Tobias, wistfully.

'I hope I get to meet him soon,' said The Prof.

'Me too. You said on the telephone that you have made progress in deciphering the riddle?' Something about Champagne? The phone connection was terrible,' Tobias admitted.

'Yes, we have strong reasons to believe that the antidote is contained within a bottle of Champagne resting within the famous chalk cellars of France,' The Prof declared.

'We think the neck of the bottle must be sabred with a sword and the contents allowed to spray onto a victim,' GJ added, unable to contain his enthusiasm.

'Have you seen one of those things in action? It is very cool!' Snuggles exclaimed. He simulated the action, complete with sound effects as the imaginary bottle top was displaced and the contents fizzed out.

'How did you reach that conclusion?' asked Flanders, bewildered.

'Gavin and I made a Champagne tower and I sabred a special bottle of sparkling wine to celebrate Eff and Kate's engagement,' said The Prof.

'The bottle was the Champagne we took to Luna Tribus and gave to Ellie and Ro,' said Snuggles.

'A very special bottle indeed!' remarked Tobias.

'I was sipping my aliquot when lines from the riddle came to mind. Then I was off!' The Prof shared.

Tobias smiled at Eff and Kate, revealing his infrequently seen razor sharp teeth and said, 'congratulations!' They blushed. Hands intertwined, they were the picture of romantic love.

'Shall I take you through the riddle in light of my new ideas?' asked The Prof. Tobias reached inside a pocket within his robe, unfolded his copy of the riddle and smoothed out the folds. 'Let's go line for line. Please check my logic.'

Flanders, the closest friend Tobias had, hung on every word. He had watched his friend drift away into a headspace that had ultimately led them to the moment the order had been waiting for. He sensed this would be the last chapter in their history together on Earth and wanted to play a useful role in it.

'What do you think?' asked The Prof, when he had finished.

'Without sounding unduly pessimistic, whilst I agree with your interpretations, I fear it will be like trying to find a needle in a haystack,' Tobias responded. His chin whiskers twitched, in an agitated fashion.

'Why is that?' asked GJ.

'I am familiar with the chalk cellars of the Champagne region. They are vast. Bottles stored within their depths are incalculable in number,' answered Tobias.

'He's right. We could spend the rest of our days searching aimlessly there,' said Flanders.

Tobias stood up and pressed the corner of an ornate frame around a landscape painting; causing it to slide away, revealing an ultra-modern touch screen monitor.

'Map of Champagne region,' he instructed verbally, triggering an immediate response.

The Prof gasped in awe. He rubbed his palms together excitedly and said, 'now that is cool! I need to get one of those!'

Tobias pointed out the various villages that comprised the region.

'I see your point,' Eff acknowledged, as the scale of the problem became more apparent.

'There has to be something we've missed that will narrow down where we need to look,' Tobias insisted. He spoke to the screen again, and a typed version of the riddle appeared. All minds went to work, desperate for a new perspective. He eventually pointed to one of the lines and read it out loud:

'Find the masters apprentice daughter at the understated place of coffee and toffee and sit in her lazy chair and stare, or find the resplendent place of oranges and search the labyrinths if you dare.'

'Do you think this is the most important line?' GJ checked.

'Not necessarily. It has caught my attention as it makes me wonder if there may be two solutions as to where to find the antidote.'

'The "or" has always stood out to me too,' The Prof agreed.

'Hang on a minute!' Flanders blurted, now pacing. Tobias, sitting back at his desk, glanced up at him quizzically. 'I'm wondering if the place of oranges is referring to the famous orangeries of France?' Big Timmy scrambled over to the serious, tall Malinois and said, 'what's an orangerie? Will we find juicy fruit to eat there?'

'I love oranges!' cried Snuggles.

Flanders laughed and said, 'orangeries are buildings; status symbols, built on the finest of estates. They are forerunners to the more modern conservatories and greenhouses you are most likely familiar with. They were designed to create warmth and direct sunlight within, so exotic species of plants and trees could thrive. Due to my passion for architecture, I am aware of a few in the Champagne area.'

'This is fantastic news! It sounds like we need to go there and explore as soon as possible. When do we leave?' asked GJ, suddenly standing. Tobias laughed and said, 'hasten slowly, my friend. A little more research could help us further narrow our focus. Flanders, your research skills are superior to mine. Please take over.'

He moved directly in front of the monitor and used his hands to flick between screens.

'Are you performing magic?' Menagerie enquired.

'No. It's called surfing the internet,' said Flanders, as images of elegant structures appeared in front of their eyes. He dwelled on some of them, collecting together a short list of estates in a folder. After reviewing each again, he clapped his hands together in glee and pointed to a particularly beautiful picture.

'The most famous orangerie in the region of interest is at the largest Champagne estate.'

'The "The House of Claude" located in Epernay?' The Prof checked.

'Yes.' He pulled up their website and scanned the pages. 'The labels of their vintage premium wines still bear an image of the legendary Father of Champagne, the esteemed Monk Perignon. These days, it seems that their orangerie is used to host lavish parties. Their chalk cellars stretch as a vast maze of tunnels underneath the city. This is where we must go!'

'I thought you had committed to staying in charge here? Are you offering to come with us?' Tobias checked.

'I will only completely assume that role when you leave for Ivor. Until then, I am your devoted brother. Without your leadership we would never have come to this point. I am committed to helping you complete what you need to do, before you face your destiny.'

'There's plenty of room to accommodate an extra passenger in Beauty,' stated Eff.

'Thank you, Flanders. Your knowledge and perspectives have always been an asset to me. Having you by my side means a great deal,' said Tobias.

'Matteo has been pushing for an opportunity to step up in his responsibilities. I can't wait to secretly explore the chalk cellars of Champagne!' said Flanders.

'It's a shame Gavin isn't here,' The Prof mused.

'The veterinarian winemaker?' Flanders checked.

'Yes. I didn't think there was anyone who knew more about Champagne than he did. I'm glad you are willing to help us.'

'It's the architecture that attracts me, simply the architecture,' he responded, flashing his canines in a mischievous smile.

'Why didn't Gavin come with you?' Tobias enquired.

'He instinctively felt he should go and help Mikey guard the prisoner.'

‘I’m grateful for that. Despite his obvious strengths, it didn’t feel right leaving the boy there with Master Sabi. It remains such a high stakes task.’

‘He’s not alone. My grandson, Sir Geo, went with him,’ GJ reminded the group.

‘He’s very smart; diligent too,’ Octy vouched.

‘We can always call Gavin if we need his opinion on something. I bet he’d love to be consulted,’ The Prof noted.

‘How do you propose we approach things from here?’ Tobias put to the group.

‘Like we always do. We eat, we sleep, then off we go,’ said GJ.

Looking remarkably chic in a well-cut grey suit, worn with a crisp white open neck, linen shirt, The Prof walked boldly into the tasting room of the House of Claude leading an enthralled entourage. Eff and Kate, Tobias and Flanders, equally well dressed, posed as exclusive clients of the flamboyant Champagne aficionado leading them.

Kate had basked in the opportunity to select their fine garments from one of the many stylish Paris establishments where they had briefly detoured for that purpose.

‘You could have simply transformed our regular clothes like you did for the engagement party,’ The Prof had commented, when this component of the plan was being discussed.

'What sort of fiancée would I be to rob my beauty of a shopping trip to Paris? She told me it was her fantasy to go there one day. Why not today, when it's so close?'

Kate had pinched herself as they flew over the Eiffel Tower and glimpsed the Gothic magnificence that was the Notre-Dame Cathedral. Strolling along the famous Avenue des Champs-Elysees loaded with shopping bags, had made her feel like she was starring in a movie.

Minimal acting was required from The Prof's party. They embraced their roles in the masquerade as educated wine enthusiasts, on a personalised tour. The Prof kept them genuinely captivated by a steady flow of facts. He effortlessly imparted his extensive knowledge with the perfect English schoolboy accent he had retained from his youth. Octy, having turned invisible, confidently executed his part of the plan, heading off stealthily on a reconnaissance assignment underground.

His eyes adjusted seamlessly to the relative darkness of the cellars. He slowly moved deeper below the surface, descending an intricate wrought iron, spiral staircase. It was not dissimilar to the one in Kalan's palace on Kaleido. At the bottom he paused briefly and listened. A group of visitors were nearing the end of their tour, having been escorted through the vast network of subterranean galleries. He set off in the opposite direction. Octy had always been able to sense magic and his focus was entirely on that now, convinced that Master Sabi would have left traces of his work.

Octy passed seemingly endless corridors of ancient riddling racks and in turn, more modern cube-like gyro palettes used to achieve the same outcome. He had once helped Gavin work on bottles, shifting the debris of yeast fermentation into the neck of the bottles in preparation for disgorgement. He briefly paused to take in the structures and marvelled at how much he had learned over the years about sparkling wine production from his dear friend.

The Octavian peered into rooms full of wine bottles laying together in hibernation, waiting to be woken up and literally have their moment to sparkle. Dates handwritten on the crates revealed that some of them had been placed decades before. After rounding a sharp bend, he found himself trailing another group, accompanied by an informative male guide. His interest was piqued at the mention of the Monk Perignon.

'Our Domaine only purchased this estate in 1927, so in answer to your question, the famous monk experimented with his blending techniques and nurtured his early experiments elsewhere.'

Octy returned at once to the tasting room where his friends were now sipping a beaded pink liquid from fine rimmed flutes. He touched The Prof's arm so as not to startle him unduly and whispered, 'we're in the wrong place.'

'Regrettably, it is time to leave,' The Prof announced after tapping at his watch. Kate sighed. 'Do not despair, as this magnificent place is only a warm-up on today's itinerary. Please discard what you have not consumed, mindful that we have other tastings.' Tobias groaned theatrically, expressing reluctance to leave. With a respectful nod to the young man who had served them, The Prof led them outside and back to the flashy white mini-van that Beauty had been transformed into for their charade. As the door slid open, GJ, Menagerie and the rats jumped up from where they had been patiently waiting, crouched on the carpeted floor at the back of the vehicle.

'Did you find it?' GJ asked, optimistically, as they moved back inside.

'No. We are in the wrong place,' whispered Octy.

With The Prof appearing to drive, Beauty pulled out of the car park and headed out of Epernay. He noticed an empty laneway between adjacent fields of recently pruned vines and instructed her to turn into it. When the engine stopped, Octy explained what he had overheard.

'Fool that I am,' Flanders muttered over and over as he engaged with an electronic tablet, hurriedly withdrawn from his satchel. Having logged back on to the internet, he verified what Octy had learned. 'We must go to Chateau Dom at once. I will navigate.'

Chapter 9
CHAMPAGNE

GJ was adamant that he was not staying behind again.

'We're all coming,' Menagerie affirmed.

'We've been over this before. It's best if you wait here, in case we don't come back,' Tobias told them, sensibly.

'Beauty can raise the alarm at the monastery if we don't return in a timely manner,' said Snuggles.

'Respectfully, I think we could use all the help we can get searching for the antidote,' Flanders interjected. As case in point, he passed around a map of the establishment they were about to enter.

'He's right,' said The Prof, wide eyed.

'It's enormous!' cried Octy.

'It's dauntingly enormous! Chateau Dom has approximately eighteen kilometres of passages, the most extensive of any of the great Champagne houses,' Flanders explained.

Octy sighed and said, 'it's disorientating in the cellars. In the time I was gone, I hardly covered any ground.'

Astonished, Eff studied the maze of tunnels in the diagram. He pointed to symbols and a series of dotted lines and asked Flanders, 'is that some sort of vehicle on rails that we will use to travel through the underground passages?'

'Yes. It is a unique component of the tour that makes it a top attraction for families. The kiddies love the train ride and it means old people don't have to walk.'

'I will revert to being invisible,' said Menagerie.

'As will I,' said GJ. They practiced rubbing their gums and disappearing, repeating the process and reappearing several times.

'How are you able to do that?' asked Eff, astonished.

'Viz applied an invisibility paste to our teeth. He found it in Master Sabi's secret stash in his study,' explained GJ.

'I never knew how he did that! I only ever learned to make two separate potions; one to cause and the other to reverse invisibility.'

Tobias reached into his bag and retrieved the jar Viz had given him.

'This erases any doubt that you were especially close to Master Sabi, as Viz told us he only shared it with those he trusted. You should all apply some. I'd like you to keep the rest Eff, as a sign of my faith in you,' said Tobias.

'It means a lot to me.' The young magician applied some to his own mouth then attended to the others.

'I have to warn you, it tastes terrible!' said GJ.

'That it does!' agreed Eff.

'It's really bad!' cried Kate.

'Hopefully one day I'll be able to replicate it. Then you can help me improve on the taste,' he told her.

'Let's make it mango flavoured.'

'You're on.'

'Is there another way to hide me?' Snuggles asked Eff, screwing up his face as the magician approached him with the paste.

'Perhaps Tobias could transfigure you into a humanoid again?' GJ suggested, smirking, aware of the strong reaction it would evoke.

'I'm never having that happen to me again! It was the vilest experience of my life!' Snuggles complained dramatically, throwing up his front paws in protest.

'Bring on the disgusting coating!' said Big Timmy, flashing his teeth.

'To avoid one of us accidentally tripping on, or standing on you, I'd like to suggest you hide in my pockets. They're rather roomy,' said Flanders.

'Excellent! It will save my legs and allow a nap when required,' noted Big Timmy.

Beauty turned around and pulled back onto the main road. Flanders, riding next to Eff in the front, navigated her to their destination. There, The Prof's tour group followed him inside the foyer where he purchased tickets for the train. Filled with anticipation over what lay ahead, they headed to the plush waiting area. When it was their turn, an elegant women teetering on stiletto heels and wrapped in a silken jade dress, led them into a lift with other guests. After descending thirty meters underground, the doors opened revealing the electric train boarding platform.

She ushered the beaming newly engaged couple to the front carriage. The party of three males were shown to the one behind them. When boarding was complete, the participants were shown how to use the audio sets provided. As the English commentary began, the train slowly started moving down the Central Avenue of the Chateau Dom. Eff called over the woman. As she leaned in close to hear his enquiry, he discreetly sprayed the contents of one of his rings into her face. She adopted a blank expression then departed.

'What did you do to her?' asked Kate, shocked.

'I've ensured she won't recall meeting us. When the train returns without our group, she will simply load a new set of patrons onto it,' he explained. She kissed his cheek and said, 'it was very slick.'

The train continued along its tracks. The lights dimmed as they passed walls of illuminated sculpted images. There was a grape harvest scene, various monks, including Dom Perignon and several commemorations to famous people who had visited including a previous French President.

'The fact that there were no machines or electricity to aid those who created this vast network of tunnels is an extraordinary testament to humanity,' Eff whispered in Kate's ear, after moving one of her headphones aside.

After passing various rooms highlighting the key steps in the wine making process, the train paused. They had reached the turnaround point of the trip. Dramatic buttressed archways crisscrossed above their heads, adorned with light bulbs that outlined four tunnels branching off.

'This seems like a useful place to get off,' The Prof suggested to Tobias, seated at his side. They motioned for the rest of his group to jump off. Eff walked along the other carriages, dispensing potion from the same ring.

The group assembled inside one of the narrower tunnels. Octy, Menagerie and GJ appeared. They had walked behind the train. The Prof suggested they split into three groups; one for each unexplored tunnel. The rats jumped out of Flanders pocket and repositioned themselves on GJ's back. Menagerie moved to his side. Octy and Flanders joined The Prof. Tobias stood next to Eff and Kate.

'We need to be able to communicate with each other. In our haste, fortuitously we didn't leave the headsets on the train. How about I reconfigure them so they can be used for that purpose?' asked Eff.

'That would be incredible, as there's no phone reception down here,' Flanders replied.

'Pull the cord out of the battery pack and hold your earphones in front of you, please.' Eff closed his eyes and touched each one in turn. He then spoke into the plug at the end of his, saying, 'this is a test. When you want to speak, talk into the plug end like I am doing. Everyone should be able to hear you.' It worked perfectly.

'Nice one, Eff!' GJ responded.

'I think we should check in with each other every fifteen minutes. If any of us get into trouble, the others will realise it and come looking for them urgently,' Kate suggested.

'If any hint of magic is detected, stop where you are immediately until everyone else can join you. If we're in the correct place it could become extremely dangerous, very quickly,' warned Tobias.

GJ was the first to leave. He set out briskly down the tunnel straight opposite from where the train had disappeared. It was the least illuminated branch. He had a hunch that this might indicate it was seldom traversed and thus most likely to be hiding their prize.

'Any questions before we start exploring?' asked Tobias.

'Is anyone else hungry?' the dog asked, loudly. The echo of his voice bounced off the walls.

'Shhh!' Snuggles boomed, generating an even louder reverberation. Kate handed out oat treats from a stash in her designer handbag.

'I'm ready now!' GJ announced.

He set off confidently, deliberately pursuing narrower side passageways that took them past increasingly unused, heavily dust laden storage rooms. Most of these were being used to house old bottles of wine on wooden racks. The pungent smell of mould hung in the air. Refraining from sneezing became a frequent challenge.

Menagerie suddenly froze and pushed ahead of GJ, halting his progress. The hairs on GJ's neck stood on end.

'I'm sensing magic. You feel it too, don't you?' Menagerie checked.

GJ alerted the other groups, whispering through the end of the headset Eff had wrapped loosely around his neck.

'We hear you. We'll come right away,' Tobias responded. The Prof said the same.

'Take all the least used looking paths when you encounter branch points,' GJ advised. As they waited, his mind drifted to food, his favourite, most anxiety alleviating topic. He dropped down on the ground next to the lion in the middle of a tight corridor located between two open-mouthed storage rooms filled floor to ceiling with full racks.

The ceiling above them started to shake, subtly at first then growing in intensity. The chinking sound of glass bottles vibrating against each other grew louder. Dirt started to rain upon their heads from spaces between the mouldy support beams. Snuggles screamed and cried, 'it's caving in on us!'

'Follow me!' the lion commanded. GJ and the rats sprinted at his side further down the corridor. With a deafening explosion, shards of glass from a myriad of shattering bottles sprayed across the point where seconds before they had been standing. Menagerie pulled GJ into an empty storage room as a column of the flying debris blew down the passage. He crouched in a corner, selflessly wrapping himself over his companions, shielding them from potentially lethal shards of glass.

When the air eventually cleared, each stood up, shook themselves and tentatively poked their heads out to assess the damage. All of the lamps in the blast zone had been smashed by flying debris. Despite the dimness, there was no doubt that the passageway they had come from was now impassable.

'Are you still with us?' Tobias's voice echoed in GJ's ear, with a discernible hint of panic.

'Yes. We have survived an explosion,' GJ explained, trying to stay calm.

'Do you think it was a boobytrap?' The Prof enquired.

'Perhaps, although surely this could have happened to a cellar employee? Why would someone risk hurting innocent individuals?' GJ replied.

'Tread carefully. Some spells can be left dormant for the longest of times and be personalised so they can only be triggered by specific individuals,' Eff explained. GJ shared the information with his companions.

'We'll wait for you to join us,' said GJ.

Menagerie continued to feel unsettled with a sense of foreboding and said, 'tell Eff I have sensed dark magic down here and I'm still feeling it now!'

GJ passed on this information.

'Don't move!' Eff insisted.

'I think we're nearly to you. The air is getting dustier,' said Octy.

'Tell them to watch their feet. This is shattered glass everywhere,' said Snuggles.

The air started to clear.

'We're together on the other side of the cave in. It's extensive. We can't reach you,' Tobias informed GJ. Flanders consulted the map on his electronic tablet.

'I can see another way to rejoin the section where they are. Unfortunately, we'll need to go backwards, in order to go forwards through this labyrinth. It's going to take a while.'

'At least you have a map and a good sense of direction,' said Kate, trying to remain brave and optimistic.

‘It’s extremely unsettling being here, so I think we should start going forwards again and try to meet you further away from this dangerous area,’ GJ proposed.

‘I understand. Do be careful friends. I fear we may be playing into Master Sabi’s hands,’ Eff warned.

The animal team set off again. The distance between functioning lamps grew longer as the tunnel took them through abandoned parts of the cellar. The stench of stale air grew increasingly overpowering.

‘Do you feel like we are being watched?’ Menagerie asked GJ, in a quiet voice.

‘I do. It’s rather unsettling,’ replied the dog.

The winding path grew narrower with progressively fewer branches. Storage rooms were more sparsely distributed, with racks deplete of bottles.

‘It’s getting colder and more oppressive with each step,’ Menagerie noted.

GJ jumped, startled by the voice of Flanders checking in.

‘We should be with you very soon. Are you OK?’ the monk enquired.

‘Yes. Nothing else untoward has happened,’ GJ replied.

‘That’s not entirely correct!’ exclaimed Snuggles, trying not to panic.

‘Look up!’ urged Big Timmy, trembling. He gripped onto the fur of GJ’s front leg tightly. A thousand sets of egg yolk-coloured eyes dotted the arched recesses above.

‘Reveal yourselves!’ GJ impulsively commanded.

Four legged, furry black creatures with tails, significantly larger than the rat brothers, scurried down the walls and surrounded them.

'Don't worry GJ, we're in luck, they're relatives!' Big Timmy boomed, relaxing. He bravely stepped forwards, convinced he was correct in his assumption. He cleared his dry throat. 'Hello everyone or *G'day mates*, as we would say in the land down under.'

Taking his lead, Snuggles joined him and said in a forced jovial tone, 'we are fellow rats visiting from Caves Beach in Australia. Do you have any food that you're willing to share?'

'You are sadly mistaken if you think we will feed you. Are *you* not food for *us*?' a deep echoing voice replied.

'Attack the dog first!' commanded another voice.

GJ was saved by Menagerie who lunged forward, wrapping himself around the individual he had vowed to protect. Upon landing, he crouched on the ground around him, bracing, as a sea of fangs started to penetrate his fur. The lion roared in pain and projected his thoughts to Eff, pleading for his help.

The carpet of cannibalistic rodents grew thicker. Blood oozed from his wounds as the relentless attack progressed. GJ had never felt so helpless. Big Timmy and Snuggles, now hiding behind a broken wine rack, wondered how much agony their companion could withstand. They started shaking, helplessly listening to Menagerie's roars turn to whimpers.

On the verge of collapse, the fur of the lion started to glow lime green, highlighting the extent of his wounding. Snuggles struggled not to vomit at the sight. He hid his face in his brother's chest.

'Something is happening! A protective barrier is forming!' Big Timmy exclaimed.

The front row of feeding rats, were forced to detach. More frenzied bodies piled up on top of them, each selfishly attempting to satiate their own desire for flesh. They thrust themselves repeatedly at the barrier, to no avail. Enraged by being forfeited their turn to feast, the shrieks of frustrated, angry rodents and the gnashing of their pointy teeth filled the space. Suddenly catching the scent of the rat brothers, several sets of eyes turned and peered in their direction.

'Time to go!' Big Timmy told his brother.

'We can't outrun them!' Snuggles cried.

'We have to try to make it inside that barrier. Aim for in between Menagerie's front legs,' Big Timmy instructed.

'What if we can't get through? Is this the end?'

'It's better to fail trying, than stand like cowards and be eaten here!'

Big Timmy went first, weaving between disorientated, frenzied groups of vicious rats. Snuggles followed, convinced he was about to die.

'Use their heads and backs as trampolines!' Big Timmy yelled. He leapt from one to the next and with a final athletic pounce, plunged through the barrier, landing with a roll. To his horror, he watched Snuggles launch himself at the same time as a rat in front of him raised his head. They collided, causing the smaller rodent to hit the ground forcefully. Desperate to live, he immediately stood up and started dragging himself towards his brother.

Snuggles felt something grasp his back legs. After a forceful tug he was pulled over, face planting. He squealed in pain. Barely conscious, Menagerie was past being able to assist. Incapable of helping, GJ was struggling to breathe, his chest compressed under the weight of the limp lion. Big Timmy peeked out from around the side of Menagerie's legs. He called out, 'there's no need to be nasty chaps.'

'Leave us alone, scum!' screeched Snuggles, spurred on by the bravery of his sibling. Sensing a fleeting hesitation of the rat holding his legs, he pulled free and limped inside the barrier.

The reprieve was brief. A new wave of venomous rage commenced. An enormous alpha male the size of a small cat, boldly ran forward and started pounding his fists against the glowing barrier.

'Your feeble magic can only hold us off for a limited time. A far greater sorcerer than you foretold the coming of the snow-coloured rats from Australia. We have yearned for your flesh!'

'You are a disgrace to our species!' Snuggles replied.

'You have brought us finer fare than we were expecting, so we'll save your crunchy bones for dessert.'

'Why feed on any of us? Based on your size, there doesn't appear to be a shortage of food down here. Besides, Master Sabi doesn't care about any of you. He's using you. I implore you, be leaders not followers,' said Snuggles.

'Our friends need our help. We are searching for a special bottle of Champagne. Once we find it, we'll be gone. Find your basic decency and let us pass,' Big Timmy pleaded.

Before further words could be exchanged, a bluish, blinding incandescent haze appeared in the room. The army of menacing rats retreated to the darkness of adjacent passages. Sniffing the air and realising that the torch belonged to Tobias, Menagerie managed to roll off GJ. The pair lay on their backs, side by side, panting.

'Great timing!' Big Timmy cried, relieved. Snuggles ran to Flanders and dived into his pocket, shaking violently.

Eff circled around, seeking out the boldest of the evil rats that had elected to remain. Without hesitation he lunged at the first one he spotted and held it by its neck, with his firm fingers encircling its throat.

'Tell us who left you in waiting. What else is to come?' he commanded.

'*Only the girl in love will be able to see*,' a mocking voice spluttered from its twitching body. As it self-ignited into a ball of flames, Eff was forced to drop the dying rat.

'Ouch! The rascal burnt me!' he reacted, examining a red patch on his hand.

'Fall back now!' Tobias warned, sensing they were in imminent danger.

Hot sparks flew in all directions as the remaining rats burst into flames. The Prof swatted at his sleeve, ignited by an arc of fire. An acrid smell of sulphur and burning flesh filled the already hard to breathe air. He started coughing uncontrollably. Feeling faint, he lowered himself to the ground. Octy produced a bottle of water from one of his many pockets and pressed it to his lips. When he finally stopped gasping, the rat army had vanished, leaving behind piles of black ash.

'They weren't of this world,' Eff stated.

'That's a relief!' Snuggles exclaimed.

'I knew they were no cousins of mine!' added Big Timmy.

'The vermin knew we were coming,' GJ shared.

'I have no doubt that this is the work of Master Sabi. The only upside to this encounter is that it suggests we must be getting close to finding what we came for,' Eff replied.

'I agree. That rats dying words were from the riddle,' Flanders noted.

Octy noticed that blood was tricking from innumerable puncture marks on Menagerie's coat. His eyes were struggling to stay open.

'He's fading!' cried GJ.

'He's lost a lot of blood,' The Prof concluded, noticing the pools of congealed blood on the nearby ground.

Eff crouched at his side and blew the contents of one of his other rings into his face. Menagerie opened his eyes. Eff stroked his mane gently.

'I feel better. Thank you for healing me and saving us with the barrier.'

'What barrier?' asked Eff, quizzically.

'The green one. Didn't you conjure it?' said the lion.

'No.'

'Whatever will be next?' The Prof muttered, now rising to his feet.

'Are you sure you are alright now? You sounded like you were coughing up your own lungs,' GJ remarked, moving closer to him. He smiled and replied, 'I'm a tough old boy.'

'Where's Kate?' Octy shouted, alarmed.

Eff scanned the cavern where the attack had taken place. She was nowhere to be seen.

'Kate? Darling? Where are you?' He started to panic.

'I can still sense her,' Menagerie reported after a period of intense concentration. He pointed in the direction of a nearby sector of the maze they were yet to explore.

'I can't smell her,' said Big Timmy.

'She must be a very long way away,' Snuggles confirmed.

'We need to remain close together now,' Tobias implored, as they started walking along the passage. Flanders consulted his map.

'We must be at the deepest part of the cellars as the ground is now flat. If we keep going in this direction, we should eventually find our way back to a major branch that will lead upwards to the surface.'

Eff had never experienced fear. He trembled, consumed by worry for his future bride.

'We'll find her. I'm on her trail,' Menagerie tried to reassure him. Taking the lead, with GJ at his side, the lion moved to the front of the group. They rounded a curve in the path.

'Ouch! I seem to have run into something,' GJ complained. He rubbed his nose in pain.

'You sure have,' Tobias confirmed, having observed him forcefully bounce off an invisible wall. He focused the beam of his torch straight ahead, trying to define what his friend had collided with. A mirror-like, reflective surface was blocking further progress. In an attempt to define its edges, he moved closer and ran his fingers across its smooth surface. 'It's a solid wall. We're stuck!'

'We've got bigger problems than that!' Big Timmy stated, gulping. During GJ's impact with the structure, he had been displaced from the dog's back. From his position on the ground, close to the barrier, he had a view the others didn't. 'Focus your eyes beyond the surface. I think this is the front wall of a cage and our Kate is in there!'

He was right. A dream like, distorted, hazy image of Kate came in and out of perspective. A translucent figure was holding her limp body in his outstretched arms.

'It's Master Sabi!' Eff cried.

'She's wrapped in the sleeping cloak we used during his transport to the prison in Tasmania,' Tobias noted.

'Look further behind them,' urged Flanders.

Through the back wall of the chamber, they could see a Chocolate Labrador.

'It's Sir Geo!' Octy cried. Standing next to him, a frantic looking Mikey, was wringing his hands and pointing into the same space.

'I think they can see and are watching the same horror unfold,' Tobias noted.

'How is this possible?' Flanders murmured.

'This is the darkest of magic,' Eff replied.

Each stood gaping, unsure what to do.

'I think the wall GJ ran into is the outside of the imprisonment structure Viz and his colleagues created to contain Master Sabi,' Tobias eventually stated.

'The crafty magician has managed to reach through to us from Tasmania. He's managed to project his prison inside this underground labyrinth and use it to trap my true love,' Eff deduced.

Recognising that he now held an audience on both sides of his chamber, the jubilant magician adopted a self-satisfied gloating smile. He moved to the innermost edge and stared directly at Eff.

'You are correct, young pupil. How disappointing that you have deviated from the path you were meant to follow. You and your mother demonstrated the greatest magical potential of anyone ever born on Luna Tribus; apart from me of course! You could have honed your gifts with my ongoing mentorship.'

'We are nothing like you! Now release this innocent woman at once!' Eff commanded.

Insults started to fly. The Prof leaned in close to Tobias.

'This is really bad! Look on the floor near Master Sabi's left foot.' A ray of torch light reflected off a bluish glass surface. 'It's a potion bottle. The lid is off. It's empty.'

'What have you done to her? What was in that vessel?' Tobias demanded, after stepping up to the barrier.

'It's called a vial. Please be precise,' Master Sabi corrected in a condescending tone.

Eff was now so angry he couldn't speak.

'Let me repeat myself. What was in the *vial*?' asked Tobias calmly.

'Kate was parched, in need of a refreshing beverage. I was delighted to meet the needs of a charming young lady. I recall that the musty air within the depths of a cellar can be rather unpleasant. It can be enough to choke on. Oh yes, you almost did professor, didn't you? By the way, it's lovely to see that your arthritis has abated. I trust your other house companions are feeling better too?'

The Prof refused to rise to the provocation.

'What have you administered to my fiancée?' Eff demanded.

'It's a little something you are familiar with.' Master Sabi moved closer to him, flaunting the lifeless woman in his arms. He gently ran his right index finger across her pale forehead then dramatically rubbed his fingertips in the air. 'How wonderful. It's starting already. The grittiness comes first. A layer of fine sand appears next. Then it progresses.'

'Oh no! He's turning her into a sand sculpture like he did the others!' Snuggles screeched. Master Sabi sneered at the two twitching rat faces that were pressed against the barrier.

'You're brighter than your brother, yet rather tediously, always one to state the obvious. I wasn't sure I would be meeting you. I've been imagining what a delicious supper you would have been for my friends, whose creation was inspired by your irritating kind.'

He scanned the group in front of him, eventually focussing on GJ.

'What a joyous moment! On either side of this feeble prison, I have an annoying brown dog watching on helplessly.'

He lowered Kate onto the ground then proceeded to pace arrogantly around the enclosure. With dramatic flair, Master Sabi swept his hand down the outer wall causing it to become completely transparent. Mikey and Sir Geo were now more visible; so much so that they too appeared to be sharing the space. Beyond them, the dark Tasmanian sky was lit up by the wandering, greenish, ghostly glow of the Southern lights.

Master Sabi drew from thin air a bottle indistinguishable from the endless racks of resting Champagne they had passed. He held it out in front of him like a sommelier presenting it to patrons at a table in a fine dining establishment.

'Congratulations! Here is the prize that you and your band of heroes came here to find. The catch is simple. Since *I* have it right now, you will have to do a trade with me. Let me out of this prison and you can have the antidote.'

'You called it "feeble". If it's so pathetic, why not walk away? Surely a genius like you could overcome a single human and their dog?' GJ responded, sarcastically.

'I agree, it's sounding fishy to me,' Big Timmy joined in. 'You expect us to believe that you are trapped, despite demonstrating this remarkable ability to reach through space. You've somehow positioned your prison at the intersection of two distant locations, simultaneously!'

'You flatter me, but alas it is true. I am trapped in here. Viz and the magicians he turned against me are not devoid of talent. Their creation has walls I can work within, yet not breakthrough.'

'I seriously doubt that,' The Prof muttered under his breath. Tobias pointed to Kate and whispered, 'true or otherwise, we haven't got time to dwell on what has motivated this grand performance.' A layer of sand was forming on her pale face, which was perfectly framed by the hood of the cloak.

'Mikey must release Master Sabi right now!' said GJ. No one argued.

'Let him out, Mikey,' Tobias shouted. He gave a thumbs up before inserting a gold key into a black lock. As he turned it, the wall on the Tasmanian side disappeared altogether. Master Sabi's taut lips curled into a self-satisfied smile.

'You have made a wise choice. Before I take my leave, I'm curious to learn what you will do with my antidote. I'd like to remind you that when you release the contents of this bottle, it can only work in one space, one time.' He rubbed his spindly hands together in glee and in a crazed voice said, 'this is the most fun I've ever had in my life! Making up the rules of a game where the only winner is me, is deliciously wicked!'

'Cruel is the term I'd use. What have this poor girl and the innocent victims in Rectangulum City that you have drawn into your "game", ever done to you?' Tobias demanded. Master Sabi directed his scornful gaze at Big Timmy and Snuggles.

'My life was ruined by the arrival of the deceased canine who came to my planet with those two pesky rats. In his absence, revenge can only be achieved by causing suffering to the associates he left behind.'

Snuggles protested, waving his tiny fist in the air, jabbing like a boxer.

'Our arrival was merely a catalyst for much needed change,' he cried.

'Let's not be drawn into a war of words. We need to stay focused. Kate and the others need us to think clearly,' Big Timmy advised.

'On reflection, I don't actually care what you do. This game is over and you are the losers,' stated Master Sabi. After placing the bottle on the ground, he casually stepped across Kate, then strode confidently past Mikey. As he stepped into the Tasmanian air, a semi-opaque wall immediately appeared behind him. The wall on the French side disappeared.

'I can't believe you aren't going to stick around and see what happens next,' Sir Geo goaded his ex-prisoner as he passed.

'It's obvious, as I am fully aware of what the strongest force in the universe is.' Mikey and Sir Geo stared at him quizzically. 'I'm referring to love you idiots! Like it or not Mikey, Eff is madly in love with your sister and he'd do anything to save her. He'd even die for her which I did contemplate engineering for a while. He loves her so much he'll save her over his parents, sister and everyone else caught up in this melodramatic saga!'

He started to move down the stairs into the darkness. Unexpectedly, he doubled back and said to Mikey, 'your band of do-gooders need to learn to be less predictable and tell Eff that the standard of magic I've been witnessing is frankly embarrassing.'

Chapter 10
GUNDAGAI

Mikey watched Master Sabi stride across the courtyard below as the nightly ghost tour approached. One of his fellow guides, a serious fellow called Jonathan, was leading a group of teenage girls and their parents through the deserted interior of the church. He was nearing the prison, assembled upon a section of its roofless mezzanine. His colleague's torch scanned the walls, theatrically pretending to search for lingering apparitions.

Catching the departing form of a pale skinned, snarling man in a flowing gold robe, the party erupted into shrieks. One of the girls started to cry hysterically and clung desperately to her father's arm in terror.

'It's haunted!' someone else gasped.

'There really are ghosts!' screamed another.

An eternal optimist, Mikey smiled to himself and thought that the sighting would work wonders in attracting much needed customers to the struggling tourist venue.

'We need to focus on Kate,' Sir Geo interrupted, drawing his attention back to the wall.

The others had flocked to Kate's side and formed a protective circle around her motionless form. Her lithe body was continuing to speedily turn to sand.

'We can't move her,' Tobias advised.

'We have no choice but to deliver the antidote here,' Eff declared.

'What about the great many others who need our help?' Octy reminded him.

'I love Kate.'

'I know this woman is special to you but there are so many more lives that we could save,' Flanders reminded him.

'Even if we decide to dispense the cure for her, we don't have a sabre to release the contents! I can't believe I left Gavin's behind, inside Beauty!' The Prof exclaimed, angry at himself.

'Even if you had brought it, I don't think it's the sword we need to use. It's clearly not a "dragon" sword, whatever that means,' said Tobias.

'Releasing the cage and cork and just tipping it over her is likely to fail. Then no one will be saved,' The Prof warned.

'Perhaps if we shook it up first, when we release the cork, there will be enough bubbles to force the liquid into a spray?' Flanders suggested.

'This whole scenario feels wrong,' Tobias remarked, stepping back.

'You're right. We've been forced into a crisis that is not true to the riddle. The line that comes to mind is "only the girl in love will be able to see". Kate may be in love but in this scenario, she's totally incapacitated,' stated The Prof.

Gripped by desperation, Eff said, 'we have to act now! I know what I have to do. I'm sorry.' He started vigorously shaking the bottle.

Without another word he ripped off the cage securing the cork and twisted it out of the neck.

'Pop!'

The agitated contents of the bottle exploded into the air next to Kate's head and covered her face and neck with amber fluid. He dropped the empty bottle on the floor and hovered close to her still motionless form and pleaded with her to wake up.

'I love you, Kate. Please come back to me. I need you.'

Nothing happened.

He started to sob.

The others watched on helplessly, recognising that it would be impossible to console him.

GJ finally spoke. He stared up at The Prof and said, 'this can't be the end for her. We have to do something!'

The Prof picked up the discarded bottle and closure device. He showed it to Flanders.

'This bottle is shiny and the foil wrapped around the neck suggests it's already been disgorged.'

'You're right. Bottles like this are not normally stored in underground cellars. All the ones we've seen down here are resting. Champagne only has a cork and cage applied after the yeast is carefully removed in preparation for sale.'

'Does any of that really matter? It hasn't cured Kate. The fact is, Master Sabi tricked us. He lied to us so we'd let him out of the prison,' Snuggles argued. Big Timmy started to speak.

'It could mean that the real antidote may still be hidden nearby. Hope remains…'

'For the others, not Kate,' blurted Octy, feeling overwhelmed with distress. He had watched her grow up. His thoughts turned to Sandy and Annie; the deep pain they would experience if she perished. He glanced across the space at Mikey, who appeared bereft.

'Perhaps the real antidote isn't hidden down here?' Tobias proposed.

'Master Sabi would have needed a crystal ball to have engineered such a moment as this,' said The Prof.

'It seems to me that as soon as Kate stepped into a certain spot in this underground labyrinth, she triggered a snare that had already been left in waiting,' suggested Tobias.

'Are you saying he somehow knew we would come here and therefore set up this series of booby traps? Are our actions so foreseeable?' GJ questioned.

'We are certainly logical, intelligent and persistent individuals. After reflecting on his reaction to each of us, just now, I think it's reasonable to conclude he's studied us meticulously,' The Prof responded.

'Darn it! We've been played! You're right! He knows our personalities, our hobbies, our areas of expertise. The riddle was tailored to our combined idiosyncrasies,' Tobias concluded.

'He preyed on our vulnerabilities,' uttered Eff, through a stream of tears.

Big Timmy ran up his arm and nuzzled into his neck.

'There, there, my boy, your Timothy is here. You tried to save her. Don't ever forget that none of this is your fault. Master Sabi is a top scoring scoundrel. He's truly a villain.'

'Your mum, dad, sister and aunt are still alive and need you now. There is a chance for you to know their love too,' Octy told the distressed young humanoid.

'I can't leave her here, Tim Tims. I can't even touch her!' Eff cried. He was completely bereft. It reminded the rat of the many nights he had cuddled in close to the distressed toddler who had been devoid of his mother and desperately needing to be held

'All is not lost!' Menagerie exclaimed.

Kate's chest had started to rise and fall. She coughed, expelling a shower of fine sand. Inhaling some of the grains, Big Timmy sneezed. He jumped off Eff's shoulder to inspect her more closely.

'Our girl is alive! She's waking up!' he confirmed.

'She feels solid enough for you to take off the robe,' Tobias eventually said. He knelt down and assisted him. When it was done, Eff sat cross legged, cradling her in his arms, rocking her gently.

She opened her eyes and stared up at his crestfallen face. A single tear rolled down his cheek and dropped into her mouth.

'You're salty,' she complained, with a weak smile before closing her eyes and falling into a peaceful slumber.

Relief spread across the faces of those witnessing the poignant moment. All except GJ, who looked profoundly sad.

'Why aren't you happy?' Menagerie asked the dog.

'If Kate has been cured with this antidote, it means hope is lost for Ellie, Ro and the others who were cursed.'

'I don't believe this is over. The Prof is right. Master Sabi is pulling our strings, like we are puppets in a sick pantomime!' Tobias reacted, now furious.

'Whatever has taken place, it's time to leave. I'm ravenous, thirsty and boy do I need a giant hurry-up!' concluded GJ.

'Perhaps I can penetrate the wall so we can exit on the Tasmanian side?' suggested Eff. He looked across it to where Mikey was sitting staring at them, stroking the back of Sir Geo.

'Is your magic that powerful?' Flanders questioned.

Eff glanced at Kate and replied, 'I'm not sure. I do know that this beautiful person has constantly encouraged me to keep developing my "gifts", as she has always called them. Since I've been happier and relaxed, things have evolved.'

His thoughts drifted to Caves Beach, the special place where he felt truly free. Experiencing a deep connectivity to the soil and sand beneath his feet, the strange fauna and flora of the area and most of all the sea, he had felt a flow of energy that had made him capable of feats he had never imagined possible.

'I sense some of Master Sabi's magic still lingering here. I may be able to harness it sufficiently to lead us through the same fracture in space that he established,' he murmured to himself

Before he could act, Menagerie roared.

'What's wrong?' cried Octy, trying desperately to stay calm.

'Something evil is approaching!' he warned, extending a paw towards the passage that had brought them to the spot. 'We're not alone!'

'Perhaps it's one of the chateau workers?' Tobias rationalised. They stood facing the dark tunnel expectantly.

'Whatever it was has now gone. Did the rest of you feel it?' the lion checked, now relaxing.

'Feel what?' asked The Prof.

'An overwhelming sense of dread; like you were about to take your last breath?' offered Flanders, in a wavering voice.

'Exactly! We need to leave now!' insisted GJ. Driven by a surge of adrenaline, his basic instinct propelled him to run away. With a wildly pounding heart, he leapt towards the barrier. Eff instinctively reached out in an attempt to stop him colliding with the wall and hurting himself. It was too late, as he was already out of reach. Fortunately for the canine, he emerged into the cold Tasmanian air, skidding on wooden boards and landing at Mikey's feet.

Menagerie followed, with the rats running hot on his heels, each propelled by a similar involuntary response to flee.

'Did you do that to the wall, Eff?' Octy checked.

'I don't think so!'

'We should give it a try too,' said Octy, stepping forwards. Rain started to pour as he crossed over.

Sir Geo and GJ ran off for a hurry up, their shiny fur quickly becoming plastered to their skin. Rivulets of water began to run down Mikey's oily dreadlocks.

'Eff, you should go next with Kate,' advised Tobias. No one argued. The others quickly followed. After Flanders exited last, the barrier reappeared behind him.

Mikey rushed forward to greet Eff.

'Thank you for saving my sister! I'm so sorry I ever doubted you,' he blurted. Eff smiled graciously and said, 'I promise I'll never fail her.' He handed Kate to him then walked back to the prison. There he paused, closed his eyes, reached out his arms and placed both palms on the cold surface of its front wall. The structure started to glow with an azure haze which extended from his fingers. The intensity grew, culminating in a blinding flash of light. He bent down and picked up the small metallic cube which Tobias had carried to this location. The chalk cellars of France were gone. Mikey, clutching the beloved sister he had thought he had lost forever, stared in awe.

'I'm glad Eff's on our side,' he whispered to her.

'I've always thought that little brother,' said Kate. He handed the shivering woman back to his future brother-in-law.

'This rain is due to set in. We should go to my place,' instructed Mikey.

He led them across the grounds of the old penitentiary towards his van, an old Kombi, in the staff carpark. As they approached the exit they were distracted by loud, hysterical sobbing. Mikey paused briefly to peer through the window of the office building to see what was going on. His boss was simultaneously attempting to debrief the distressed young girls who had spotted Master Sabi. An animated trio of hard-core paranormal enthusiasts were waiting to ask questions regarding the likely identity of the figure they too had seen.

'The show Master Sabi put on tonight will never be forgotten. It will be on the cover of the local paper by tomorrow. It's the stuff of legends!' exclaimed Mikey, smirking.

Upon arriving at his vehicle, he slid open the back door so they could pile inside. Like sardines stacked tightly in a can they huddled, each passenger grateful for the warmth and sense of safety it provided.

'I like your wheels,' said Flanders, sat at his side in the front seat next to Tobias, with Sir Geo lying across their legs.

'Kate helped me restore this baby!' he revealed proudly. He slowly drove off down a narrow, dark, unmade gravel track that led out onto the main road. There he picked up speed. Trying to normalise things, he said, 'did you like the mural on the side of my van? Kate painted it for me as a birthday present a few years ago. It's why I call my van "Mango".'

'I'm sorry I didn't notice it,' Tobias confessed.

'What exactly is it of?' Flanders enquired.

'It's a collage of the local produce from around the town of Bowen. You know how the women in our family are obsessed with food?'

'Yes,' said Tobias.

'The Kensington Pride, better known as the "Bowen mango", is a local delicacy. Abundant crops of tomatoes, capsicums and eggplants also grow well up there. It is a fishing paradise too, where Spotted and Spanish Mackerel roam the waters and trawlers bring in the tastiest prawns. Seasonally, there's enormous mud crabs to be eaten too. All of these feature in Kate's artwork although it's mangoes that predominate.'

'Where exactly is Bowen?' asked Flanders.

'It's a waterfront town in the Whitsunday Region near the Great Barrier Reef in Queensland. It's where we spent our summers when we were kids, as our dad was born there.'

Eff leaned forward from the back seat and said, 'I didn't know that, Mikey.'

'Kate and I should take you there one day. We went up there on our first road trip together to scatter some of dad's ashes into the sea at his favourite beach.'

Overcome with emotion, the driver stopped speaking. The reality that his sister had almost died was sinking in.

'We should definitely do that one day,' Eff replied.

Mikey's telephone started to ring. He removed it from his pocket and passed it over his shoulder to The Prof, sitting behind him.

'Mikey?' came a familiar voice with a distinctive South African accent.

'He's driving right now. Gavin, it's me,' The Prof answered.

'Prof? How is that possible? I thought you were in France scouring the chalk cellars without me. I've been very jealous,' he replied.

'There is much to tell you. Where are you now? Who are you with?' The Prof questioned, in rapid fire.

'I'm with Annie, Sandy, Smiley, Floorplank and Honey. We're at Gundagai, on our way to Port Melbourne to get the car ferry across to

Tasmania. We're getting ready to take our turn guarding that scoundrel prisoner.' Various 'hellos' were audible in the background.

Choosing his words carefully so as not to upset anyone, The Prof replied, 'we definitely have much to catch up on. Most importantly, Master Sabi is on the loose again and we still don't have an antidote for those on Luna Tribus.'

'That is very bad, Professor,' said Gavin. He relayed the information to his passengers.

'Is everyone alright there?' a frantic Sandy called out.

'Tell them we are all together,' said The Prof, eager to put the worried women at ease. 'Gavin, it's very late here. Why exactly did you call Mikey right now?'

'You don't miss a beat old friend. Something significant has occurred here.'

'Go on.'

'I was woken from sleep by the voice of Beauty in my head, compelling me to wake up and go to the main cave urgently. I left my bed and found her there, partially submerged in her original form as a submarine. She told me you had sent her to collect us and insisted we needed to drive south at once, towards Rutherglen in Victoria in order to see an old acquaintance of ours. She was adamant it is where the antidote is hidden.'

'What acquaintance?' prompted The Prof.

'A winemaker we met when we used to do the sparkling wine competitions. Do you remember Tommy?'

'I think so. He was an intelligent, friendly, albeit intense chap; a bit like you as I recall.'

'I'll take that as a compliment. Yes, in those days only a few of us were obsessed with making Australian, French style sparkling wine using the Traditional Method.'

'With ginger hair?'

'Yes. You didn't send Beauty to get us, did you?'

'No. We left her in the carpark at a chateau.'

'Then who did?'

'I have no idea,' said The Prof, now frowning.

'We started worrying when we couldn't get through to any of your phones. Then we couldn't contact Mikey. Sandy had a chilling feeling that something bad had happened to you. In the end, we decided to go with Beauty and have kept trying to reach you every half an hour. Then you finally picked up.'

'Going to Rutherglen to find Tommy is a crazy long shot. Why would he have the antidote?'

'It's bizarre, yet I felt this tip could not be ignored. Besides, it was on the way to Tasmania and we were getting ready to depart anyway. Do you have the riddle there to refer to? I've had some thoughts regarding why it could be true.'

'We don't need to see it. We've memorised it,' said The Prof.

'I think the "apprentice daughter" might refer to Tommy's girl. The woman has done her father proud, completing Viticulture and Oenology studies in Melbourne before returning and helping him run the business. Their website indicates their unpretentious boutique vineyard is continuing to flourish,' said Gavin.

'It's all coming back to me. Tommy won many awards for his sparkling wines, yet resisted becoming overly commercialised. His business model relies on word of mouth and having a devoted following of appreciative consumers,' The Prof explained to the others.

Hope was slowly returning to Tobias, who said, 'I think he's onto something. We went down the path that was overly obvious by heading to the place of oranges and entering those labyrinths.'

'We've got nothing to lose by checking it out. We need to get to Rutherglen immediately!' The Prof concluded.

'Kate needs to rest before we can contemplate travel,' said Eff. He was still profoundly worried about her. She barely stirred as he stroked her hair.

'We're almost to my cottage. She can rest there while we make plans,' suggested Mikey.

'I feel strongly that we should join Gavin and the others immediately,' insisted Tobias.

'Why does my daughter need to rest?' asked Sandy, alarmed by Eff's worried voice.

'You didn't say where you were right now, Gavin,' said The Prof.

'We are taking a break at the Gundagai Caravan and Camping Centre. It's a short distance off the main highway, right on the bank of the river. Beauty transformed herself into the campervan of my dreams, putting the modest one I purchased to shame.'

'Something is wrong with my Kate!' Sandy exclaimed to her mother.

'I'm sure we'll know more soon, darling. She's safe with Eff and the others. Regardless of what's happened, I know we are always better when we are together. Fortunately, I have a serious supply of my beloved Cornish pasties in the Esky. They could be heated in a flash and all will be well,' Annie insisted.

'Do we need to come and get you?' Gavin enquired.

'Tell them to stay where they are! We'll join them soon,' insisted Tobias.

'Stay there. Gundagai is only a few hours away from Rutherglen,' The Prof replied.

Mikey turned into a driveway and stopped the van outside his residence.

They exited. The cold air caused Kate to stir. She opened her eyes and smiled at Eff. She wrapped her arms around his neck and drifted back to sleep. The dogs, rats and Menagerie ran around the yard enjoying the fresh air. After weeing on various trees and shrubs they returned to the van to find that the others, apart from Flanders and Tobias, had gone inside the house. They watched Tobias remove Orizuru from his coat and unfold her paper form across his outstretched hand. Having witnessed the monks return to the monastery on the back of the graceful crane, Flanders grew excited about the possibility of taking a flight.

‘I guess we’ll need a few trips,’ GJ commented.

Tobias held the corner of the parchment, triggering Orizuru to unwrap herself. She flapped her silken wings, opened her long-lashed eyes and took in the scene. Tobias told her what had happened.

‘I need your help,’ he concluded.

She flicked her wings vigorously, causing two of her feathers to detach. They landed on the ground and spontaneously started to rotate, so fast, they became a blur. When their movements stopped, two pieces of paper were left in their place. Each grew larger, before folding in half. In a series of synchronised, choreographed folds, two other cranes took shape.

‘We need to help our friends. Follow my lead, children,’ Orizuru instructed. She started rhythmically flapping her wings. They mimicked her actions and grew in size until they were as large as their parent.

‘When you are ready, climb onto our backs,’ she instructed Tobias. He sent Flanders inside to retrieve the others.

‘I’m sorry that we have to move Kate again. Rest assured that a soft bed is waiting for her as we travel to Gundagai,’ he told Eff, when he returned carrying her.

Tobias organised them into three groups. Mikey and Sir Geo climbed aboard one of the birds with The Prof. Eff and Kate alighted a second one, with Octy and the rats. Tobias and Flanders climbed onto Orizuru last, taking GJ and Menagerie with them.

‘Hold on to our feathers,’ Orizuru instructed, preparing to take off.

‘We haven’t told you our required destination,’ said Flanders, politely.

'We were created by The Oneidon to take our riders wherever they need to go…anywhere and to anytime.'

GJ peered over her shoulder and watched the ground disappear. As the birds levelled out in flight, the only sound was the hypnotic flapping of their wings. Feeling safe and secure, he drifted off into an exhausted sleep, thinking about Ro and Ellie. With all his heart he hoped that they could still be saved.

Having sensed a change in speed, Mikey woke up. He peered over the edge of the warm, soft wing where he had been slumbering. Lying at his side, with his head resting on his knee, Sir Geo let out an enormous yawn. Pale blue light was starting to appear in the dawn sky as the crane started to descend. She gently dived towards a winding strip of brownish water. The Murrumbidgee River gradually appeared below like a lazy slumbering snake. The landscape was dominated by four bridges; two new carriageways for motor vehicles and more impressively, the historic, crumbling Prince Alfred Bridge and railway viaduct that spanned a vast flood plain.

Mikey jumped off as soon as they landed. His companions followed. Their crane had brought them to rest outside Beauty, a shiny silver campervan. As he approached the door, two whiskered faces appeared in the window.

'They're here! They're here!' Honey and Floorplank echoed in unison. The door swung open and Gavin appeared, rubbing his gritty eyes in disbelief at the majestic bird. Smiley appeared at his side and flashed an enormous toothy grin.

'I can't believe you are here!' Gavin told The Prof, shaking his hand.

'Tobias is behind this rather extraordinary transportation service,' explained Mikey.

'Where are the others?' The Prof questioned.

'You are the first to arrive,' answered Gavin.

'You old boys should go inside and wait. We'll do the meet and greet for the rest of the gang,' Mikey offered, with a cheeky wink. They gratefully moved out of the bitter subzero cold, away from the icy breeze gusting off the water.

Several minutes passed as Mikey, Sir Geo and Smiley stood patiently waiting. Determined to be helpful, Honey and Floorplank stubbornly insisted they stay with Mikey, shivering within opposite fleecy lined pockets of his jacket. Fortunately, it wasn't long until he heard fluttering wings above. He spotted Big Timmy and Snuggles still curled up together, lying close to Kate's neck. At her side, Eff opened his right eye lazily, then closed it again. Octy poked his fellow passengers, each reluctant to leave the cozy warmth. With his persistent coaxing, they were soon safely inside the van.

'You should take the little rats inside the van. There's no point in all of us freezing,' Mikey told Smiley. They departed.

Mikey and Sir Geo continued to search the sunrise expectedly, waiting for Orizuru to appear.

Time passed.

More time passed.

Mikey started to worry. Eventually Sir Geo voiced his unspoken concern.

'They should be here by now.'

The Chocolate Labrador went over to the nearest crane who had folded herself into a shrunken paper square. He started to nose her then asked politely, 'do you know where Orizuru is?'

There was no response. He repeated the question to her sibling. Mikey leaned down to pick up the slips of motionless parchment. As he did so, the delicate material disintegrated, then disappeared.

'Now I'm really worried!' he told the dog.

'I don't think they're coming,' said Sir Geo.

They retreated inside Beauty to update the others. As they opened the door, the smell of warm pasties greeted them. Kate looked better, now awake and being fussed over by her mother and grandmother. Eff looked up from a mug of hot chocolate, frowning at Mikey's news.

'It's ominous,' remarked The Prof.

'We should stick to the plan,' Sir Geo urged.

'I agree. We should start moving. Tobias knows where we are heading,' stated Gavin.

'Would you like me to start moving while you finish breakfast?' Beauty enquired.

'Yes, thank you,' Gavin replied.

'Someone needs to pretend to ride in the front seat. I'm happy to do it,' said Mikey. He picked up the remains of his pasty. Sir Geo, now never far from his side, followed him outside and jumped into the cabin next to him.

'How long will it take to get to Rutherglen?' Mikey asked Beauty.

'At the permitted road speeds, I estimate that we should arrive later this morning, around ten o'clock. Gavin expects the tasting room will be open then.'

Orizuru circled over the sprawling grounds of the Belgian Malinois Monastery. Expecting to be on the tail of the other two cranes in search of the true antidote, Tobias was shocked when her wing tipped and he recognised their unexpected location. GJ and Menagerie woke up as he stirred. Before any words could be exchanged, the smell of pungent smoke filled their nostrils. Flanders woke up in a panic. GJ violently sneezed.

'I have brought you where you needed to go,' Orizuru announced. She descended swiftly then landed in a grassy clearing, upwind from the monastery. Without further discussion her passengers jumped off her back. They ran towards the magnificent residence that had been the only home the two monks had ever known. Out of control, crackling flames were leaping high above the front entrance. Alarmed residents, some of them screaming, ran from the heavy wooden front doors.

'Look up there!' cried Flanders, pointing to a cloaked figure standing on the roof, cackling in delight. It was Master Sabi. He disappeared from view as a rotund, frenzied monk rushed towards them, struggling under the weight of a bulging sack containing aged scrolls. Others ran by, gripped by a terror that made them oblivious to the return of their leaders and the unexpected presence of a brown dog and lion. Some had scorched robes, others sooty faces. A few were moaning in pain from areas of burned skin. One of them elbowed the sack of the struggling librarian, causing one of the scriptures to fall onto the ground. Tobias picked it up and handed it to the owner. A look of relief crossed his ruddy face.

'You are a sight for sore eyes!'

'What has happened here, Nicolas?' Tobias demanded.

'We are under attack! Brother Matteo ordered an evacuation but many remain trapped inside. A large area of the cathedral ceiling has collapsed, blocking their escape.'

'Flanders, do what you can to help our injured brothers who have made it outside,' Tobias instructed. He left to attend to the small gathering of frightened monks. Some of them were lying motionless on the ground.

'What can we do?' asked GJ. He was standing with the lion, each feeling the distress of the monks, some of which were now howling.

'We need more help. Take Orizuru to The Oneidon. I'm going to try to get inside and free any survivors.' He started to walk towards the burning building.

GJ and Menagerie ran back to where Orizuru had landed and found her flicking ash from her wings.

‘Please return to Ivor and bring The Oneidon here,’ instructed GJ.

She lowered her lashes and replied, ‘I can only go where my rider needs me to go.’

‘One of us needs to go with her,’ said GJ.

‘I made a pledge to never leave your side,’ the lion reminded him.

‘We don’t have time to argue. In the chalk cellars you repaid your life debt to me. So please go now, friend.’

Menagerie leapt onto Orizuru’s back and asked to be taken to The Oneidon. As she prepared to take flight he closed his eyes, concentrating.

‘Master Sabi is in the bell tower. Get him!’ the lion shouted to GJ.

The Chocolate Labrador bolted towards the monastery where the inferno was spreading at an alarming pace. He ran to the back of the building in search of the villain and pawed open the heavy wooden door in the base of the tower, fortunately left ajar. It was cold, damp and silent inside, a welcome contrast to the heat and smoke. He sniffed the air repeatedly and after catching a hint of the magician, approached a winding staircase. Upwards and upwards, round and round he ran. Half way to the top, the panting dog paused on a landing to catch his breath.

GJ’s eyes were drawn to a door, outlined by a flickering orange light. He pushed it open cautiously and padded outside onto a viewing deck. Immediately overcome by acrid smoke, he dared to linger only briefly, appreciating the widespread nature of the spreading flames and destruction. Back inside, he ascended again. Having made it to the top, he stood still, with raised hackles. Smiling jubilantly, Master Sabi stood adjacent to the enormous bell.

Consumed by anger, GJ leapt forwards and overbalanced his enemy. He plunged his canines into his bony arm and pinned him to the stony floor with his body.

'You have gone too far!' the dog barked.

His victim shrieked in agony, then quickly recovering from the surprise attack, mounted his own response, flinging the dog across the enclosed space. He stood up and cradled his oozing arm.

'I could say the same about you! You pesky brown dogs never give up!' he sneered, enjoying watching GJ struggle to stand.

'Was it really necessary to come and burn this magnificent place down?'

'Tobias has been a solid adversary from the moment he joined your band of trouble makers. This is his punishment.'

'You can belittle us, bruise us and burn us, yet we will prevail!'

'That's very poetic, GJ. Perhaps you should be a bard?' remarked Tobias, stepping into the light.

'I should have known you'd turn up. You're never far from the action are you…hybrid?' Master Sabi stated, glaring at the new arrival. Tobias was taken aback. 'Yes, I know what you are. You really are nothing more than an animal, barely more evolved than the pure canine here.'

Before either could react, the magician turned and jumped onto the smouldering roof of the monastery. GJ growled. Filled with rage, he followed him across a horizontal beam, before lunging at his target.

With his teeth now embedded in Master Sabi's left leg, he pulled him down onto the hot surface.

'Get off me!' he protested, choking for breath in the smoke-filled air. In order to meet his own need for oxygen, the dog was forced to detach. The process allowed his victim to roll forcefully to one side, out of range of his assailant. The dog spat out a combination of the fabric, hair and blood of his enemy and prepared to resume the chase.

It was Tobias's turn to make his move. He ran past GJ and forcefully wrestled their nemesis to the ground. Master Sabi wriggled and squirmed, almost pulling himself free. The dog blocked his retreat by sitting on his torso, attempting to pin him to the tiled roof under his full weight. The attackers were strong but their opponent, despite his asthenic form, was superhumanly stronger. Writhing and pushing like a frenzied serpent, he skilfully managed to repeatedly try to free himself from the determined grip of the duo.

GJ howled in pain, as thrashing like a rabid animal, Master Sabi fought back, successfully thrusting a long bony talon near one of his eye sockets. Tobias instinctively came to his aid. He momentarily released his grip on Master Sabi so he could check on his friend.

'I'm alright. Get him Tobias!' GJ urged, oblivious to the blood that was trickling from a gash, on the side of one of his eyebrows. The monk resumed his pursuit of the now fleeing villain. Driven by dark fury, the magician accelerated across a section of crumbling roof then confidently climbed up onto an intact section of wall above the central cathedral, whose ceiling was continuing to give way. Like an advancing spider, his white knuckled fingers gripped onto prominent stones protruding from the ancient wall.

From his elevated vantage point, Master Sabi's streaming red eyes darted around, scanning for a safe route to escape. He spotted a long metal service ladder in the distance that would take him to the ground. Too weak to execute a flying spell, it was the only way out. To reach it, he recognised that he must drop down again and traverse the already partially collapsed, previously resplendent stained-glass roof. He took a deep breath and leaped.

GJ and Tobias watched his cloak billow behind him as he jumped. Caught up in the moment, they continued their pursuit.

'This is really bad!' GJ proclaimed, noticing tiny cracks were appearing around their feet with each step as they ran. A fracture line was fast forming along the last intact section of stained glass. It was extending with every step of the three figures, each desperate to get to the ledge with the ladder.

'It's not going to hold for much longer!' Tobias warned, as the roof started to give way.

No one was spared. Steps away from his destination, Master Sabi commenced his descent, free-falling into the fiery void below. GJ snapped his strong jaws together, halting his fall by clamping onto one of his arms. Tobias managed to grip onto the back legs of the Chocolate Labrador, miraculously steadying the three of them by anchoring himself on a solid, smouldering cross beam with his other hand.

Chapter 11
RUTHERGLEN

They dangled precipitously.

'Why would you try to save me?' Master Sabi demanded, meeting the eyes of his rescuers.

'Good question,' GJ thought to himself, unable to reply, as to do so would mean losing his grip.

'It's because we are better than you,' Tobias shouted from above. 'We have no evil in our hearts. It's who we are, who we will always be.'

Master Sabi seethed. With a final mocking smile, he wriggled violently, successfully dislodging himself from GJ's precarious, slippery, saliva coated, anchor point. GJ and Tobias stared in disbelief as the ungrateful magician fell to his death. They watched his body crash onto the debris strewn, stone floor below, before quickly being overcome by the ravaging fire. They watched his sardonic, twisted grin fade to a neutral expression as the flames consumed him.

Tobias recognised that he was tiring and turned his efforts to pulling GJ up onto the beam at his side. They rested briefly, hyperventilating. Just as GJ was starting to recover, he felt a strong dark presence. An orange-red, ghostly form ascended from the fire. The formless figure paused in front of them and met their gaze. Inside their heads a voice reached out.

'Until next time,' it said calmly. With a flash it was gone. Thunder cracked and the skies opened, bucketing a torrent of much welcome rain. Water droplets splashed their soot covered faces.

'Let's get out of here,' GJ uttered, battling his own fatigue.

'We'll have to go back to the bell tower,' instructed Tobias.

Together they made it to safety.

'What was that?' asked GJ as they commenced their descent down the stairs.

'I have no idea. I think it was living inside Master Sabi and was forced to leave his body when he perished.'

They exited into a chaotic horror scene caused by the inferno. He Tobias found Flanders trying to ease the pain of a distressed monk with significant facial burns. Having ripped his own robe into swathes of material, he was dipping the rags into a bucket of water and using them as cooling compresses.

'Report,' said Tobias, taking charge.

'There is only bad news. Most of our brothers have perished. Almost everyone who made it out has sustained burns.'

Tobias scanned the area and noted that few of the survivors were standing. Those that could, were huddled together in the rain, wailing, watching the final destruction of their monastery. He spotted Nicolas sitting on the sack of scrolls he had saved. He was inconsolable, mourning the loss of his home and the senseless loss of life.

'Nothing is salvageable now,' said Tobias gravely.

'We must be grateful that the rain came. It is helping take the heat out of the burns,' said Flanders, graciously.

'Where is Matteo?' asked Tobias.

'He didn't make it. He ran back inside to wake those that were sleeping in their beds when the fire started.'

'Exactly how many survivors are there?' asked GJ.

'We number less than two dozen,' Flanders replied.

Drawn to a familiar sound, Tobias looked skyward. The fluttering of wings grew louder. Those that were capable, stared up in awe at the approaching flock of cranes. In the lead was Orizuru, with The Oneidon appearing beside her slender neck. Menagerie was at his side.

'I fear we are too late,' the Head of the Compasse told the lion. They disembarked close to where Tobias was standing. The Oneidon motioned for the other birds to land behind them. GJ shared what had taken place. Few words were needed as the scene of devastation told the story.

'My heart is with you brother. I am sorry that I could not prevent this tragedy. Menagerie says this is the work of Master Sabi. Is that your conclusion?'

'Yes. We never stood a chance. He played us like a fiddle with his conniving ways and daunting magic.'

'Where is he now?'

'Where he cannot hurt anyone again. We watched him die,' said Tobias.

'There will come a time for us to discuss what has transpired. For now, I see that many are in need of care and shelter. You are all welcome in Ivor.'

Flanders convened in hushed tones with his surviving, devastated brothers, conveying the offer.

'No one is questioning that leaving Earth is now desirable. Many believe this is our destiny,' he reported back.

'Is that the same for you?' The Oneidon checked.

'Yes, although one day I wish to return and rebuild.'

'I understand. Please start helping your brothers mount the birds.' Flanders departed. 'What of you, Tobias? Will you be joining us?'

'Not yet, as I have unfinished business here.'

'The antidote?' He nodded. The Oneidon stared into the glowing embers of the decimated building that was their backdrop. 'All seems devoid of hope here and yet you fight on?'

'I will never succumb to darkness!' he cried.

The Oneidon placed an arm around his shoulder and with obvious admiration said, 'all strength to you, my brother.'

Flanders walked past them leading the still sobbing Nicolas. He boosted his rotund companion up onto one of the cranes then doubled back to speak with Tobias.

'We are now all aboard. You're not coming with us, are you, my friend?'

'Not yet.'

'I'll take care of them. Make sure you come and join us soon, as we will need your guidance...especially me.'

'You are their leader now. I have been drifting away from the order for a long time.'

'You have transcended that role and have others who need you. Go and help them!' They embraced.

The cranes lifted off into the smoky haze with the pollution acting as a filter for the sun's powerful rays, producing bursts of light reminiscent of a kaleidoscope.

'It reminds me of a Luna Triban sky. Perhaps it's a sign that our friends will be saved?' GJ commented.

'I like your company,' said The Oneidon.

'There's nothing like a brown dog to maintain optimism in the face of defeat,' explained Tobias.

'Could we borrow one of your cranes to take us to Rutherglen?' requested GJ. 'We believe it's where the antidote is hidden and our friends are expecting us to join them there.'

He pointed to a remaining crane at Orizuru's side and said, 'go now.'

'Thank you. We will depart soon, after the dead have been properly laid to rest,' advised Tobias.

The Oneidon remained and helped Tobias, GJ and Menagerie prepare a grave. No one spoke as the bodies were laid to rest, stacked in layers within a large fire pit. The Head of the Malinois order led them in a simple prayer as the cremation proceeded.

'This is all my fault,' Tobias uttered, when he had finished.

'No. I am to blame; Geo and I. We have meddled in the affairs of a world far from our own. So many have paid a price for this,' the Chocolate Labrador lamented.

'Both of you need to listen to me and listen well,' The Oneidon commanded, his face now stern. 'We are standing together at a crossroads of darkness and light battling for victory. This is the way of all worlds and the way it has always been. This is not a moment to doubt yourselves. It's appropriate to be sad but do not allow it to paralyse you.' He touched the brow of the dog and hybrid and said, 'you'll feel better after I freshen you up.'

Each felt a surge of energy. All traces of smoke were gone from their skin and Tobias was wearing a fresh brown robe of the Compasse order.

He ushered them towards the cranes.

'You need to eat too.' He handed them a bag of Agar. 'Tsuru will take you where you need to be. When you are ready, she will bring you home to Ivor. I wish you well.' He mounted Orizuru and flew away.

Mikey pretended to steer Beauty down a gravel driveway. The sun was casting a golden glow over the trellised vines that rustled in a gentle breeze in the adjacent fields. They stopped in a cul-de-sac at the end, outside the entrance to a tall pale shed with a skillion roof. A corrugated iron portico covered the front access door. Attached to it was a sign painted in a simple clear font that said, 'The Shed - Tasting Room'.

Eager to stretch their legs, the passengers piled out of the campervan.

'It's not what I expected,' remarked Mikey to Gavin.

'That's because you are used to the flashy establishments that predominate in the Hunter Valley. I always respected the fact this was an understated, modest operation. What you will experience is a superlative example of small batch production. The owners only have a few parcels of land under vine of their chosen cultivars. They are lovingly tended and all of the grapes are hand-picked,' he replied. He pointed to the meticulously planted rows of grape vines, each designated with a sequential letter of the alphabet.

'I love the way their wines are named after the rows where the vines are located. For example, their famous Sparkling Chenin blanc is called "The DE". Their Shiraz Durif is "The KLP".

Sandy and her mother approached the entrance and read a smaller sign attached to the wall.

'They are closed today,' reported Annie.

'That's most unfortunate,' The Prof responded.

'Perhaps we are in luck? Company is approaching,' Gavin replied, referring to a person and dog, walking towards them from the paddock. Octy rendered himself invisible.

As Gavin headed to meet the staff member, Tsuru landed on the other side of the building. Tobias waited until she folded herself into a piece of parchment, before placing her inside the pocket of his robe.

With GJ and Menagerie flanking his sides, he headed towards the group assembled outside the shed.

'Have you found the antidote yet?' GJ enquired, running forwards with his tail flapping enthusiastically towards Sir Geo and Smiley. There was much sniffing and licking.

'Where did you come from?' asked The Prof, rushing forward and greeting Tobias. They shook hands.

'You look different. Is that a new robe?'

'Yes. Much has happened and most of it is terrible,' he replied, solemnly.

'You look out of place and we have company approaching,' Eff noted. He touched Tobias on his sleeve, closed his eyes and outfitted him in jeans and a sweatshirt.

'Thank you,' Tobias acknowledged gratefully.

'You should render yourself invisible too,' The Prof instructed Menagerie.

'Let's go and meet the dog!' Sir Geo suggested to his canine companions. He bounded ahead to greet the four-legged creature who was now running towards him. GJ and Smiley sprinted to catch up. Sir Geo, having arrived first, started sniffing the unknown canine.

'Steady on mate!' came the nasal twang from the overwhelmed Kelpie. Sir Geo backed off. 'What are you lot doing here? We aren't receiving visitors today as there's lots of work my humans need to do.'

'I've just read the sign. Sorry, I didn't realise you'd be closed today,' Gavin interrupted politely. The dog nearly jumped out of his skin.

'You can understand what I'm saying?'

'Yes,' Gavin responded.

'What is your name?' asked GJ.

'I'm Menny.'

'That's an unusual name,' Gavin observed. The dog continued to be stunned by their ability to communicate.

'Menny, Menny,' his owner called, interrupting their conversation. An attractive young woman dressed in overalls and wearing muddy gumboots approached. Her long mane of chestnut hair was tied back in a low ponytail. She smiled. 'I'm sorry to tell you that we're closed today.'

'That's a shame as I've brought a load of close friends with me and promised them the best sparkling wine in Australia; apart from mine of course! I'm Gavin, an old acquaintance of your father's. I assume from your likeness to him that you are his daughter, Jennifer?' He politely extended his wrinkled hand, which she shook firmly.

'Please call me Jen. How exactly do you know my dad?'

'I met Tommy several times when we were competing in wine shows, both in the sparkling categories.'

'Are you still a winemaker?'

'Sadly, I'm not. I do miss it dreadfully. I was extremely proud of my Sparkling Shiraz; a perennial winner.'

'I love Sparkling Shiraz, although I prefer some Durif in my blend.'

He shivered in the cold and said, 'that's precisely the wine that I have brought my friends to taste. Any chance of a few minutes of your time so we can warm up and try it?'

She smiled and said, 'if you give me a few moments to get organised, I can invite you inside and remind you of the endless work it involves.'

'Now that's the truth of it! It's a labour of love,' admitted Gavin.

'Stick around long enough and I'll put you to work disgorging a few bottles for me.'

'It would be an offer hard to refuse.'

'I'm glad you came by. It's been lonely since dad retired. I'll meet you at the front,' she added, cheerfully. Menny remained with him and the other dogs, while she disappeared into the loading dock at the back of the shed.

'This is Menny,' Gavin told the others as he stroked his ears.

'That's an unusual name,' The Prof noted.

'Not really, when you realise it's nothing more than a shortened version of the word "Meunier", as in Pinot Meunier, one of our grapes,' the dog explained.

'Of course! It's the third of the grape varieties used to make Champagne,' Gavin told his companions, chuckling.

Sandy went to the campervan to check on Kate, who was yet to emerge from her bed. She returned with her daughter.

'Are you feeling better my darling?' Eff enquired of his fiancée. He hugged her and planted a gentle kiss on the top of her head.

'Much better. Not even a hint of graininess remains on my skin,' she reported, forcing a smile.

'I suggested to Eff that we should go on a roadtrip to Bowen when this is over. What do you think about that, big sister?' asked Mikey.

'I'd like that. What I like better is the fact you have finally accepted him as part of our family.'

The dogs continued their own conversation as they waited for Jen to reappear.

'How is it that your humans can understand our language?' asked Menny.

'They have special abilities,' said GJ.

'It's very rare. I've only ever met one other with the same skills.'

'Really? Who?' Sir Geo questioned, stopping in his tracks. They all paused and stared at the Kelpie.

'You're being a bit intense. What's so interesting about what I said?'

'The fact you've met someone before who could converse with you is of enormous interest to us. Can you tell us about that individual?' requested Smiley.

'It was last year. We always take on seasonal workers and there was a funny old man who worked with us for a few months. He was very helpful to the mistress; much more capable than he looked. He worked hard with the harvest and seemed very knowledgeable when it came to blending the base wines.'

'What was his name?' asked Sir Geo.

'Sabi.'

'We have news!' Sir Geo announced excitedly, leading the dogs towards the rest of their contingent. He blurted the information extracted from Menny.

'We're in the right place! I know it! Let's go and get that antidote!' Smiley proclaimed.

Jen unlocked the front doors and invited the party inside. Gavin introduced the winemaker to his eager companions. Her kind eyes rested upon Kate, who was still looking pale.

'You don't look well,' she observed, astutely. Kate nodded and said, 'I've been rather ill.'

'Come inside and lie down on the settee while I set up some glasses. If you'd prefer tea to wine, I can provide that too.'

Kate smiled gratefully and walked into the shed with Annie, Sandy and Eff. Octy and Menagerie following closely behind, invisible. The rats scurried after them and found places to hide so they could observe what they hoped would be a defining moment in history.

Spurred on by hope and in a fatigued, frenzied state, GJ took off, running around on the nearby grass doing zoomies.

'Your dog seems very wound up about something,' Jen commented.

'Don't worry, he'll behave as soon as we go inside; won't you GJ?' Gavin called out to him.

'Come GJ,' said The Prof. He stopped chasing his tail and walked over and sat down at their feet, resting on his back legs, adopting his most angelic stance. Sir Geo and Smiley took his lead and lined up looking equally fetching.

'That's very impressive behaviour,' she remarked.

'I was a vet before a winemaker and believe dogs understand more than you'd think. Talking to them normally works well with our boys,' Gavin told her. They all went inside.

Sir Geo and Smiley continued to cross-examine Menny about 'Sabi', attempting to extract information relevant to their search.

'I didn't have too much to do with him. We only spoke when we needed to. He wasn't a dog man, if you know what I mean. On reflection, I don't think he liked me one bit, so I avoided him. It might be best to get one of your humans to ask the mistress about him.'

Having overheard the discourse, Gavin followed the recommendation.

'I assume your father's retirement means you have a lot more work to do yourself these days?'

'I've been lucky to have a stream of capable workers continue to come through these parts. It means I can get help with the laborious tasks and focus on the fun stuff which I'm more than capable of doing alone.'

The Prof, whilst continuing to listen intently, wandered over to the nearest row of riddling racks and expertly handled an inverted bottle of developing wine.

'I used to love assisting Gavin make his wines. If I wasn't helping escort these good people on a wine tour, I'd have suggested we stop here for a while and give you a hand. I'd forgotten how soothing it is to nurture the bottles as the contents magically develop.'

She laughed and watched him, observing his excellent technique.

'Nice work! I can see that you've been taught well. I agree, wine making is magical. I love it! Feel free to keep working on that row.' To her delight, Mikey joined in too.

'I grew up helping Gavin too. I almost studied winemaking myself,' he told her.

'What did you do instead?'

'I became a scientist. I'm currently involved in an animal research project in Tasmania.'

Feeling relaxed, Jen moved away to a serving area on the other side of the workroom.

'Shall we do the tasting now?' she enquired, after a short delay.

Gavin responded appreciatively, motioning for the others to play along.

Jen assembled a row of cold bottles on a high counter between herself and the guests. A stainless-steel spittoon was already resting at each end of the bar. She removed a tray of glasses from a shelf underneath it and made each gleam with a linen cloth, before placing them in a tidy row. She donned a set of short white gloves and held the end of the first tapered bottle elegantly at its base. The sound of fizzing pale golden liquid cascading into the glasses, made Gavin beam.

'This is my favourite wine at present. See if you can guess what it is,' Jen instructed the group. Eff, genuinely enthralled to be sampling what he later described as 'potions that induce pleasure', brought authenticity to their pretence. Tobias, Sandy, Annie and Mikey, accustomed to the procedure, joined in as fellow avid participants. Acting out his role perfectly as a wine connoisseur, Gavin inspected, swirled and sniffed the contents of his glass dramatically, prior to finally pressing the delicate rim of the flute to his lips.

'I believe this to be a rather divine sparkling Chenin blanc. Am I correct?' he checked, after a short delay to savour the flavour profile.

'You're spot on! Do you like it?'

'I love it! I should never have stopped making wine!'

'If you don't mind me asking, why did you?' Jen enquired.

'My body started to fail me. It was my back principally. It meant I couldn't keep up with the work it entailed and I struggled to find good help with the more complex tasks.'

She agreed that exceptional workers were hard to come by.

'The problem is that the finances of running a winery make it impossible to give permanent work to keep them. When you do find someone extraordinary, they often don't stay. Last year, we had the most wonderful assistant until one day he simply disappeared.'

'What was it about him that you found most helpful?' Gavin pressed.

'That's easy. It was his blending skills for the sparkling wines. He had a natural flare for it. I called him 'The Alchemist'. He was like a wizard. As a result of his talent, I named one of last year's vintages after him.'

She motioned to The Prof who was slowly meandering through the racks, seeming to innocently sip at his drink, and said, 'you'll find "Alchemist's potion number one," on the back row on the left. Sabi and I were both very proud of it.'

'What's in it?' asked Gavin.

'Predominantly Shiraz, with a touch of Durif and splash of Saperavi.'

'Three grapes,' said Gavin with a knowing look at Tobias.

'I've not heard of the last one,' Mikey confessed.

'It's an ancient grape native to the European country of Georgia, the birthplace of winemaking. It has the rare quality of having both red skin and flesh.'

'I'd forgotten about it. A teinturier grape!' remarked Gavin.

'Very good!' Jen remarked.

'Wine making and potion making are both fine arts. It was no coincidence that all those years ago, Master Sabi based himself at the vineyard in The Hunter Valley. He would have been drawn to it,' Eff whispered to Tobias.

The Prof continued to explore, with GJ remaining at his side. Filled with the anticipation of finding the antidote any second, the dog's tail had started enthusiastically thrashing from side to side.

'I feel we're getting warm! Be careful not to bump into any of the racks,' he warned the dog.

Gavin continued the pretence of them being on a wine tour.

'Do you like this Chenin blanc? One might describe this vintage as refreshingly acidic, with notes of ripe stone fruit and yeasty, bready characters. This grape is notably cultivated in South Africa, where I was born. It's also classically found in the Loire Valley in France. As we are fortunate to be experiencing firsthand, Jen can certainly give those places a run for their money with this superb wine.' She beamed while the others listened, hanging on his every word.

Jen poured the next wine and again asked Gavin to comment. He examined the sample then said, 'you have created the most divine example of Australian Christmas in a glass! This is iconic Sparkling Shiraz and I love it! It's so rich, ripe and full bodied. It's absolutely delicious!'

'Possibly even better than yours?' Mikey questioned, flashing a cheeky grin.

'An old man knows when to concede defeat. This is brilliant, Jen!' said Gavin, meaning every word.

Eff was particularly impressed with the sample and immediately committed to purchasing some. He too congratulated her, saying, 'it's better than anything we recently tried in France.'

'When were you there?' she enquired.

'It seems like yesterday,' he replied.

'This could be a statement wine for your wedding, Eff. Red is the quintessential colour of love and passion,' Mikey suggested. He nodded. Jen offered her congratulations when she heard that he had recently become engaged. She went to check on Kate who was feeling better. Her ashen pallor had resolved.

'Would you like to try something now?'

'That would be lovely.'

'Rutherglen is famous for making dessert wines from the muscat grape. What you need right now is the sweetness of the coffee and toffee to give you a lift,' suggested Jen. The onlookers struggled not to respond to the specific mention of the words 'coffee' and 'toffee', mentioned in the riddle.

'We're definitely in the right place!' GJ told The Prof, still actively searching the racks.

Kate sampled the sticky, brown liquid offered and commented that it was beautifully luscious. She stood up and joined Eff at the bar as they sampled the next wine, the Sparkling Shiraz Durif, Gavin had alluded to. Feeling fatigue set in again, she returned with the glass to the couch to rest. Annie, sat down next to her.

As the tasting progressed, Smiley and Sir Geo followed Menny around the shed, hoping to find a clue that would take them closer to the antidote.

'Your dogs seem to be bringing out the best in my Menny,' Jen noted, in between pouring and clearing away more samples.

'Thank you. It often feels like we can understand exactly what each other are saying,' Gavin replied, managing to keep a straight face. Eager to start searching himself, still sipping his wine, he moved towards an impressive glass trophy case fixed to the wall, adjacent to the entrance. The shelves were brimming with awards in various formats, mostly trophies. At the far end of the cabinet, resting next to a huge shiny chalice, was a wine sabre. Unlike his own, the handle was forged to resemble the body of a dragon and the blade was housed within an ornate blue and silver carved scabbard.

'That is a magnificent sabre, Jen. I love the dragon! Where did your father get it?' he enquired, loudly. All ears pricked up at the mention of the word dragon.

'He brought it back from one of his trips to Europe. It means a great deal to me.'

'May I take a closer look?'

'Sure.' Engraved along the silver blade was a message:

'To Jen - may your passion for winemaking last forever. Congratulations on your first Methode Champenoise! Love Dad xxx.'

Gavin continued to sip his wine and returned to the tasting bench.

'I have found a row of very special looking bottles over here,' The Prof stated, loudly. 'Come and have a look Eff and be sure to bring Kate. It might be an even better vintage for you to purchase to help celebrate your nuptials.'

The couple joined him.

The Prof pointed out a series of bottles that were unlike any others in sight. They contained no visible sediment. There were no temporary crown seals. The bottles had been disgorged, ready for sale, stoppered with a cork and cage that was wrapped in foil. Eff slowly waved his hand across the necks of them.

'They're pulsing with magic!' he confirmed. Kate reached out and without hesitation picked out one of them.

'This one is special. It's shining extra brightly.' She handed it to Eff to inspect. It looked the same as the others to him.

'Are you sure my darling?'

'Yes. Completely.'

He handed it to The Prof who placed it in his satchel.

'What's going on over there?' Jen interrupted, having clearly watched him steal the bottle. She left the bar and moved angrily towards them.

Anticipating trouble, Eff opened his jacket and removed a tiny wafer from a blue envelope. He placed it on his thumb. He pressed it into her mouth as she opened it to protest. An expression of fear fleetingly crossed her pretty face. It was replaced by a smile. She gazed into his eyes before collapsing. He caught her effortlessly and carried her across to the settee where Kate had been resting.

'When she wakes up in a few hours she won't have any memory of our visit,' he explained.

Kate rearranged the pillows under her head and covered her slim form in warm blankets, leaving a hand crocheted patchwork quilt tucked up under her chin.

'Then we had best be cleaning up so there's no trace of anyone having been here,' Annie suggested.

'I'll help you with the dishes, mum,' offered Sandy. Octy reappeared and assisted them.

Gavin removed the sabre from the cabinet.

'It feels bad taking it, when it has such sentimental value,' he told The Prof.

'May I hold it for a moment?' asked Eff. He examined it's contours then moved over to the counter and asked Sandy to find a simple bread and butter knife that would not be easily missed. She went to the adjacent kitchenette and found a drawer full of cutlery. Eff placed one of his hands upon it and the other on the sabre. He closed his eyes and felt a flow of magical energy extend from his fingertips. When he lifted his palms, there were two swords. He gave the duplicate to Gavin to place in the cabinet and said, 'one day we'll come back here and return the real one.'

The Prof placed the precious item in his satchel with what was deemed to be the antidote.

'Time to leave,' said Tobias, eager to be on his way to Luna Tribus.

GJ went outside to retrieve the other dogs who had followed Menny outdoors to chew sticks. When he returned, the Kelpie ran inside to be with his mistress. Unable to wake her up, he became inconsolable. Eff administered another wafer. Tobias helped him lift up the now unconscious dog and place him at her side on the settee.

As they walked to the exit, GJ said, 'who is coming with us to Luna Tribus?'

Menagerie, now visible again, padded forward first and stood at his side.

'I'd like to go with you,' said Annie, unexpectedly. GJ licked her hand.

'Why now?' asked Sandy.

'I thought I was approaching the end of my life and now I'm having a second chance. I regret being too sensible. I've often wished that my Glen and I had lived to see the world that blessed us with so many wonders, including an extended family.'

'I feel the same,' said The Prof.

‘I’m going too for the same reasons,’ added Gavin.

‘Then I’m going with you. Someone needs to keep an eye on you!’ Sandy exclaimed.

‘Eff and I made a pact to be together when the antidote was administered,’ Kate reminded them.

‘You’ll need me to run surveillance as my area of expertise is spying,’ Smiley insisted, flashing an enormous toothy grin.

Mikey sighed deeply.

‘Someone needs to be sensible. I will stay and keep an eye on things at Caves Beach with Becky.’

‘I will remain with you,’ Sir Geo announced. Octy looked proudly at the dog he had raised. Sandy cast a similar expression at her son and said, ‘you are growing into an impressive man, very much like your dad. He would have been proud of you, as am I.’ She wrapped her arms around his neck. ‘We’ll be back to tell you about it and I feel sure that one day you’ll get your chance to go. I know it.’

‘I hope so, particularly now that I’m going to have a brother-in-law from Luna Tribus.’ He gave Eff a giant bear hug and told him to look after everyone.

‘Are you coming too?’ Annie asked Octy.

‘Yes. I’d like you to see Octavia, then we’ll come home together,’ Octy promised.

‘Where are the rats?’ Menagerie enquired, alarmed.

‘I’m certain they came inside with us,’ Annie recalled.

Gavin locked the door behind them. The air outside the heated shed had a distinct chill. As they approached the campervan four furry faces appeared in the window.

'You took your bleeding time!' Snuggles complained when Beauty clicked open her side door.

'What happened to you?' asked GJ.

'We stupidly went out the back to poke around in the cargo bay and became locked out. Beauty let us in so we didn't freeze to death,' Big Timmy explained.

Honey and Floorplank curled up their lips indignantly.

'You probably didn't even notice that we were missing!' they cried in unison. GJ looked apologetic and said, 'you are right. We didn't notice until now. I'm so sorry. We got carried away looking for the antidote.'

They piled inside.

'Did you find it?' asked Snuggles.

'Of course! Are you rats coming with us back to Luna Tribus or staying here?' asked GJ.

Honey and Floorplank made it clear they wanted to go wherever Mikey and Sir Geo were going. When told that they were staying on Earth, they tried hard to conceal their disappointment. Big Timmy and Snuggles struggled to decide what to do; torn between the family of rats that had brought them happiness in recent years and the other important individuals from the previous chapters in their lives.

Recognising their dilemma, GJ said, 'you should stay here. Geo would have wanted you to take care of things at Caves Beach. You don't need to worry about me, as I'm a grown up now.'

'I'll watch over him for you,' Menagerie promised.

'We'll be waiting when you get back,' said Snuggles.

'Don't let Eff and Kate get married while you are away. We need to be there,' said Big Timmy.

Tobias had remained silent, pondering his own divided loyalties.

'Are you coming with us or is it time to return to your brothers at the monastery?' The Prof requested.

'There is no monastery. Master Sabi burnt it to the ground while my brothers were slumbering. Most of them perished in the inferno. The rest have travelled with The Oneidon to take shelter in Ivor with the Compasse.'

There were gasps and expressions of distress.

'I'm so sorry, Tobias!' cried The Prof.

'As am I. Yet, despite your grief, you came here to help us,' said Eff.

He nodded and said, 'at least Master Sabi is no longer a threat to anyone. He too perished in the flames. I must see this through to the end before I can start to process the tragedy. Besides, these events are inextricably linked.'

'How do you foresee us returning to Rectangulum City?' Eff enquired.

'That's a good question.' He turned to Menagerie and said, 'when Orizuru flew you to find The Oneidon, what path did you take?'

'She took us back the same way we came here. We passed over the snow monkeys then circled up into the wormhole. I exited the portal inside the concealed section of the White Corridor which led me straight to him.'

'We will go back the same way. Tsuru can only carry a few of us, so I think it's best if the rest of you fly in Beauty and stay close to her, especially as we approach the wormhole,' stated Tobias.

'Beauty will need to transform into a suitable vehicle for that flight,' said The Prof.

'None of her usual forms are right for that. The jet is the closest I can think of, but the wing span will be too great to fly into a wormhole,' Octy advised.

'I have a solution that will only require some minor tweaking,' said Eff. He asked them to go outside for a few minutes. He entered the front seat and spoke to her about his vision. He touched the steering wheel and focussed, willing energy to flow from his surrounds. A purple glow enveloped the campervan. When it dissipated, she had changed into the familiar black limousine.

'We can't drive to Japan,' noted Gavin, confused.

'I know. Beauty has some new tricks up her sleeve,' said Eff mysteriously.

'I've never been in a limo. Perhaps you could drive us to the bus station?' said Mikey, awestruck.

'We can manage more than that,' replied Eff. He ushered everyone into the vehicle, pausing to confide in Tobias the specifics of his transport plan before they entered the front seat.

Beauty pulled away from the carpark. Effortlessly, Eff transfigured the straight driveway into a concrete runway.

Hold on tight!' she urged, quickly accelerating to a scene blurring velocity for those attempting to peer out of her windows. Like a dart she took flight, gaining altitude then shooting across the sky.

'We'll drop those of you who have elected to care for our Caves Beach homes directly there,' Eff advised, speaking over the divider to those in the back.

'This is astonishing!' cried Mikey. To his disappointment, no sooner had they levelled out in flight, the descent began.

'One day we'll go for a longer ride,' promised Eff, taking delight from his reaction.

'We're coming in to land,' Octy announced. The wild sea and choppy waves drew nearer, crashing into the jagged rocky shore. It was raining lightly as Beauty's wheels touched down on the bitumen road near the surf life saving club, adjacent to the upper entrance to the cave facility. It was midweek and there was no one to be seen. Sir Geo, with Big Timmy and Snuggles now riding on his back, disembarked first. They spotted a perfect rainbow over the ocean. Mikey exited the limousine with Floorplank and Honey, who ran off in search of Becky. Eff left the front seat and faced him.

'I'll look after your family Mikey. It really is the honour of my life.'

'Correction, you'll look after *our* family Eff and I know you will.'

Chapter 12
RECTANGULUM CITY

When GJ stirred from his nap, the sky outside Beauty was an ominous grey. Even with the heater blasting, a chill penetrated the air inside the limousine. Beauty was travelling high and fast, pulling through a system of thick cloud cover. She started to shudder, then rock.

'Watch out for the hail and ice!' Tobias warned. Sensing his alarm, she replied, 'we are climbing into the mountains beyond Nagano almost to our destination. I think it would be prudent to set down in the valley at Jigokudani and wait for the storm to pass.'

'I agree. Besides, we need to land somewhere, long enough for me to mount Tsuru and lead us to the wormhole,' said Tobias.

'As much as I want to keep moving and get back to Luna Tribus, perhaps this inclement weather is an omen that a proper break is needed?' Octy suggested.

'Some of us have been awake for several days in a row,' GJ admitted, yawning. Menagerie agreed.

'Let's do as you suggested,' Eff told Beauty.

Dusk was approaching as they circled the valley of the snow monkeys before touching down in a deserted carpark near the tourist entrance. Tobias tentatively rolled down his window. He shivered, as gigantic flakes of perfectly formed snow were blown in by a gust of whistling, ferocious wind.

'I propose that a couple of us go exploring and see if there is a safe, comfortable place to shelter. I remember seeing a guest house on the other side of the valley when we came here previously,' Tobias suggested.

'I'll come with you as I don't feel the cold,' Octy reminded them.

'I'm definitely going with you! I do feel the cold but I'm busting for a hurry up!' GJ announced. Eff opened the back door and watched him run towards a tree. The snow was falling fast.

Careful not to slip on the treacherous icy surface, despite Eff releasing a traction spell onto their feet, the four of them were forced to inch along a path down into the valley. They crossed a wooden bridge that flanked a completely frozen stream. On the other side, a steep set of stairs made of carefully positioned stones led upwards. Holding on tightly to a wooden rail, Tobias led the way. At the top they found the lodging he had remembered, built precariously on the edge of a cliff face. A worn, barely legible sign declared it to be the 'Orizuru Onsen'.

Octy scratched his chin in reflection and said, 'I wonder if this is where The Oneidon took the name for his crane?'

'Probably,' reflected Tobias, intrigued.

'It's abandoned,' GJ cried, failing to hide his disappointment. 'I was imagining a roaring fire. All I want right now is a full belly and to curl up and sleep.'

Eff moved ahead of them and climbed a second, shorter set of crooked steps that led to a covered foyer. Icicles were hanging from the rafters of the wooden ceiling. He peered through a window and noticed a faint light in a room discernible in the distance. With strained ears he detected music. The lulling of flutes made him feel serene and overwhelmingly somnolent. He doubled back to provide a report to his companions.

'We may not be alone after all. I'm going to explore inside to see if I can find anyone or at least anything to help us.'

'The weather is deteriorating. We need to find shelter urgently. This is going to have to be it,' Tobias concluded, sensibly. Certain that Eff and Tobias could deal with whatever might be encountered, GJ and Octy suggested they return to the car and escort the rest of their party towards the inn, before things deteriorated further.

GJ took the lead, bounding down the stairs and picking up pace as he started to cross the bridge. Octy followed more cautiously. In the middle of the bridge the Chocolate Labrador lost his footing, skidding at speed across a patch of black ice. Before he could warn his friend, the Octavian overbalanced too.

'Urrrrrgh!' the out-of-control Octavian wailed.

'Thump!'

Their slide was broken by a wall of soft fur.

'Steady on there, we've got some senior folks with us and you almost took them out!' a deep voice shrieked. Octy tried to stand and regain his grip on the railings of the bridge. He looked around, attempting to identify the owner of the voice. Several sets of golden-brown eyes, barely visible in the near darkness, had encircled him.

GJ relaxed, having recognised the familiar scent of the snow monkeys.

'G'day mate,' he said, in his broad Australian accent. 'We're friends of The Oneidon and were on our way to his wormhole when the weather turned for the worst. We're seeking shelter for the rest of our group who are waiting in the car.'

'You should use caution in sheltering in that onsen. That place does not feel right tonight,' the largest monkey, called Akira, warned.

'We thought it was a regular lodging for travellers?' GJ checked.

'It has been closed for renovation for several months. Until tonight we were the sole residents bathing in the terrace over there,' another monkey reported.

'We saw a light on and heard music playing, so perhaps you are mistaken? Maybe someone is residing there?' Octy surmised, respectfully.

'A worker perhaps?' GJ suggested.

'Who or what is up there right now, is not familiar to us,' stated Akira, firmly.

Having heard the commotion, Tobias appeared. Goro, the oldest monkey in the pack, a greying, stooped, massive Macaque, stepped forward next to Akira and examined the Malinois. He verified for others in his troop that he had previously met the humanoid, who was a friend of The Oneidon. The monkeys relaxed and escorted GJ, Octy and Tobias to the carpark. He opened Beauty's snow covered back door and updated the occupants who were huddled together in the sub-zero temperature.

The helpful monkeys assisted their safe passage towards the onsen, guiding them along the path that was now concealed with fresh snow. A bone numbing icy wind whistled down the valley as they crossed the narrow bridge. As they were heading up the steps, a red lantern switched on. Eff was waiting to greet them with a diminutive elderly woman at his side. Her gnarled hand tightly gripped an ornately carved wooden stick. She was stooped over from the ravages of severe arthritis in her back; so crooked that her eyes could barely meet the gaze of her guests. The monkeys, led my Goro, ran forward and encircled her, sniffing and jumping up and down screaming.

'Are we safe?' GJ enquired, trying hard not to smirk. The tiny lady before them was far from the menacing threat his mind had been conjuring.

Akira relaxed and said, 'calm yourselves. It is only Hisa, the grandmother of the owner. She must have refused to leave.'

As the cacophony subsided, the woman reached out with her tiny wrinkled hand and gently patted the head of the nearest young monkey.

'I've ascertained that we are welcome to stay overnight if we tidy up after ourselves. She is willing to share her limited provisions,' Eff announced.

Hisa shuffled ahead of them into the building. Without using words, she signalled for them to remove their wet shoes. They followed her into the kitchen where she stoked a struggling fire before proceeding to fill a kettle with melting snow to boil. Annie sat down on a stool beside the flames and relaxed, feeling comfortable in the familiar scenario and eager to assist. The two old women had little need to chat. Annie took her cues that cups needed to be laid out, broth prepared and soba noodles boiled.

Sandy and Kate were tasked with procuring sets of robes from a massive cupboard, one for each of the humans and humanoids. Hisa attempted to demonstrate how the traditional Ryokan attire, called a Yukata set, was worn. Two spacious family rooms were opened, each with their own private indoor heated baths known as onsens, separated for privacy by paper shoji screens.

Individual woven straw, tatami sleeping mats were laid onto the floor and each covered with a light futon mattress and blanket. The rooms became progressively more welcoming, the disarming atmosphere completed by flickering tea lights scattered around the room inside miniature lanterns.

As she had been orientating them to her home, Octy and Menagerie had reverted to their invisible form. As soon as Hisa departed, they reappeared and assisted Sandy and Kate complete their preparations.

'It's a very tranquil place,' noted Octy.

'Where is GJ?' asked Menagerie. He bounded off in search of his friend. He found Eff, Tobias, Gavin and The Prof standing in the main foyer peering out a window, laughing. Beyond the profuse cascade of condensation droplets that were running down the window, he spotted

GJ rolling about, periodically flicking water out of his ears as he frolicked with half a dozen tiny monkeys. Together they were taking a bath in a steaming outdoor hot spring located on the terrace.

'The water is very inviting. Now that the work is done, I'd like to give it a try too,' said Octy, having followed the lion. The Octavian opened the door and without hesitation, lowered himself into the pond.

'Onsen means bath,' The Prof recalled.

'There are large private ones in your room,' Menagerie explained, prompting the onlookers to go and explore the facilities. He pushed open the door and joined his friends outside.

'A hot soak to rewarm, food then bed would be a perfect end to this day,' said Tobias. He entered the tub first.

As he was drying himself in a fluffy towel, he caught a waft of a delicious, subtle spice. He quicky donned one of the navy and white patterned, Yukata robes and heavy Tanzen outer coats Sandy and Kate had set out. He tied a wide Obi belt around his middle and warmed his feet in a pair of white Tabi split-toe socks.

'I love these clothes. So much so, I'd like to get a set for home,' The Prof remarked later, when he entered the dining area similarly attired, as the last to arrive.

Bowls of flavoursome noodles were welcomed like gourmet fare. Each guest expressed sincere gratitude to their hostess for her hospitality. She smiled warmly, appearing to take pleasure from caring for them in a manner consistent with the Japanese Ryokan tradition.

In their fatigued, now relaxed state it was easy to forget that they were still on a vital mission.

Outside, the snowfall grew progressively heavier. After eating, GJ returned to his new happy place in the warm water outside and started taking grooming tips from an old monkey. Gavin had almost nodded off during the meal and Annie was fighting to keep her eyes open. After quickly drinking her soup, Kate retired to her sleeping mat in the room for the women. Sandy washed the dishes and went with Annie to join her.

'We should try to get some rest too,' The Prof suggested. Octy and Gavin yawned and went with him to their room.

'I will take the first watch,' Tobias announced, reminding himself that they were not on vacation. Eff volunteered to relieve him in a few hours. As he departed, the young magician said, 'if we see a break in the weather we should take it, regardless of the hour.' Tobias agreed. Menagerie was soon napping in front of the fire.

As the kitchen emptied, Tobias went in search of GJ. He was curled up in the foyer.

'The monkeys will watch the outside of the building for us. They are still sensing an ominous presence. I'm on guard duty here. I'll wake Menagerie in a few hours to take over from me.'

'I'm on first watch too,' said the monk, yawning.

'Then we should keep each other company, so neither of us falls asleep.'

'It's warmer in the kitchen,' said Tobias.

They returned to the fireplace where he poured himself a cup of Matcha green tea from the brewing pot that had been left on the kitchen table. He settled into an armchair with GJ laying on his feet. As he stared into the flickering embers his thoughts drifted to the fate of his brothers, particularly those who had perished in the fire. He hoped their death had been swift, without undue suffering.

Intermittently the sound of a lump of snow falling off the roof and breaking up on the ground broke his reverie. He was so lost in his grief that he failed to notice the old woman standing at the door observing him. She was gone when Eff appeared four hours later to relieve him. He departed, eager to rest.

Eff stoked the fire. He refilled the pot with water to boil for fresh tea before sitting down at the table waiting for it to be ready. Snow continued to fall heavily, causing him to frown. He was desperate to get to Rectangulum City and there were no signs it was abating.

The dregs of his third cup of tea were growing progressively cooler when he was jolted to full alertness by the screaming of frightened monkeys. A second round of their blood curdling cries raised everyone from their slumber. Eff, GJ and Menagerie bolted to the foyer to investigate. Dawn was breaking, offering a limited view of the chasm below their lodging. In the distance, the walls of the cliff faces were crawling with spooked monkeys.

Akira bounded to the door of the onsen and called out for Tobias. He unbolted the locked door and went outside to converse.

'You must leave now! A dark force is descending on our valley.'

A sense of foreboding gripped the group.

'At least it's stopped snowing,' stated GJ, trying to remain upbeat.

'We'll have to borrow these robes. Our clothes are still soaking wet,' said Annie, having darted into the kitchen to inspect the drying rack where she had laid out their garments.

'Is it right to leave Hisa behind?' asked Sandy, as they were preparing to head to Beauty.

'We should at least thank her for her hospitality and say goodbye,' replied Octy.

'I haven't seen her since we went to bed,' Annie reported.

'She's no longer here. I'm certain of it,' said Menagerie having searched for traces of her presence.

The high-pitched screams continued, escalating in intensity as in single file, the group carefully headed towards Beauty, wading through deep powdery unpacked snow.

'She's completely covered! It'll take hours to scrape off the ice,' Kate moaned when she saw her.

'I've got this,' said Eff. The snow instantly melted underneath his hands as he waved them over her surface.

'Your hands are like a hot iron on a plate of vanilla ice-cream!' she remarked, impressed.

'Good job, Eff. It reminds me of that ice wall on Phalago,' noted Tobias.

'It's a handy trick,' replied Eff, smiling.

'As soon as I am airborne, follow closely,' Tobias instructed. He removed the parchment that he had taken care to relocate inside a pocket in his new robe.

'Tsuru, please take us to The Oneidon via the wormhole above. I need you to watch out for Beauty and her passengers. They will be following closely and need to come with us to Ivor.' He jumped onto her back as soon as she had completed her transformation.

The crane took off and circled overhead, patiently waiting for Beauty to take flight. The limousine engine turned over without missing a beat. Like a helicopter, Beauty ascended vertically, progressively gaining height. The crane flew around the vehicle in tight circles as their climb continued.

'I wonder how far up the wormhole is?' Eff asked The Prof.

'It seemed a long way to the ground when we came out of it,' GJ answered.

The sound of distressed monkeys was no longer audible.

They continued to rise.

'I hope the old lady is alright,' Sandy remarked.

'The fact she was there seemed creepy to me,' Gavin confessed.

'I did like her soup with the strong umami flavours. I wish I'd thought to get the recipe,' said Octy.

'It was strange that we struggled to communicate with her. It's like our polyglots weren't working effectively,' noted Annie.

'We were too tired to even notice,' said Menagerie.

'As I said, she was creepy.'

'It feels like we are in an elevator inside a skyscraper,' remarked The Prof.

'I've never been in one that moves so fast you have to pop your ears to relieve the pressure!' Gavin remarked.

'Is that a wormhole hovering there like a magnificent golden cloud?' Kate requested.

'Yes Kate, it sure is!' GJ exclaimed.

'This is it, friends! We're off. Goodbye Earth!' The Prof cried as Beauty followed the crane into the glowing portal.

She halted as soon as they were inside the White Corridor.

'As you disembark, take care with your eyes. The starkness of the white light can be overwhelming,' Beauty advised her passengers.

Octy opened the front door, almost scraping its edge on the side wall. Eff exited the driver's seat and opened the back door. He assisted Kate, Annie, Sandy, The Prof and Gavin from the vehicle. They followed GJ and Menagerie, who had spotted Tobias picking up the folded piece of parchment that had been his ride.

'This is extraordinary!' Annie voiced.

'It feels eery, like we are nowhere,' remarked Gavin.

'We are in a private area of the White Corridor only accessible to the Compasse,' Tobias explained.

'Which direction should we go in?' asked Eff. Tobias didn't know.

'Follow me. I'll take us to the end of the corridor where I found the door to Ivor,' said Menagerie.

'I don't think this passage is wide enough for Beauty,' Octy observed as he watched her start to roll after them. Eff turned around. He opened his backpack and removed a tiny bottle containing a powdery purple potion. He placed a tiny dose onto his palm then blew it across her bonnet. She started to shrink until she was sufficiently small enough for him to pick her up. Before placing the miniature limousine into his bag, he said, 'you have earned a rest. I'll deliver you back to Kalan soon.'

'That was cool!' Kate blurted. She was feeling back to her usual self and starting to marvel at seeing her fiancée behave so confidently. He had always seemed worried about demonstrating his magical gifts, concerned what others might think and the implications of not blending in on Earth. She wrapped her arms around his neck and lightly kissed his forehead.

'It's time to fully embrace who you are,' she told him. He intertwined his fingers in hers and they started following the lion.

The starkness became less prominent as they moved further from the door used to enter.

'We're getting close! I can detect the scent of Flanders and another, who I presume is a Compasse monitor,' advised GJ.

They walked faster. Footsteps drew nearer.

'Is that you, Tobias?' came the familiar voice of Flanders. He moved forward, towards his greeter.

'Yes. We believe we have found the antidote.'

'The Oneidon has stationed us here, awaiting your victorious return.' He introduced his companion, named Maxime. Tobias did the same with his party.

'We should go directly to The Oneidon. Follow me please,' Maxime insisted, using a serious tone. Tobias didn't fail to notice his troubled expression.

He led them towards a door at the side of the corridor.

'I didn't use that one when I came to get help,' noted Menagerie.

'You are correct. We are going directly to the Office of The Oneidon and this is the fastest way to get there. Time is of the essence.'

They exited directly into the Cathedral of Ivor. The central hub was buzzing with activity. A sea of hooded occupants scurried across it, before disappearing underneath one of the many archways that radiated out from the enormous, high dome. The individuals were so engrossed in their duties that few seemed to notice their arrival. At the far end of the space was an area The Prof correctly identified was off bounds. In front of it, burly attendants were constantly scanning the gathering.

'The mood is very different from when we first came. It seems bustling, unlike when we were cross examined here,' GJ remarked to Tobias.

Maxime strode purposefully towards the guards who greeted the monitor with a simple nod, before standing aside. Maxime knocked on the smooth, pale door, delivering a series of patterned taps that triggered the barrier to melt away. It reappeared behind them as soon as they were inside.

The contingent crossed a meeting room. In the centre was a long oval table, rimmed by ornate high back chairs. Maxime stopped outside another door on the opposite side from where they had entered. After a further series of taps, it too dissolved. He ushered them inside a low ceilinged, cozy study. The walls of the office were covered in images of totally unfamiliar places, objects and living things.

The Oneidon stood up from his desk where he had been reading a massive tome. He scanned the group.

'It is as it should be,' he responded simply, greeting the visitors in turn, correctly identifying each of them without needing an introduction. He interacted as if they had long been acquainted.

'You are now a man, Eff. I have watched you walk within our walls since you first peered inside as a curious child.'

Tobias was eager to know the fate of his brothers who had sought refuge from their burnt monastery.

'They are settling in well. Flanders has performed impeccably in providing support in your absence.' He went on to describe the various activities they had been allocated in order to facilitate their transition, ending by saying, 'you will see for yourself in the course of time. For now, there are those that need you more. I have grave tidings. Kalan and Viz grow ever more concerned about the situation in Rectangulum City. Many more victims affected by Master Sabi's poison have started to crumble.'

‘We must go to them right away,’ Tobias responded.

‘As you wish. I will escort you there myself.’

As they walked, Tobias briefed him on the events since they had parted. Annie, Sandy and Octy followed silently, with The Prof and Gavin staying close behind them. Eff brought up the rear with GJ and Menagerie. His fingers were again tightly interlocked with Kate’s. He struggled to control his mixed emotions. Despite his fears they might be too late to help, he felt excited to be bringing his beloved to his birthplace for the first time. He couldn’t wait to introduce her to his parents and sister.

The Oneidon dropped back to talk to him.

‘Do you want me to take us to your favourite exit outside the palace wall?’ he enquired, flashing his pointed teeth mischievously. Eff chuckled and replied, ‘so you knew about it.’

‘Of course! We have always diligently monitored your activities within the White Corridor, always serving to ensure your safe passage through our system of wormholes. That is our purpose.’

Eff looked perplexed and said, ‘how was it that my guards never found a way to Ivor?’

The Oneidon chuckled and replied, ‘you have your magic and we have ours.’

‘Let’s take the fastest route,’ GJ interrupted, keen to keep things moving.

‘Over to you Eff,’ said The Oneidon, having arrived at the door under discussion.

He tightened his grip on Kate's hand and led them outside, emerging from the wormhole he knew well at the outskirts of the city. The checkpoint was still standing, although now abandoned. It appeared unchanged from when he had last passed it, leading his aunts and grandmother away from the place of his birth. He set off to find a concealed door in the city wall. Having located it, he touched a lock that had not been there previously. It fell apart allowing them to pass into an alleyway behind a residence.

Cognisant of the fact he was leading those older and less agile than himself, he called for a brief rest. Three rotating, coloured moons turned slowly in the sky casting a blanket of light. The humans stood enthralled, staring up at them.

'Welcome to Luna Tribus. You are now in Rectangulum City,' he told the new arrivals to his home.

'I had forgotten how beautiful it is here,' GJ remarked.

'There's nothing that prepares you for a moment like this,' replied The Prof, tearing up.

Eff frowned as he stared at the sky.

'What's wrong darling?' Kate enquired, sensing his worry.

'It's not right here. The moons are turning too slowly.'

Octy concurred, his antennae twitching.

'Are we really where we need to be?' Tobias asked The Oneidon.

'Yes. This is unexpected and disturbing.'

'We should keep moving. Whatever else is happening here doesn't change what we need to do,' urged GJ.

They set off again, with Eff slipping into a commentary, analogous to what a tour guide might have provided.

'We're heading straight for the palace. It's quite a distance. Along the way, you'll be able to see how the average citizen lives.'

'Is it always this empty?' The Prof enquired.

'No. This part of town is the merchant quarter and is usually teaming with activity, regardless of the moon phase,' replied Eff. The buildings were secured with shutters pulled down over windows and closed doors.

The moons started turning to dark shades of the primary colours with muted red, blue and yellow rays blending together to cast gloomy, muddy shadows over the lifeless buildings they passed.

'It feels like a ghost town,' Gavin remarked.

'I hope Master Sabi didn't do something to the citizens that we aren't aware of,' said Eff, voicing his worst fears.

They walked on. The sky's hues continued to shift again, favouring a pastel palette. Like a veil being lifted, the towers came into view, outlined by the brighter back light.

'You've just experienced the closest thing we have to sunsets and sunrises here,' Eff explained.

They turned into the Central Promenade.

'What is that!' cried Kate, reacting to the scene before them. A series of vast rectangular structures were emerging, each covered by mirrored panels that were starting to shimmer, reflecting the bluish glow of Caeruleus, the moon now dominating.

'It's like a stunning mirage in an alien desert!' Gavin blurted.

'That's the palace,' Eff admitted, proudly.

As they drew closer, the details caused more comments. Kate was particularly taken with the decorative jewels embedded between the panels of the marble walls.

'Don't just look up friends, feast your eyes on the space below!' The Prof exclaimed. They had arrived at the top of a set of wide stairs. Eff became distraught as he turned his gaze to the vast palace forecourt.

'I think we've found the missing inhabitants,' noted GJ.

The scene was chaotic and overcrowded. They descended the stairs and weaved their way towards the palace gates, passing groups of friends and families huddled together. Many were crying. Others appeared numb. Men stood close together clutching sacks containing their precious belongings.

'Stay close to each other. Distress and volatility go hand in hand,' Tobias advised.

'What is happening here?' Eff asked one of the men.

'It's the end! The moons are going to fall out of the sky!' cried the panicking individual. His trembling wife sat on the ground at his feet clutching a whimpering baby. The woman's eyes bulged as she looked up and recognised who was addressing them. A burst of hope filled her heart.

'Have you returned to save us?' she asked.

Struggling to contain his own fear, Eff dropped Kate's hand. He bent down and gently touched the baby's cheek and with a tiny surge of magic, caused her to stop wailing. She smiled, revealing a prominent front tooth and started to gurgle. For the first time in his life, he understood what it meant to be a true leader. He stared into the desolate eyes of her mother.

'We are here to do what we can to help. Never lose hope in your heart that goodness will prevail. I believe that this is not the end but the start of a new beginning,' he uttered humbly. He stood up and beckoned for the others to follow him towards the palace's inner gates.

The Oneidon raised his eyebrows at Tobias. They had both overheard his heartfelt reassuring gesture and sensed it had come from a selfless place of true empathy.

'Could it be that his trip to Earth has made him realise who he is?' The Oneidon questioned.

'True love has unlocked his authenticity,' Menagerie interjected, before Tobias could respond.

Eff weaved through the crowd, trying his best to look inconspicuous. It was impossible, given the eclectic nature of his companions: a brown dog, a golden lion, an Octavian, a robed Compasse hybrid and an entourage wearing identical, distinctive onsen attire. By the time they reached the guards at the front of the imposing gates they had drawn the attention of the crowd, who had started chanting his name.

'Halt!' interrupted a bawdy guard, dressed in an ivory and gold uniform. Sandy immediately recognised the palace insignia from Eff's uniform that he had been wearing when he was washed up onto her beach. It was a surreal moment.

'At ease officer,' Eff replied, commandingly. The guard stepped forward to evaluate whether he should comply.

'Who seeks to enter?'

'It is I, the son of Praeceptorum Elektra and Prince Ro of Kaleido. Please open the gate so we can end this crisis.'

'Apologies! I didn't recognise you,' the officer responded, averting his eyes respectfully then signalling to a fellow officer to comply with the request.

'Don't leave us!' cried a tiny frightened boy behind them. GJ turned back to investigate the source of the voice. He licked the terrified looking child who squealed in delight before facing his mother and saying, 'it's him!' He turned back to GJ, reached out bravely and stroked his silky fur. 'You're so soft!'

'We're not leaving you. We're merely departing for a moment to attend to some important business,' GJ reassured him.

'Can you come back and play later?'

'Of course!'

The dog ran to Menagerie's side. The gates started to close behind them. As they set off again, they heard the boy say, loudly, 'he's returned! Geo the Space Explorer has come to save us!' GJ bounded back and corrected him, proudly saying, '*GJ* the *Earth* Explorer, actually!'

'I can't believe they know of our Geo,' Annie remarked to Sandy as they moved away.

'Geo's arrival here changed the course of history,' Eff told her. He reminded The Prof that he too, had played no small part in the chain of events. 'There are various versions of the "Geo" story. Amongst those who were not fans of my grandfather, thanks to our Big Timmy, the story of "Geo the Space Explorer" has become the stuff of legends!'

The noise started to abate as they passed into the inner confines of the palace. An empty terrace stretched out ahead of them. A subtly moving, opalescent membrane had been erected over a section of it.

'I assume that is where we'll find my parents?' stated Eff, pointing at it.

'Yes. They are in the private formal garden of the praeceptorum,' said Tobias.

GJ started to bark. He bolted like an eager racehorse out of the starting gates, in the opposite direction from where they were heading.

'It's Kalan!' declared Menagerie, before running after him.

GJ jumped up and almost bowled over the king.

'I was starting to worry you weren't coming. Do you have the antidote?'

'Of course we do!' cried the Chocolate Labrador.

'We must move quickly. There's not a moment to spare,' he replied seriously. The trio walked towards the others. Kalan was overwhelmed with relief as he surveyed the group. Tobias introduced The Oneidon.

'It is truly an impressive rescue party you have assembled!' he told the dog.

‘These aren’t exactly the circumstances under which I would have liked to bring my fiancée home for the first time,’ Eff stated, placing his arm proudly around Kate’s shoulders. Kalan congratulated the happy couple.

‘I can’t believe you are here!’ he told The Prof.

‘It was time I visited your world before I died, taking my regret to the grave with me,’ he responded dramatically.

‘That’s why we’re here too, isn’t it Gavin?’ stated Annie. He nodded.

‘None of that rubbish! You’ve got years in you yet,’ Kalan reacted.

‘Master Sabi targeted the three of them as part of his revenge plan. He used emanators to deliver a nasty potion that almost killed them,’ Menagerie explained.

Kalan looked shocked. Eff patted the lion’s mane affectionately and said, ‘fortunately, Menagerie was able to detect and neutralise the toxin.’

‘Skydog is unfortunately still infested with the devices. It’s now uninhabitable,’ The Prof explained.

‘There are others who may never live to age another moment,’ a serious voice interrupted. It was Viz. Eff introduced the strangers to him then said, ‘are you responsible for the slowing of the moons?’

Viz looked surprised and replied, ‘you give me more credit than I deserve. That kind of magic defies my understanding. Why did you think I was behind it?’

‘I have always respected your power and it’s what I would have tried to do, if I’d been here.’

'Why darling?' asked Kate.

'To buy time for those who need it. Slowing down the moons slows down time here.'

'How do you know that?' Viz asked, perplexed.

'I don't know for sure. It came to me as I started speaking. When did this phenomenon start?' Eff checked.

'Not long after Tobias, GJ and Menagerie departed,' advised Kalan.

'It was right after the first of the cursed victims completely crumbled into particles,' Viz recalled.

'Who was that?' Tobias enquired.

'We've concluded it was a young attendant called Andra. She was busy taking a tray of food to the terrace when the process started,' Kalan recalled.

'What is the purpose of that barrier?' asked Eff.

'The practically minded healers of Pluvia Silva suggested it. They brought it with them to isolate the precious sculptures from the potentially devastating effect of wind,' Viz explained.

'We had assumed that the slowing of the moons was some kind of visual countdown; a harbinger to the end of the spell, created by Master Sabi,' Kalan explained.

'Who could have performed this kind of magic?' asked GJ.

'Why did they elect to be helpful?' added The Oneidon, joining the conversation for the first time. The Compasse leader had hung back, unobtrusively listening.

'We'll have to figure it our later,' stated Viz, staring at the moons overhead. The frightened cries of the crowd had grown louder and were now audible in the background.

'They have almost stopped turning entirely. I'm worried if they stop completely, that we'll be frozen in time forever,' shared Viz.

'Where is the antidote?' requested Kalan.

'I have it in my bag,' replied The Prof.

'Come with me,' said Kalan. He led them towards the garden where most of the victims were concentrated.

'There are additional afflicted subjects in the throne room and many others are scattered throughout the palace. Where do you want to release it?' he checked with the group.

'Near Ellie and Ro, as they are the ones most linked to Geo. Master Sabi admitted to me before he perished that his attack was a direct, vindictive retaliation for the perceived crimes of the dog,' said Tobias.

'Perished?' Viz checked, shocked.

'Yes. Tobias and I watched him die,' said GJ.

'Why isn't Geo with you? Where are the rats?' asked Kalan, worried.

'We have much to tell you,' said Tobias.

'It will have to wait. I suggest that only the individual who will administer the antidote should go inside the garden. I am worried that in their fragile states, even walking too close to one of them could cause the sand to crumble,' Viz shared.

They paused outside a flap in the translucent shimmering barrier over the garden. Annie reached out and touched the sheer fabric.

'It's very beautiful.'

'It's spun silk. We made it ourselves,' said Multis, appearing with Unus.

'You are the ones who saved my Big Timmy's life!' cried Annie, recognising them from his descriptions. They started chatting.

The Prof removed the dragon sabre from his bag. He secured it in his right hand. In the other, he held the bottle of sparkling wine he had been dutifully protecting since the moment it had entered his possession.

'Perhaps you should do it, Gavin? My arthritis has not completely resolved. The stakes here are high.'

'You were always better at it than me. This is your moment. I feel it,' he replied. The Prof laughed nervously.

'What are you talking about?' asked Viz.

'He's going to use that sword to chop the neck cleanly from that bottle without it shattering. You'll see. It's very impressive!' explained Kate.

'Sabrage? Seriously?' said Kalan, incredulous.

'Are you sure your conclusions about the meaning of the riddle are correct?' Viz checked with Eff.

'I am hopeful but cannot be sure. What I do have is faith.'

'Of course it's the antidote! Off you go Prof. A dose for one will be an antidote for all!' cried GJ.

'I am ready. Where will I find Ellie?' The Prof checked.

'She's over near the far wall where she rests with Ro. They are sitting together on that bench,' Kalan instructed. He opened the flap and pointed to the figures in the distance.

'I need you to touch the bottle and make all the liquid, particularly in the neck, turn icy cold,' The Prof instructed Eff. The glass frosted under his touch. No one spoke after this. Each observer watched on solemnly as The Prof walked away from them. With mounting tension and fear he cautiously weaved between eerie sand sculptures, in search of Ellie and Ro.

He easily spotted the children he had never had. He had watched them walk along the beautiful Caves Beach, laugh at his dining table at the Skydog, wed in a casino in Las Vegas and enrich his life in ways he had never dreamed possible.

'Hold on,' he whispered almost inaudibly, fearful that his speech might trigger their disintegration. He removed the cage and cork from the bottle and placed them on the ground. He gripped the wide base firmly in his left palm and held it on its side, tilted slightly upwards. He took a deep breath, then swiftly and with bold determination, slid the silver and blue weapon powerfully along the seam of the bottle, careful to ensure the departing neck sailed over the heads of the seated couple and the contents remained directed towards them.

With perfect execution and magnificent grace, the head of the bottle was sent flying. A shower of millions of carbon dioxide bubbles intermingled with majestic crimson fluid was expelled, spraying Ellie. He stood back, relieved to have successfully dispensed the cure.

Nothing happened. His heart continued to beat wildly. The others watched on with anticipation.

'Come back to us!' he cried.

Tears started to trickle down his wrinkled face as the lacunae passed.

In desperation, he was debating pouring the rest of the bottle onto her head when colour started to creep into her rough face. Her neck was next, then her arms. As life returned and her first inhalation of air commenced, the process started to begin on her beloved Ro. The Prof watched Ellie open her eyes and blink away fine grains of sand. He basked in joy as he watched them lean in and complete the passionate kiss that had been interrupted by darkness. Oblivious to having lost time and almost their lives, Ro pulled her close and they embraced.

'Hello,' said The Prof, causing them to face him. Bewildered by his unexpected presence, they blushed like guilty teenagers interrupted during a stolen kiss. Astonished, they surveyed the garden, watching sand sculptures turn into humanoids and feeling the stares of old and new acquaintances they had not been expecting to see.

As soon as he felt it was safe, Kalan rushed forward towards his wife Christina. Izzie stretched and laughed as GJ circled around her ankles, chasing his own tail. She spotted Eff and walked towards him. Tobias went to find Aquilegia and returned with her at his side.

In the happy frenzy it would have been easy for the revellers to be oblivious to what was going on around them. Out of the corner of his eye, GJ spotted two familiar figures standing behind one of the fountains, unobtrusively observing the jubilation. He skulked closer, trying to overhear their conversation without drawing attention to himself.

'They finally got there,' a hunched, elderly female commented to her robed male companion. She dabbed sentimentally at her misty eyes with a lace handkerchief. 'I do so love a happy ending. What an incredible merry chase we've led them on!'

'It was touch and go for a while. I thought they were doomed when the evil rats tried to eat them,' he noted.

'They are remarkably loyal to each other and those brown dogs are so tenacious.'

'The canines are less predictable than the humans and humanoids. They kept us on our toes. My all-time favourite move was when Geo led that contingent to their deaths through the underwater wormhole!' the man exclaimed.

'All of them would have perished without our intervention,' she reminded him.

'Now we can add matchmaker to our credits. There's no way I'm going to miss Kate and Eff's wedding! I've already made them a gift.'

'What is it?'

He removed a sketch book from his robe and showed it to her. She flicked through the many filled pages.

'Ro inspired me to start making my own mud maps. To pass the time watching them I have been most productive. I do love to travel and these are meaningful souvenirs of where this assignment has taken us. I'm sure they'd treasure one of my works.'

'You won't be able to give them a present. That would be a step too far! You know the rules,' she insisted.

'Perhaps!'

'Don't tell the mistress but I never doubted that the forces of light would prevail over her dark agents.'

'It could have gone either way. Regardless of the outcome, we're going to have to fabricate our reports so we don't appear to have unduly influenced the result.'

'We can hardly be accused of being biased. I burned Tobias's monastery to the ground!' She nodded and said, 'I am so grateful you humoured my request to spend time with the heroes at that run down onsen. I wanted so desperately to interact with them up close. It's impossible not to like them.'

'You can't ever tell that to anyone! We would be in serious trouble!' he warned.

'Along similar lines, we must never confess to giving them more help than we should have. It's been fun. What is next?' she checked.

'We have to go home and wait for orders. I could use a break as that Master Sabi routine was getting dull.'

'If I don't drop the Hisa routine soon, I'll never stand upright again.'

'Why are we still taking their forms?'

'We're really tired,' she responded, yawning.

'There's one last thing we need to do.'

'What?'

He clicked his fingers. The moons started to pick up speed.

'That's much prettier,' she replied.

'We agreed that if the moons stopped turning altogether that we'd have left this planet like this for eternity. They really did get here in the nick of time,' the man cackled.

'It's good for us. This way there is more scope for future mischief.'

They disappeared.

Menagerie, had also heard every word of their conversation. He shivered, having recognised what they were. GJ padded to his side.

'We've been played,' the dog told him, feeling exasperated.

'We have.'

'Why would anyone choose to use heroes, villains and brown dogs, in such a foul, complicated fashion?'

'I do not understand the ways of eidolons.'

Book Five of Geo the Space Explorer, *Temptas,* will reveal more about the devious role of eidolons in orchestrating conflict between good and dark souls.

Carole Foot has been obsessed with imagining other worlds and realities since before she could read and write. She firmly believes that life is too short to be held back by convention and that anything is possible. Her vivid imagination and capacity to invent extraordinary people, things and places is finally captured in these epic tales. Carole comes from a modest childhood in Australia. She excelled in a career in critical care medicine before deciding to take the plunge and pursue her passion for writing. She hopes her stories will be sources of entertainment, joy and instil hope that good will always conquer evil.

Liz Hickson knew as a small child that the secret to a happy fulfilled life was one that comprised lots of travel to faraway lands and many dogs. It is no surprise that she now finds herself the author of fiction books inspired by her many real travel adventures and the Chocolate Labradors who continue to be a constant source of joy and reliability. Liz has always sought to be her best version, constantly striving for happiness and meaning, in at times, a difficult life journey. From her childhood in The United Kingdom, to a high-powered career in clinical medicine that took her to Australia, she is now in a chapter where health, authenticity and her own dreams, have resulted in stories that explore true friendship, other realms and the nature of darkness.

Find out more about the authors, their real lives and more **@geohickson**

www.ingramcontent.com/pod-product-compliance
Lightning Source LLC
LaVergne TN
LVHW091531060526
838200LV00036B/570

* 9 7 8 1 7 6 4 3 6 0 8 2 1 *